MW01181645

Dropping
the Other
Shoe

Samara,
Thank you for
coming out to Girls Night!
I hope you enjoy
the book!
Quinn Halladay

Dropping the Other Shoe

a novel

Quinn Holladay

iUniverse, Inc.
New York   Bloomington

Dropping the Other Shoe

iUniverse books may be ordered through booksellers or by contacting:

iUniverse
1663 Liberty Drive
Bloomington, IN 47403
www.iuniverse.com
1-800-Authors (1-800-288-4677)

Because of the dynamic nature of the Internet, any Web addresses or links contained
in this book may have changed since publication and may no longer be valid. The
views expressed in this work are solely those of the author and do not necessarily
reflect the views of the publisher, and the publisher hereby disclaims any responsibility
for them.

ISBN: 978-0-595-53402-9 (sc)
ISBN: 978-1-4401-1531-8 (dj)
ISBN: 978-0-595-63460-6 (ebk)

Library of Congress Control Number: 2008944272

Printed in the United States of America

iUniverse rev. date: 01/12/2009

To the people in my life whose relationships inspire me ...

Mom and Dad

Taylor and Kim

Kathy and Zach

Prologue

Twenty-eight years. Twenty-eight years, six months, and three days, to be exact. That's how long I've known what I wanted to do. I've known what I wanted to do my entire life. Some people think it's an exaggeration, but I knew when I was three years old and would hum my favorite commercial jingles rather than the nursery rhymes I was learning in preschool. I knew in the seventh grade when my science project was an experiment testing people's recall of commercials. And, I knew the first day in college when I chose to major in marketing. I wanted to write slogans and create company brands.

I woke up every morning eager to get to class because it meant I was that much closer to my dream job. My best friend, Andrea (who goes by Andy), groaned every semester, as I would register for 8 AM classes and then get up early to prepare for them. We had drawn each other as roommates out of the freshman lottery system. The summer before school I experienced apprehension about living with a stranger for an entire year, but it melted away the minute I walked into our dorm room and saw her wearing the same outfit as I had on—T-shirt, khaki shorts, and flip-flops. I knew immediately we would get along.

That's not to say we weren't different. Andy had spent most of her adolescence in boarding school, while mine was spent hanging out with friends, playing golf with my father, and working after school. Her parents had hired movers to pack and unpack her boxes so that she was completely moved into our room within an hour. My father, mother, and sister helped me carry every single box into my room, and then stuck around to help unpack for eight hours. Her parents sent her gift certificates to go to dinner with friends in lieu of their visiting, and my parents would drop in to see me every parents' weekend and every birthday. My parents even started visiting for Andy's birthdays. I think Andy appreciated the closeness of my family, and it wasn't long before she was adopted into our circle.

Ten years later, and Andy and I were still living together, though our apartments had dramatically improved over the years. Now I actually had space for a chair, desk, and bed in my room, contrasted to our first post-college apartment, where my room was only large enough to contain a twin bed.

Even with the changes, I still woke up every morning, eager to get into work—my first job since I finished my master of business administration in marketing. My office holds a coveted window that overlooks downtown Houston and the bustling city below. Over the last year and a half, I have been putting in my time working on more senior associates' projects. But I am ready to run my own project. I want to put a team together and pitch my own vision rather than a watered-down version of mine or someone else's entirely.

I needed to step up my game to make that happen, so during the last year I started working longer hours, and I swore off men. The latter was unintentional at first. Andy said that I was using work as an excuse and that life can't be so easily compartmentalized. But after I realized how much I had hurt Josh, I couldn't get into a relationship with another guy and end up treating him the same way.

Josh and I had become friends in college after Andy introduced us. He was a good friend and the roommate of her boyfriend, Drew. Drew and Andy as a couple were a staple during our college years, although the cutesiness of their names almost prevented them from dating. Andy would break out in a rash when their names were paired together in introductions and people would remark how precious it was. She eventually got over it, and the four of us solidified into a group, going out a few times a week—a pattern that increased in our last year of school when jobs and responsibilities loomed around the corner. Josh or I would occasionally bring a date or fling into the group, but it never lasted. I remember one guy saying rather bluntly that I let him remain on the outside, and it wasn't going to change, at least not for him.

As affectionate as we were with one another and as much as we liked each other, Josh and I did not date until after graduation. When we finally got together, it became serious quickly and lasted a couple of years. In the second year of our relationship, I began to narrow in my focus, solely worried about the progression of my career. It was gradual at first, but I began to ignore my role as the girlfriend. As my absence and withdrawal from him became more obvious, neither of us could continue to pretend things were fine. Going from friends to a relationship back to friends was not easy. Given my horrible behavior, I was grateful that Josh was willing to try. In the early days after our break-up, we crossed over the friends' line, and we probably still get a little closer than most friends. We are making a concerted effort to fully make the transition—at least I like to think so. I didn't realize until some time had passed how much I relied on his support and belief in what I was trying to achieve in my job.

That's where I needed to focus.

And that's why I walked into my boss's office at Smithson, York, and Associates. One of my colleagues had experienced contractions in her second trimester along with elevated blood pressure. She was doing fine now, but her doctor wanted to take precautionary measures. That meant no coming into work and absolutely no travel. She would be still be working but was stuck telecommuting from her bed at home. It came at a time when she was about to make a pitch to a client in California. The firm was now in a bind, trying to determine who to send to Los Angeles in her place. It was a relatively new client account, making the partners extremely nervous about having to transfer it to associates so early in the contract.

I walked into Bill's office after hearing the chatter running through the firm and asked to be put on the project. I knew for whatever reason that I was flying under my boss's radar and needed to get on his screen. This was my opportunity to become more visible and increase my chances of being considered for the promotion at the end of the year.

Though I had been optimistic, I was still surprised when he agreed. My enthusiasm was knocked down a notch when I found out that another junior associate, Simon, would be going to California as well and that the project was now being overseen by Ben, a partner.

I wasn't going to let either of them spoil the rush I felt as I walked back to my office. I wasn't going to think about my nerves and how I could actually feel them jump when Ben zeroed in on me. And, I wasn't going to think about how Simon was Ben's go-to person on most projects.

I was going to focus on my work.

Chapter 1

*T*he shades rose on the windows, and the fluorescent lights that had been dimmed now hummed brightly in the room. As the room began to fill with the combination of sunlight and artificial light, the suits around the table waited expectedly for the silence to be broken.

Henry, the president of the company, clapped his hands together. "I've been waiting twelve years for this." He stood up and walked around the table. "Kate, this is exactly what I've been looking for. I cannot wait to get these concepts underway over the next few months."

Henry shook my hand vigorously. His energy seemed to infuse liveliness into others as they began talking animatedly among themselves. A few pulled Simon aside for questions.

"I am so glad to hear that we're on target with your expectations." The relief of a successful pitch to our newest account washed through me.

"My dear, if you were any closer, I might think you've been walking around in my mind." The warmth Henry exuded put me at ease as we chatted about next steps and how I would recommend implementing the marketing strategy. Out of the corner of my eye, I could see Simon watching our exchange. His desire to be in our conversation was palpable. I just hoped the people he was talking to didn't pick up on his disinterest in them.

John, Henry's second in command, walked up to join us. "Could we convince you two to join us for dinner tonight?" He motioned toward Simon to include him in the invitation.

I glanced around, taking in my surroundings. The restaurant had an intimate feel, with only a handful of tables. I fidgeted with the strap on my bag to draw energy from my nervousness. Dinner with our clients was different than the office setting earlier in the day. Their continued home court advantage was throwing me off my game.

We were standing near the bar waiting for our table. When the hostess came to get us, Henry and another business associate, Stephen, led the way, followed by Simon. John turned and guided me through the tables by placing his hand on the small of my back. My back immediately arched away, but I forced myself not to jump and draw attention to the two of us. I had to concentrate not to flinch at this unwelcome gesture.

My attempt at remaining calm was unsuccessful, as my reaction caused me to bump into a nearby chair and knock it off-balance. I covered my eyes to avoid watching the ripple I started. After the crashing noises stopped, I peeked through my fingers to see Simon's pants were soaked through the crotch area. "I'm so sorry." I averted my eyes and bent down to pick up some of the silverware that had fallen from the table.

A couple of waiters were scrambling to clean up the mess I had made. Diners were turned toward the scene, since the clanging of water glasses, silverware, and chairs hitting the floor captured their attention. The fire in my cheeks was beginning to pulse through the rest of my body. "I'm so sorry," I muttered again.

"It's fine." Simon took the napkin that the waiter handed him. As the commotion subsided, the restaurant returned to its indifference.

The waiter directed us forward. I carefully maneuvered through the tables, John's hand noticeably absent this time. Simon who was immediately in front of me shook his head.

The waiter handed us our menus as we settled into the *u*-shaped booth. John slid into the booth, so that I was between him and Simon.

"I should have warned you when we started working together. I'm a terrible klutz, and it seems to happen at the most inopportune times." I tried to lighten the mood of the table. Thankfully, Henry seemed to find the whole situation amusing, chuckling to himself.

"Is there ever an opportune one? Really, it's fine," Simon mumbled under his breath where only I could hear. To the others he appeared focused on the menu open before him.

"Do you mind if I order for you? I want to be sure you get the most out of your experience here." I turned to realize that John's question was posed to me.

I tried to read his face to see if he might be joking, but his eyes were genuinely searching mine for an answer. My jaw clinched behind the forced smile as I uttered, "Okay." *He's my client. I can forgive small annoyances.*

I scanned the menu to see what I might be missing out on. Satisfied that he would not be able to go wrong with his choice, I shut it and turned my attention to the group. "Come here often?"

"It's pretty close to our office, and we enjoy the ambience," John quickly replied, missing my meager attempt at humor.

The waiter filled our table of five with enough appetizers for ten people. Although my choice in food tends to be conservative, in work settings I try to remain open. I accepted the plate handed to me by John, served myself, and then passed it on to Simon.

I took a bite of a sliver of something—I hoped it was meat covered in sauce. I immediately began to cough. As I reached for my water, I

3

inadvertently knocked it over. John reached across, catching the glass midair and most of the water before it spilt.

I swallowed, catching my breath. "That was a bit spicy."

"I should have warned you."

"Nice catch."

"Definitely seems to be a handy trick around you."

As dinner progressed, I couldn't help but notice the conversation focused on John. Even Henry would start a story, only to be cut off by John. He would attempt to pick his story back up, but gave up when John would interrupt a second or third time. While assertiveness is an admirable quality, his behavior came across as surprisingly disrespectful toward his boss. At least Simon's derisive glares toward me lessened through the evening. I wasn't sure whether it was our clients, the food, or the realization that he was coming across better than I was that removed the tension he had been visibly carrying.

"It was really kind of you to give us a ride back to the hotel. I hope it wasn't too out of the way." I stopped in the lobby. John had given his car keys to the valet rather than dropping Simon and me at the front door. His coming in with us could only prolong the evening, and I was ready to curl up in my bed and watch some late-night sitcoms before falling asleep.

"No problem. Could I convince you to have a drink with me in the bar?" He looked straight at me, not even attempting to include Simon in his invitation.

"It was great to meet you. I'll be in touch." Simon turned and walked toward the elevators, leaving me standing speechless in front of John.

"It looks like it will just be you and me." John reached out to guide me by my elbow to the hotel bar.

"I really need to get to sleep. I do have any early flight." I removed my elbow from John's grasp, halting the momentum toward the bar.

"Is that an invitation?" He looked lasciviously toward me.

My stomach began to turn. I repressed what I wanted to say—how I could not stand him and how I would be perfectly happy if I never laid eyes on him again. My work and my job were more important, and carefully navigating this without offending him in any way was a must.

With as much charm as possible, I responded, "John, I am flattered by your attention." And, trying to let his ego remain intact, I added, "Under different circumstances, I might entertain your offer. But you must know I cannot act in any way that could put our business relationship in jeopardy. Your company is too important as a client to our firm. I do hope you understand."

He seemed to mull over his options before landing on one. The lechery quickly left his eyes, replaced with a steely focus. "I cannot fault you for putting my company first. I should let you get to your room. I'll be speaking with you soon, Kate." He extended his hand.

I breathed in relief and shook his hand.

"Oh, shit! Oh, shit!" I fell out of bed, the sheet twisted around me. I picked up my phone. "How is the battery dead?" I followed the cord to the outlet. "You have got to be kidding me." I then noticed the switch controlling the electricity flow to the outlet. "So much for the alarm on my phone," I sighed.

I began throwing clothes into my luggage. Then, realizing I needed something to wear, I began pulling clothes back out. I continued to pack and dress at the same time. "Ohhh," my foot was catching in my underwear as I tried to pull them up. "Ummph." I landed on my side. "This is brilliant."

I managed to finish dressing without any additional bruises and hailed a cab to the airport. When I made it to the gate, the plane was still waiting.

"Attention, passengers for Flight 274 to Houston. The inbound aircraft is on the ground. We are waiting for the passengers to deplane and the plane to be cleaned. As soon as we get the all clear, we'll be boarding."

Some grumbling sounded through the gate area. I looked at my watch. We were already thirty minutes past our scheduled departure time. Lately, the flights have been delayed more often than not. For once, I was grateful for the delay. I tried to slow my breathing from rushing through the airport.

I set up a makeshift office while we waited to board. My computer was perched in my lap, and my diet Sprite, cell phone, and BlackBerry were sitting on my carry-on. I stared at my e-mail for five minutes, futilely trying get through the sea of unread messages overflowing my inbox. I was trying to block out the absurdities streaming through my mind from the night before, shuddering at the image of John's face.

Simon sat down next to me. "I left a message for Ben earlier, and he just called me back. He wants to sit down with us first thing Monday morning to go through our notes from the meetings the past couple of days."

I jumped at the sound of his voice, nearly knocking my computer off my lap and causing my makeshift desk to tumble over. I was hastily grabbing at stuff. "Sure, okay." Ben Covney was the senior consultant over the project that Simon and I had been sent to L.A. to oversee. I didn't bother asking Simon why he hadn't told me he was calling Ben.

"What's wrong with you? You seem a little jumpy." He was wiping away the little bit of my drink that spilled on him. Simon pushed his glasses onto the bridge of his nose as he warily took me in. His wire rimmed glasses often drew my attention, because he had a habit of frequently adjusting them.

Twice in two days. I really should come with a warning sign. "Nothing. Sorry."

"I can't believe you were so dramatic at dinner." He ignored my apology and redirected our conversation to the night before.

"I can't believe you didn't wait for me this morning. We could have shared the cab. I'm sure our client would have appreciated our sharing the expense."

"I didn't know what your plans were this morning. You may have had company, and I didn't want to disturb you."

"Seriously, Simon, did you really think I would have company?" I didn't let him answer. "It sounds like you would have preferred that I flirt a little for the sake of business. You know, I'm sure there were some there last night who would have responded better to you than me."

He shifted uncomfortably. "I think our work speaks for itself."

"I agree, which is why I tried to engage Henry in the conversation, limiting my interaction with John … no thanks to you."

"All I know is he seemed pretty focused on getting you alone."

"Jealous?" Realizing that question may not have come across as I intended, I clarified. "They knew there were two of us behind the presentation. I just did the majority of the talking in this case, so I'm sure that is why he directed most of his questions to me."

"Uh-huh." Simon clearly did not agree with my assessment.

"Listen." The PA system was on again with new instructions for passengers. "They're finally calling us to board," I said as I pulled myself together. I was sitting a few rows in front of Simon on the aisle. I settled into my seat, and once the others on my row had filed in, I let the whirring of the jets put me to sleep.

Chapter 2

*I*t was Saturday. With Josh and Buddy, my two-year-old black Labrador retriever, in tow, I drove out to my parents' house for a belated graduation celebration of my little sister. Josh Forrester and I had been friends since college, and he loved hanging out with my family. It had not been a hard sell when I asked him to come with me for the afternoon.

As we turned onto my parents' street, I felt nostalgia for my childhood. I loved the immediate feeling of comfort I had when I saw the canopy of trees over their street. With the warm weather of Houston, it was rare that the trees were not green. Even during winter, my parents' neighborhood always seemed green. The canopy was something I could count on, a shelter from the treeless midtown section of Houston where I now lived.

When we pulled into the driveway, we could see my father and sister's boyfriend, Shawn, taking practice golf swings in the backyard. Buddy bounded from the car and ran toward them, propping his front paws against the waist-high fence so he could peer over. He then began barking playfully at them for attention. I unlatched the gate to let him through. Once his excitement subsided, I hugged my father and Shawn and left them to their swings.

"Hey Mom," I said as I walked into the kitchen, setting my sister's gift on the counter.

She looked up from the stove. "Hey, sweetie." She hugged me and kissed me on the cheek. "Where's Josh?"

"He got caught outside with Dad and Shawn. Where's Caroline?" I looked out toward the living room.

"She's still up in her room getting dressed. She got a late start this morning."

I smiled at this. My sister had been this way since we were little. She was always rolling out of bed at the last possible minute, and usually a few minutes after that. But you couldn't help but forgive her with her rosy cheeks and tousled, wavy blond hair. She always looked like she just walked off the beach. We couldn't look more different or be more different in personality. My hair was jet black and straight as could be. About the only thing we shared were our bright, blue eyes—that and our height, as we were both five feet, nine inches.

"Hey," she burst into the kitchen, blond hair bouncing in its ponytail. "Did you see Dad and Shawn? They've been out there all morning."

"Yeah, Josh got sucked in."

"You brought Josh?" A smile spread across her face as she went to peek through the shutters before coming over to the counter.

"I didn't think you would mind." I bumped my hip into hers. My family had immediately liked Josh the first time I brought him home during the time we dated. I knew they still harbored hope that we would date again, though they did a pretty good job of not actually saying anything. "So how are you feeling?" I was still trying to absorb the fact that my baby sister had graduated from college.

"It doesn't really feel any different. I don't think it has quite hit me yet. I am really excited about tomorrow, though."

"Where do you go first?"

"We fly into London, tour around there for a couple of days, then to Paris, then Germany, Belgium, Italy. Hopefully, we'll have time for Greece. We spend a couple of days in each city or country, I guess, according to Shawn's schedule, but I wouldn't be too upset if we get off schedule."

"Sure, you love each other now, but let's see about after you get lost and haven't showered in days," I teased.

"This trip is nothing compared to when we did our summer with Habitat for Humanity. We really smelled at the end of the day. This time we will just be walking around."

"Maybe the real worry is throwing Shawn off his schedule."

"I know he is trying to be relaxed about it, but he can't help himself with his lists and making sure we have time for everything." Caroline was grinning at him through the kitchen windows. "I definitely cannot fault his intentions."

They had been an odd fit from the beginning. Shawn had a plan for just about everything, while Caroline seemed to get there in the most roundabout way with little planning or forethought. The one thing they both had in common, and what I knew made them right for each other, was a playful sense of humor. They seemed to really like one another and laughed easily together. I would be jealous of them if they weren't so cute together.

"How was L.A.? When did you get back?" Caroline directed her attention back to me.

"I got in Thursday night. It was good. Work was fine." I picked up a grape from the bowl on the counter and popped it into my mouth. "I did go on a date while I was there."

"With who?"

"Oh, nobody, just some guy I picked up in a bar." I winked at Caroline. Mom had turned around to face me, trying to mask her shock, leaving somewhat of a strained expression on her face. "Oh, okay, he picked me up." Caroline tried to hold back a chuckle but couldn't keep it in.

"Kate, is that really safe to go out with a perfect stranger?"

"It's no different than the perfect strangers that I usually go out with here. If it makes you feel any better, I gave the details of where I was going to Andy. I told her if I did not check in with her by a certain time to call the police." I donned my most serious expression.

"No, that does not make me feel any better. What was Andy going to do from halfway across the country?"

"She could make a call to the police just as easily as she could in the same city."

"Well, I'm glad that you are home and safe." She squeezed me tight.

"Mom, she's kidding. She's just trying to get you upset." Caroline rolled her eyes.

"There was no date, but we did go to a really great restaurant," I continued. "The food and atmosphere were amazing. I had this chicken and pasta with white wine sauce that almost melted in my mouth."

"You are the only person I know who goes to a great city and has more details about your entrée than the people you were with," Caroline said with frustration.

"I am just spending more time on the details that are worth noting."

"It could have been a great opportunity for you to meet someone while you were out there. You know, one day—"

"I'm happy on my own. Besides, I was there for work. I know you and Mom have this desire to see me coupled."

"It's not that." She looked to our mother for assurance.

My mother continued for her. "We just don't want to see you closed off."

I knew I was becoming defensive. "I'm not closed off. I'm happy how things are—my friends, my family. I'm good."

"Is it about time to fire up the grill?" My father was entering through the back door followed by Shawn and Josh.

"What have you been doing out there?" Mom asked.

"Working on my golf swing," Dad responded in a mock serious tone.

"I'm so glad we have regressed to our gender roles, with the women in the kitchen getting the meal ready and the men outside doing nothing." Mom retorted.

"We would happily fulfill our role as men, but the last time I hunted squirrels in the backyard, you were upset. I'm damned if I do, damned if I don't. I tell you, Hayden women are tough to please. Shawn, Josh, are you sure you two know what you're doing getting involved with these two?" Mom playfully swatted him with the dish towel.

"They just won't leave us alone. I've tried to get rid of this one," Shawn responded as he walked over to Caroline and put his arm around her waist.

"You know how lucky you are?" I interjected in sisterly defense.

"If you don't, just ask one of the Hayden women," Josh joined in.

"I'll have you know we had a fine role model to look up to, and surely you wouldn't insult the lady of the house, provider of your lunch this afternoon," I taunted Josh.

"So how can I help, Ms. Hayden?" Josh ignored my attempt to bait him.

"You could carry the plates into the dining room, and Kate, you can set the table."

"Well, since you asked so nicely …" I grabbed the utensils and led the way to the other room.

"Now I get why you are so willing to come over to my family's," I said.

Josh was setting the plates on the table. "Besides the free food?" He smiled.

"That's too obvious."

"Well, then, why else?"

"You have an audience, or rather accomplices, willing to help in teasing me."

"I don't know what you're talking about. I never tease you. I only treat you with the utmost respect that you deserve, and I never try to engage others in teasing you."

"You shouldn't lie so readily or so easily. I do have a knife in my hand."

"I'm more scared of those pointy-toe shoes you have on with the three-inch heel than the butter knife."

"You like?" I held up my foot for his admiration. "I'm so glad you noticed."

"You do realize we are just having a casual lunch with your family." Josh was looking fresh in khaki shorts and flip-flops. With his sandy blonde hair and green eyes, he looked like he should be in a J. Crew ad. And at six foot three, he still towered over me, even with my three-inch heels.

"Yeah, so? There's no reason I can't dress fashionably."

"I will never understand why you force your feet into those things. You are going to have the ugliest toes when you get older, all crunched up." His nose crinkled as he contorted his hand to show what my toes would look like. "So, no, I do not like your shoes."

"Whatever." I placed the last set of silverware on the table.

"Wow. That was a great comeback."

"I'm not going to indulge you, participate in your games. I like my shoes and that's that. No need for me to defend them to you." I held up my head as I walked back into the kitchen, acting miffed.

"Your father has the meat on the grill," Mom said. "It should only take a few minutes, so you can go ahead and start carrying the rest of the food into the dining room."

"You heard her, Josh." I looked over at him.

"She was talking to you," Josh said, shaking his head.

"All right, children. I used *you* in the collective sense. That means all of you can help." She pointed her finger at the four of us.

"Thanks for getting us dragged into this. I thought we were being honored today," Caroline said in protest.

"Mom expressly said when she told us about lunch today that we were not to let you get a big head and start resting on your laurels just because you're a college graduate now," I teased.

"Now, Caroline, you know I would never say such a thing," Mom countered.

"Don't worry. I would never get that idea around here with this group. I know I need at least another degree before I can do that." Caroline picked up the pitcher of margaritas to carry to the dining room. Shawn followed her lead, picking up the pitcher of water.

"You're helping mankind and the greater good," I countered. "That is way more impressive than my MBA. I look like I'm just out for more money." I wanted to convey to my sister how proud I was of her studies in social work and involvement in volunteer programs.

"Besides, it wouldn't matter how many degrees you had, sweetie." Dad joined the conversation as he came in carrying a large tray of steak and grilled chicken. "There's no room for big heads in this family."

"What is all of this talk of more degrees? I thought you were taking time off to travel around Europe and then were going to start work at Women 2 Aid," Mom added.

"I am, but you never know what can happen."

"Yesterday, she was talking about getting her master's in social work. The day before that she was talking about getting her MBA, and the day before that she wanted to study public relations," Shawn added.

"I'm just trying to keep my options open," Caroline replied. "And thanks for ratting me out." She playfully jabbed at him.

"Speaking of options," Dad started. I knew he was directing this at me. "How is the promotion coming at work?"

I knew my parents were asking because they cared, but sometimes I didn't think they truly understood what it was like to work for "the man" and how it can be a long process before anything happens. Mom authored children's books since before we were born. She had a brief career at a local newspaper, but after penning her first book, she quickly found a publisher. She then ended her career at the newspaper and had been writing books ever since.

My father, on the other hand, began his own bioengineering company with a friend immediately after finishing their master's degrees. They started out as a two-person shop, with my mom pitching in to help with the administrative functions when she could. They had grown into a successful operation with a large staff of engineers and now dedicated administrative and sales staff.

"I don't know." I paused before adding, "I'm putting in the hours, but I probably won't know anything for another six to eight months at least. They won't make any decisions until we get closer to the end of our year and they've had time to review more of our billings and business development."

"I can definitely attest to her putting in the hours," Josh said. "Every time I try to get ahold of her, she is at the office working. It's been a rare weekend lately that she is not there." He gave me a reassuring look. "So how about we get the food into the dining room? I think I might start to look like Buddy if I don't actually get to taste the food soon." Buddy had drool hanging from his mouth.

I was happy for the distraction and would have to remember to thank Josh later for his change of subject.

We all settled into our chairs around the table. My parents sat at either end of the table, and Caroline and I sat diagonally across from one another. We were a family of routine with which spots we sat in, and Shawn and Josh had become accustomed to their seats as well. Before Shawn or Josh, if Caroline or I brought a guy home, those were their designated chairs. Even Buddy took his normal spot underneath my feet at the table. During lunch, the conversation stayed mostly on Caroline and Shawn's trip to Europe. It occasionally drifted back to my work, but every time Josh would redirect the conversation with another question.

"Are you sure you can't stay longer?" Mom asked as she and my father were walking us to the door.

"I wish we could, but we need to get going so we have time to stop by our places and then get to the stadium," Josh said. "Kate has graciously agreed to accompany me to an office thing. We have a box tonight for the Astros game. I had to twist her arm though to get her to come."

"Are they playing the Cardinals?" Dad asked.

15

"Yes." Josh nuzzled Buddy's ear with his hand. "It should be a good game."

I turned to my mom. "I'll probably be able to come by next weekend. I know you'll be in withdrawal with Caroline and me out of the house."

"I don't know. I think we might be throwing a party with all of our friends to celebrate," Dad deadpanned.

"I was talking to Mom, and careful—I might think you don't like having your kids around." I jabbed my father in the arm.

"You know that's never the case." Mom gave me a hug. She then gave Josh a hug and said, "Come back and see us soon."

Dad enveloped me in a bear hug. "Let me know if you have time for golf, and we'll go out and hit some balls."

"I will."

"Even if Kate can't get away, let me know and I can get us a tee time at the club." He shook Josh's hand.

"Sounds good."

"See ya later." We waved and walked across the lawn to Josh's car. My parents waited until we were driving away before they closed the door.

⁓

Josh gave me an hour to get ready and be at his place. We walked to the stadium since our apartment building was only a few blocks away. It was the longest distance I would willingly walk in my shoes.

"Kate," Josh's boss extended his hand, "It's good to see you again."

"It's good to see you too. Thanks for having me tonight."

"Well, how could I turn Josh down after he told me what an avid baseball fan you are?"

"I grew up watching baseball. I think my father threw all his interest in baseball on me since he never had a son."

"She knows more stats than most guys I know," Josh chimed in, "and she's the only woman I know who TiVos *Sportscenter*."

"Just one of the guys? I would almost believe that except for the shoes." He added in a hushed voice. "My wife has me pretty well trained to notice shoes. Now please help yourself to food and drinks and enjoy the game. And Josh," he said even more quietly, "our clients are here, so be sure to spend some time talking to them."

Josh worked for a banking group that dealt strictly with mergers and acquisitions. The clients at the game had used Josh's group for their last three acquisitions.

"Will do," Josh said, and we headed toward the drinks.

"Who are the clients?" I asked.

"The three men standing in the corner up close to the glass," he answered.

"Do you want to get a couple of drinks and then get the schmoozing out of the way?" I whispered. Then I followed up quickly with, "Do you want me to tag along or hang back?"

"I want it to seem casual at least for right now. So I would appreciate if you would come over and meet them. I know you will become worthless when the game gets started."

I smirked, knowing he was right.

"Let me ask you this very important question. This food looks great and all, but can we get a hot dog later?" I looked at him expectantly.

"Don't worry. I was under no illusion that you would want this fancy food."

I linked my arm in his and we headed over to his clients. We chatted with them for about fifteen minutes, discussing the old-timers and newbies on the Astros. After fulfilling Josh's quota of small talk, we found a spot to watch the game.

"Thanks for BSing with them." Josh smiled.

"It's the least I can do in exchange for luxury seating at a game."

"Let's head to Sammy's for a couple of drinks after the game."

I nodded. "Do you think it would be all right to bring a dog in here?"

"You're like a little kid not wanting to get in trouble."

"I'm just looking out for you. After all, I am a reflection on you."

"As long as it's of the food and not the canine variety, I think it's fine."

The game passed quickly. Josh spent some time talking to the clients, but he came to check on me every ten minutes or so. The Astros ended up losing 6-4, and we walked to Sammy's while most of the crowd weaved in and out of traffic through the parking lot trying to locate their cars.

"Grab a table. I'll get us a couple of drinks," Josh said, as he made his way to the bar.

"Sure." The bar was pretty empty after the Astros loss, so I had my choice of tables. As I was waiting for Josh to come back with the drinks, I noticed a woman staring at me. I started to think I was just imagining it because there was no way someone would be that blatant, but she didn't seem to be looking away. I was trying to look anywhere but in her direction. Josh came over to the table with the drinks, so I focused all of my attention on him.

"How did the business go?" I asked. "You seemed to talk to them for quite a while."

"It went well. They were quite impressed with you."

"Well, obviously." I rolled my eyes.

"But I feel pretty confident they'll renew their contract with us to handle their next acquisition. We actually talk details about the contract on Monday."

"That's great! A toast is in order." We raised our glasses. "To you and your smooth talking."

We watched the game highlights on the flatscreen in the corner. I let out a yawn, not even trying to suppress it. "I think one is my limit tonight."

"I won't take offense to that." Josh faked a yawn.

"You shouldn't. It was a long week. I'm sorry I'm such a bore." I looked at my watch, "It's not even late."

"It's okay." Josh got up from the table to close our tab at the bar. I pulled out some money, holding it out to him. He shook his head. "You can get it the next time."

Out of the corner of my eye, I could see the woman who had been staring at me earlier gesturing in my direction. I tried to ignore it, but then she began to wave at me. I finally gave in and gave her a head nod.

From her table, about ten feet away, she asked, "Is that guy your boyfriend?"

Like any woman in my situation, I lied. "Yes."

"For how long?"

I was shocked. "Does it matter?"

"Well, there is nothing that I can really do, but ..." as she pulled out her card from her wallet, "... if it doesn't work out, can you pass along my card?" She got up from her seat and placed it on the table between us.

I couldn't think of anything acceptable to say.

Josh returned to the table and motioned to the woman. "What was that about?"

"Nothing." I grabbed his arm. "Let's go home." I ignored the business card on the table and headed toward the door. "Wait." I sighed.

"What?" he stopped. "What's wrong?" He looked at me expectantly.

"She was leaving her card on the table for you. I know it's ridiculous, but she didn't know we weren't together. And even if I am just your faux date, doesn't that entitle me to your monogamy at least for the night?" I felt sheepish.

Josh smiled. "Come on. Let's go." He grabbed my hand and pulled me out of the bar.

Chapter 3

I got into the office a little after seven Monday morning. I was just booting up my computer when Simon came in.

"Ben's ready to see us," he said, not bothering to look up from his BlackBerry.

Good morning. How was your weekend? What, me? I had a good one. Saw my family and caught a baseball game and a movie. I know, I slacked off this weekend. I'm sure you were up here all weekend.

Simon had been fairly cordial over our business trip. There were rough spots, but I thought we were becoming collegial. Back in the office, his coldness toward me had returned in full force.

"I just need a few minutes to get settled," I replied.

"We'll be in the small conference room waiting when you're finally ready." Simon looked up to meet my eyes and, in an uncomfortable gesture, shifted his glasses before leaving my office.

Really? I mean, really, is it necessary to add the finally?

I took a deep breath and pulled my notes out of my bag. I checked my inbox to make sure there were no urgent e-mails waiting. Then I grabbed my BlackBerry and headed toward the conference room.

"Good morning," I said as I walked into the room.

"Good morning, Kate," Ben echoed. "If you wouldn't mind, since you're up, could you get me a cup of coffee?" Ben and I had worked together at Smithson, York, and Associates for the past year and a half. However, most of our exchanges from the first day and those since had been limited to "hi's" and "how are you's."

I took a deep breath. "Sure." *Did your legs break?* At least we were beyond the cursory greeting. I handed him the coffee. My eyes dropped to his hand; it had not escaped my attention that recently a vacancy had turned up on his ring finger. He focused solely on his work and kept personal details private. This privacy, especially now, only caused the rumors to swirl.

"Simon was just briefing me on your extracurricular activities while you were out in Los Angeles. I'm glad you had time to wine and dine our clients," Ben said.

I looked at Simon, who was scrolling through his BlackBerry, not even acknowledging me so I could give him my discreet but effective death stare. "I can't believe that you two have nothing better to discuss than my whereabouts in L.A., and I feel so lucky to have had an escort on the trip," I tried to say in a light tone as I took my seat.

"Why do you think I sent you both?" Ben quipped, pausing before adding, "But, I was just telling Simon that he should follow your lead. You can't work twenty-four, seven, and it's okay to enjoy your travel."

Not exactly what I was expecting. "I went to a nice dinner that included Simon, and I was in my room only moments after he would have been in his."

"I was unaccompanied to my room," Simon remarked, with a smirk that spread to his eyes that vanished immediately when Ben looked at him.

I cannot believe he would imply that I would sleep with a client. Would you look up from your e-mail and actually say something to me directly? Are we really playing such a childish game?

"So let's get started." Ben had moved on. "Kate, walk me through the first day."

Simon Rothfield was another junior consultant vying for a promotion. He had been Ben's golden boy on projects for the past few months, so I was a little surprised Ben asked me. After about ten minutes detailing our tour of the client's facility, followed by observations of some of the workers and meetings with senior management, Ben seemed to be satisfied. "In general, any issues come up why you were there?" he asked.

"No, I feel like we were well prepared. I do think they will be expecting a rather aggressive turnaround time."

"I sent you an e-mail outlining a schedule that I think should put us well within their expectations." Simon, who had been quiet until now, added to the conversation.

"I have not had a chance to look at the e-mail. Did you copy Kate on it?" Ben asked.

I was already scrolling through my e-mail, not seeing anything from Simon.

"No, I'll be sure to forward it to her."

"Why don't we spend some time this morning going through that timeline and also determining who will take the lead on the various tasks? We don't need to bore Ben with that though," I said.

"That sounds good. Send me your plan when you have reached an agreement, and I will look over it." Ben got up, then stopped, as though trying to think of something to say. "Sounds like you both did a good job last week," he finally added, but was gone before either Simon or I could muster an ingratiating response. *I hate these games.*

"In the future, we should probably copy each other on any e-mails we send regarding the project," I said.

"Here's a copy of the timeline I proposed. Do you have any problems with this?" Simon asked.

"I want to look through it to make sure all of the major steps are covered. I also need to compare it to my calendar to see if I have any conflicts. It shouldn't take me a minute, but I need to go back to my computer to be able to do so."

"I'll wait here."

"We could both just go to my office. It will be quicker."

"That's okay." Simon had returned to thumbing a message on his BlackBerry.

I debated about what to say next, but after traveling with him I felt more comfortable in being direct. "Have I done something to offend you?" I said, willing him to look me in the eye.

"Kate, it's nothing personal, but you and I both know we are up against each other for the senior position this year. Working together just throws the competition right in our faces. And honestly, I'd rather not get to be friends or like each other because it just makes the situation more awkward."

"Simon, I cannot believe it could be more awkward than it is right now. You won't even address me. Did it occur to you that things could change and they could promote both of us? Or that us being able to work together under these circumstances is some sort of a test?"

"Are we actually having a talk about the relationship?" he asked in a tone dripping with sarcasm.

"I just don't want to be miserable every time we are put on a project together. I can't believe this is pleasant for you. But if it's how you want it, that's fine and I will leave it alone." I got up and headed toward my office, and to my surprise, Simon followed me.

It ended up taking us about an hour to go through and coordinate our schedules, but we managed to civilly coexist for sixty minutes.

The rest of the day was spent with the creative team brainstorming ideas to reenergize the marketing campaign for an energy drink that was in direct competition with Gatorade, the current leader in the market. Post-it notes and markers were strewn across the room with white boards full of ideas. I was trying to merge them into a cohesive concept.

I felt like I had a pretty good handle on where we were going with it, so I packed up my laptop and papers and shoved them into my bag. When I turned off my office light, my side of the office suite was pitch black. I used my hand to feel along the wall while my eyes adjusted. When they finally did, I saw Ben standing in front of me.

A scream escaped before I could stop it. His expression registered his amusement.

"You scared me." I pressed my hand to my chest.

"I would assume that you don't normally go around screaming when you see people." He stood to the side to let me pass.

"Have a good night."

It took my entire drive home for my heart to stop racing.

"Hey, I'm home," I said as I set my keys down on the entry table.

Buddy was jumping all over the place. "I know I'm a horrible doggie parent." I knelt down to pet him, trying to avoid getting head-butted. "I have no idea what I'm going to do when Andy moves out," I mumbled to myself. She had become the only reason I wasn't overridden with guilt from leaving Buddy at home when traveling and working late.

"Hey, I remember you," Andy said, emerging from her room. She had already changed from her work clothes into pajama pants and a tank top. Her brown hair was pulled back into a short pony tail.

"It smells good in here," I said as I headed toward the kitchen.

"I cooked."

"How lucky am I?"

"Who said it was for you?" She paused. "Okay, well it is for you, but only because I haven't seen you in, like, a week."

"How was work?" I pulled out a bottle of water from the refrigerator and stepped out of my heels.

"Oh, you know, the usual. Just trying to reinvent ourselves for the third time this year. Because rather than try to stick with something, we take the jumping ship strategy." Andy worked in the marketing department at corporate for Goldman's Department Store; the conglomerate name was something that I could never remember. "This is one of those times that it would really help to have some people with economics in their background to understand that there are factors outside of how good our image is that can affect our consumer profile."

"I can tell you agree with the new direction."

She smiled wryly.

"Is Drew coming over?" I asked.

"Nope, it's just us girls tonight."

Buddy had begun a slow whine.

"You have time to take him for a run. I just put it in the oven, so it will be another hour before it's ready."

I walked over to the oven, leaning down to see what was in it. Andy was cooking her lasagna and had garlic bread waiting to be toasted. "I think I need to burn some calories before dinner."

I changed, put the leash on Buddy, and headed out for a quick run. It was an unseasonably cool day in Houston in early September. It felt good to work up a sweat.

I grabbed the mail on my way back up to our apartment. Buddy and I walked to the stairs to avoid putting him in contact with his fear of elevators. Buddy pulled me a little harder as we got closer to the stairs, and I lurched forward. I looked up and saw Josh bending down to pet Buddy's head, now realizing why Buddy had hurried to the stairs.

"Hey," I said, a little out of breath as I pushed my hair away from my face.

"How was your run?" I couldn't tell if he was asking me or Buddy, but then he looked up at me and smiled.

"It was good—quick but good."

"And I assume you reclaimed the neighborhood." Josh patted Buddy again as he stood up.

"Yes, I think he peed on every tree and plant within a two-mile radius. Where are you off to?"

"Going to the gym and then for a run myself."

"Andy made lasagna. We'll probably have tons left over if you want to stop by later."

"Tempting, but I have some dinner plans already." He smiled.

25

"Hot date?" I asked.

"Would I have any other? I have to get going though so I can get my work out in."

"You'll have to give me the details later." I waved.

"I always do." He waved and then turned and jogged off.

Buddy and I ran up the stairs, and I unclipped his leash as I opened the door to the apartment. "Do I have time for a shower?" I asked as I entered.

"It still has about twenty minutes to cook and then it will need to cool," Andy replied.

"I ran into Josh on my way back up. He has a date tonight."

She gave me a quizzical look.

"Don't say a word. I'm getting into the shower." I brushed off her look.

After my shower, I put on a T-shirt and yoga pants. I wandered into the kitchen as I twisted my wet hair into a bun. "You do realize when you start living with a guy, it is very likely that we will not see each other for a week," I said to Andy as she was pulling the lasagna and bread out of the oven. I moved to pull out a bottle of wine for us to drink with dinner.

"I agreed to marry Drew, but I didn't necessarily say I would live with him," Andy said.

"I'm pretty sure he is expecting a wife who actually lives in the same house. I mean, some men just have the most unrealistic expectations." I made a face.

"Do you think I can convince him that we should each have our own bathroom?" Andy asked, looking slightly anxious at the thought of sharing a bathroom.

"Are you worried about him seeing you get ready … seeing 'the magic happen'?" I paused. "Or is it the ick factor?" I laughed, struggling to get the cork out of the bottle in one piece.

"Could you take me a little bit seriously?"

"I could, but where is the fun in that?" Taking in her expression, I softened. "Okay, okay. Well, Drew seems pretty reasonable and may even appreciate having the extra room himself."

"Maybe. I'm just not sure how to broach the subject. 'I want to share my life with you, but not my bathroom.'" Andy giggled.

"Just tell him how much hair you shed, how it clogs up the sink and shower," I said as I took a sip of my wine. I moved over to the cabinet to pull two plates down and grabbed some forks. "Do you want any salad? I could throw one together."

"I know I should, considering I'm in wedding training, but I'll just go with an all-carb-dinner tonight. But seriously, how do I relegate him to the guest bathroom?"

"That's probably a little trickier." I poured some dog food in Buddy's bowl and refreshed his water.

"I think the lasagna has cooled enough." Andy cut into it and placed a steaming portion on each of our plates.

"Hey, look on the bright side—bathroom issues aside, at least you know how your name will sound with his last name."

"That's true. But I like mine. I am used to how it sounds. 'Andy Strighton.' Has a good ring to it, doesn't it?"

"Well, you don't have to change it." I grabbed the wine and our glasses. She grabbed the plates and bread, and we headed into the living room.

"How was your date with Josh this weekend?" Andy teased.

"Stop it! You know it wasn't a date. How long have we all been friends?"

"I've been *friends* with him for nine years." She drew out the word. "But you two, I'm not sure what I would call it. You spent the whole day with him—he went to lunch with your family, and then you went to a work event with him."

"And I'm going to another work event with him this weekend. I'm just doing a friend a favor so he doesn't have to take a random girl to one of those things. It doesn't make me more or less of a friend than you."

"Maybe that's the problem." Andy blew on the lasagna before taking a bite.

"There's a problem?" I raised my eyebrow. "I was unaware."

"You are each other's fillers, which puts you in this safe, comfortable place."

"Fillers?"

"I mean, when is the last time you really put yourself out there with a date?"

"I went out with that guy—"

"Who you knew you would never see again. You know you always have Josh there to rely on. And, I am not coming down on you," she said, reading my face. "He does the same thing—taking you to his work stuff, having you fill in as his faux date."

"I wish he was gay," I said dejectedly.

Andy spewed a little of her wine and quickly used her napkin to blot the couch. "I'm glad this is white. I'll pass that along to him." She laughed.

"It would make things so much easier. People would leave our relationship alone."

"Hint taken."

"Do you know how hard it is to find a decent guy?"

"Are you looking?"

"Yes." I knew Andy's question was rhetorical, but I answered anyway. As soon as I did, I knew I set her up.

"There's one right in front of you." Andy couldn't help herself in pointing it out.

"He's my friend, and I thought you took the hint."

"I'm just curious why you seem to have a one-date-wonder trend going on."

"You mean the ones who don't know how to engage another person in the conversation? What is it with men and their inability to ask questions?"

"I don't know. It must be that men who are able to ask questions are married … since they are the ones who can get out the 'will you marry me' ." Then she paused, contemplating her words before adding, "I'm pretty sure Josh can ask questions."

"Uh-huh." I took a sip of my wine.

"Okay, okay. Switching topics. Did you look at the pictures I sent you of the bridesmaid dresses?"

"No, I'm sorry." I winced. "I haven't had a chance yet."

"I just so happen to have some magazines for us to look at and the print books for this season's Vera Wang and Monique Lhuillier bridal and bridesmaids dresses."

"Now the truth comes out. The lasagna, no Drew, all a ploy."

"I know I have to come up with some way to get you to look through all of this girly stuff." She teased. "I could turn a game on in the background if you need me to or pull up shoes on saks dot com so you can plan out your shoe choice."

"No, that's all right. You have my full attention." I moved the stack of wedding stuff closer.

In the background, Andy found reruns of *Sex in the City*. We spent the next couple of hours flipping through the pages and flagging any with potential dresses we liked. By the end, we narrowed it down to three dresses, two Vera and one Monique.

Chapter 4

I was sitting in my office with scraps of papers and drawings strewn across my desk. I was trying to assimilate all of the ideas that had been tossed around in yesterday's and today's meetings. My phone rang, piercing through the silence in the room and causing me to jump out of my thoughts and back into my chair.

"This is Kate," I said into the phone.

"Another late night?" Josh's voice came across the line.

"Hey!" Smiling, I leaned back in my chair. I looked out the window, seeing the lights from the buildings and cars. It was pretty dark already and most of the foot traffic had changed from the professional to the younger bar crowd. "What time is it?"

"Nine."

"What? Really! I lost track of time trying to get through"—I picked up some loose sheets of paper—"some stuff. What's going on?"

"I wanted to know if you would be interested in grabbing a bite."

"I'd love to, but I really need to finish what I'm working on tonight." I scrolled through the e-mail that was up on my computer screen. "Thanks, though. How was your day?"

I heard a soft knock on my door and swiveled in my chair to see Ben standing there.

"Hey, I'm going to have to call you back. Okay?" I hung up the phone without waiting for his response. "Hi."

"How does your schedule look next week?" Ben asked.

I pulled up my calendar on my computer, though I already had it memorized. "I have a couple of meetings later in the week, but for the most part I scheduled desk time."

"Simon had another project come up, pulling him to Atlanta. I need you to come with me to Chicago in his place. Here are some background materials you can read through, and there are more documents in the file room. I'll give you more details on the flight there." He was mentally running through a list. "I'll forward the flight and hotel information to you so you can make your reservations. Sound good?"

"Sure. How long is the trip?"

"We leave Sunday night and come back Wednesday night."

"Okay."

"I'll see you at the airport on Sunday," Ben said over his shoulder as he walked away.

After he left, I stared at the twelve-inch stack of paper he left on my desk and knew there were more just like it in the file room. I always felt unnerved after my interactions with Ben. I didn't know whether this came from my competitive side, where I wanted to impress a senior consultant—and partner, for that matter—with my work, or if it was the attraction toward him that I was suppressing. He had a confidence that bordered on arrogance, but it was attractive because it was regarding his work. He was good at what he did, and he knew it. It didn't hurt either that he was good-looking. He had dark hair with flecks of gray and deep, chocolate brown eyes.

I picked up the phone and hit the speed dial. "I know I was rude."

"Not the first time I've encountered your kind," Josh said.

"And hopefully not the last."

"Are you calling me back to tell me that you will take me up on my offer?"

"I wish. I just got more work piled onto my desk ... literally." I was thumbing the edges of the papers now stacked in front of me.

"You do have to eat at some point."

"If I leave now I won't come back, and I'm too lazy to lug it home."

"I can pick something up and bring it there. We'll eat for thirty minutes and then you can get back to work."

"I can't really refuse an offer like that. Are you sure?"

"I'm not going to beg you to take me up on my offer."

"I get it. I'm grateful. Call me when you get here, and I'll meet you in the lobby."

Thirty minutes later, my e-mail buzzed with a text from Josh. "I'm pulling into the garage." I grabbed my keys and badge and headed down to the lobby.

"Hey." I opened the door to let him into the lobby and grabbed one of the drinks from everything he was carrying.

"Hey." Josh gave me a quick kiss on the cheek. "You look nice. I don't usually get to see you in ..." He was motioning to my clothes.

"They frown on wearing pajama bottoms or sweats to work, even after hours."

I swiped my badge so we could get back upstairs.

"We can either eat in a conference room or my office."

"It doesn't matter to me."

"I'm assuming you'll want my undivided attention, so let's use a conference room." I led Josh down the hall and flipped on the light. "So how was your date the other night?"

"It was fine as far as first dates go."

"Will there be a second date?"

"I doubt it."

"Why's that?"

"There was nothing there." He was pulling containers out of the to-go bags. "The conversation wasn't exactly flowing."

"How did you meet this one?" I reached for the plastic silverware he was holding out to me.

"Met her at the gym, spotted her for a set, got her number, and went out for dinner. You know, the usual."

"Oh, my gosh." I put my hand to my eyes. "It's so cliché, Josh." Then almost knowing there was no point, I added, "Well, maybe now you can be friends."

"I have enough estrogen-dominant friends in my life, and not to be rude, because I usually leave that for you, but I could not have another conversation with her. It would be torture." Josh looked pained.

I knew he hated saying one mean thing about another person. "So how did you leave it?" I took a bite out of the box with chicken and rice.

"I dropped her off and said I'd see her later."

"Will you guys never learn? Now she is probably out talking with her friends tonight saying what a great time you two had last night and checking her voice mail to find out when you will be seeing her again," I said with food in my mouth.

"You will never get tired of this lecture. I didn't say I would call her, so she has no reason to be checking her voice mail."

"What's that?" I pointed with my fork to a small box sitting in the middle of the food containers.

"I was wondering when you ..." Josh trailed off as the door creaked opened. Ben was standing there, propping the door open with his foot.

I almost dropped the food in my lap. "Oh, hi."

"Sorry to interrupt. I just thought the light was left on. I didn't realize anyone was in here," Ben said, looking at Josh.

"Ben, this is Josh Forrester. Josh, this is Ben Covney. He's a partner of the firm." Josh stood up to shake his hand.

"It's nice to meet you. Kate spends so much time up here that it's nice to put faces with the names of people she works with."

"We don't mean to take her away. I'll let you get back to your dinner." Ben half-smiled and backed out of the door. He hesitated.

"Kate, if you need to spend some time at home, I can try to find someone else to fill in next week."

"No, that's not necessary. I've already started prepping for the project, and I'm looking forward to it." *Please do not take this away from me. You haven't really gotten a chance to see my work yet.*

"All right then. Good night."

After Ben closed the door, Josh turned to face me. "Wow, he's …" He trailed off. "I'm sorry if I said something I shouldn't have. I was really trying to put a plug in for how hard you work." Josh looked worried.

I leaned across the table and put my hand on his arm. "Don't give it another thought. I can't read him, but I definitely do not get warm and fuzzy around him. I wish I could tell if he was a jerk or socially inept or something to make him seem a little more personable. Right now he pretty much makes me jump every time he walks into a room." *Or scream*, thinking back to my encounter with him in the hall the night before.

Josh began clearing off the boxes from the table, throwing them into the plastic bag. "I'll let you get back to it."

I got back to my office and texted Josh to thank him again for dinner. "You have got to be kidding me." The stack had tripled since I had been in the conference room. A Post-it note grabbed my attention. "Came across a few more documents—a branding survey, focus group notes—that weren't in the file room."

"A few?" I said to myself. I untucked my shirt, took off my heels, and curled my feet up underneath me in my chair. I picked up the first document and started reading.

Chapter 5

I woke up shivering. Buddy was curled up against me, but he wasn't providing enough body heat. I tugged at my blanket to pull it higher over me. With his body weight, I was unsuccessful, and he wasn't budging. Then it occurred to me why it was so cold—*Drew*. I quickly jumped out of bed and scurried to find my robe, usually reserved for winter. I grabbed a pillow off the couch and jacked the air conditioner fifteen degrees higher as I passed by. I threw Andy's bedroom door open without even knocking and hurled the pillow at the bed.

"What the hell?" Drew grumbled.

"Yeah, it apparently froze over last night."

"What's all the commotion? It's still the middle of the night." Andy peeked her head out from under her pillow.

"Drew had the AC turned down to fifty."

"Drew Petersen, this is not your apartment, remember." Andy was kicking at him under the blankets.

"Admit it. You slept like a baby. Never slept better," Drew replied, already falling back asleep.

"Yeah, I slept so well I got up before my alarm went off."

35

I stood at my door, debating whether to get back in bed or head into work early. Buddy had repositioned himself with his head sleeping on my pillow. "Make yourself comfy." I tugged his tail. He lifted his head, but let it fall back in the same place. With Buddy taking over the bed, I decided to shower and go into work early. When I arrived, the office was empty. I turned on all of the lights. The sun was just starting to shine in through my windows, lighting up the room. It was nice having the quiet in the morning and getting to wake up a little before the office went into full swing.

"You were here when I left, and it looks like you've been here for a while this morning." Simon surveyed the papers I had spread all over my office in various piles. "Did you even go home last night?"

"Yes, I went home. Glad to know my appearance looks refreshed."

"Well, if I didn't know better, I would think you were vying for a promotion."

"I couldn't fall back to sleep this morning, nothing more." I smiled, knowing there was probably some truth to his comment.

"I heard you got saddled with Chicago." Simon was perched on the corner of my office desk now.

"Yep, just trying to get through all of the background on it." I glanced at the stack that did not seem to be shrinking.

"I could send you my notes. They may be of some help."

I must be experiencing some other personality of Simon. "That would be really helpful. Thank you."

"We could go through them if you want."

Where was this new Simon coming from? Maybe he was taking my advice or trying to keep his competition close. He was definitely in my "frenemy" category. "Would you have time tomorrow? That will give me more time to get familiar with it."

"Sure, just stop by when you're ready." He backed out of my office and turned down the hall.

"Thanks, Simon." I found myself staring after him, thoroughly confused by his gesture.

I spent most of the morning reading, and by the afternoon my eyes had glazed over, so I took a break and walked down to the kitchen area. Some of the administrative staff were engaging in idle conversation about a partner, but I couldn't quite catch who they were talking about before they moved on to some celebrity gossip. I looked at my watch. It was almost five. I knew most of the office would be clearing out soon. I grabbed a bottle of water from the refrigerator and went back to my desk to read some more.

The next morning I felt pretty comfortable with everything I had gone through, so I took Simon up on his offer. We spent two hours in the small conference room. He was giving me background information, and I was asking him questions that I had marked in the pages I had read. "Simon, I really appreciate your doing this." I was gathering my laptop, notepad, and pen to return to my office.

"You're welcome. I knew it was a lot to get through in a few days. Glad I could help."

When I got back to my office, I settled in my chair and found myself thinking about the next week and the business trip with Ben. The phone rang. I moved to pick it up, knocking the phone off the receiver in the process. "Hello, hello," I quickly scrambled.

"Kate, this is Luke Harrison."

I couldn't stop the words from coming out of my mouth. "Are you kidding?" Our mothers had been trying to set us up for as long as I could remember. I had been hearing his name for the past five years.

He ignored my question, skipping straight to the point. "I hope you are doing well. I know this comes as late notice, but I was wondering if you would be available on Saturday night to attend a benefit at the Museum of Natural Science."

"It's Thursday." I found myself losing brain cells and stating the obvious.

"I understand if you are unavailable."

"I don't know what this says about me and my availability, but okay, I'll go. Will you be picking me up?"

"Yes, I'll be there at 7:30."

I gave him directions to my place, and just as I was ending the phone call, he added, "It's black tie by the way." *Of course it is.*

Andy and I had nicknamed Luke "Oakie" a while back. His friends and family lived in River Oaks, an affluent part of Houston. The houses were historic, and ever since I was little I loved driving down the streets. Somehow the flowers always seemed to be in bloom. He and his friends had the obligation of attending various events in Houston. After hanging up, I went online and scrolled through some dresses and shoes, thinking I could make my shopping more efficient when I went to find something.

On Friday I left work early for some retail therapy, and now I had an excuse with the benefit on Saturday night. The Galleria was packed with people avoiding the heat. The floor-to-ceiling windows were reflecting the sunlight, forcing me to keep my sunglasses on until I walked through the doors. As I entered the department store, I knew I wanted to find a dress but decided to take a slight detour through shoes. The right shoes could really narrow down the choices for a dress.

"Hi, Kate," Tina the saleswoman greeted me with a hug.

"Hi." I smiled, trying to hide the cringe I was feeling. *I'm not a hugger, much less with people I don't know that well.*

"Haven't seen you too much lately." Tina pulled back.

Obviously enough if you know me by name and hug me. "I've been swamped at work."

"We've gotten a lot of fine shoes in, so look around and let me know if you want to see something." She went back to her desk.

"Thanks, I will." She was great about letting me look without hounding me.

I found three different shoes to try on. "Can I see these?" I showed them to Tina.

"Absolutely, I'll be right back." She jumped out of her chair and headed back into the storage room.

She was back with four boxes in a few minutes. "The black ones run small, so I brought the nine just in case."

The first ones I tried on were black, strappy, three-and-a-half inch heels. I could always use another pair. The second pair was a nude pump that I could wear to go out and to work—the practical choice. The third shoe was a Christian Louboutin red satin peep-toe pump.

"I saw these online the other day. They're beautiful." *And I love them.* I paused a moment, admiring them in the mirror. "I'll get them."

"Great. I'll be right back." Tina hopped up from the cushy stool.

"Do you need my card?" I started to reach into my bag.

"No, I have your information," she said over her shoulder.

I ignored the sign about my over-shopping. I knew I would be wearing these Saturday night regardless of my dress.

When I got to the apartment, I walked into Andy and Drew's domestic bliss. Drew was flipping through a book, while Andy was leaning over his shoulder.

"Hey, guys." I threw my keys onto the table and walked toward them in the kitchen.

"Been shopping lately?" Drew asked sarcastically.

"No, I just like to take old shopping bags and put my clothes in them. It makes them feel all new again. Want anything to drink?" I asked, grabbing a bottle of water.

"I'll take some water." Drew held out his hand.

"There are some more bottles in the fridge," I said, closing the door.

"Children, it's Friday. Can we all just get along? I'm in a good mood. Play nice."

I threw him the bottle and grabbed another one out of the refrigerator.

"So, what's the occasion?" Drew motioned toward the bags.

"I was beginning to accrue some savings and wanted to put a stop to that." I unscrewed the cap to my water. "Sorry, I have pent-up sarcasm. I'm going to a benefit tomorrow night and picked up some shoes and a couple of dresses." I hopped out of the chair I just sat down in. "Speaking of which, I wanted to get your opinion," I said, turning to Andy.

"Let's see."

"I have to show you the shoes first because they set the stage." I was rummaging through the bags.

"Do you have a newspaper? I need to read some sports to counter the estrogen overflow." Drew was looking around the kitchen. I pointed behind him. "Kate, you, my friend, are a conundrum. I expect this from Andy, but you talk sports stats and then go all girly about shoes." He leaned back to grab the paper from the counter. "I think it's better to not even try to understand." He started flipping through the paper.

"Honey, I think that's for the best." Andy patted his knee and turned her attention to me.

"I gave into my weakness and bought these." I pulled the red Louboutin pumps from their box.

"They're amazing!" Andy took one from my hand. "It's so cruel that we don't wear the same size." She looked over at Drew and stuck out her lower lip. "Not that you ever take me anywhere worthy of my wearing them."

"Where do you want me to take you?" Drew asked.

"You two have this argument every weekend. We could just fast forward to you staying in, cooking, and watching a movie."

"Are we that predictable?" Andy flopped onto Drew's lap. He acted annoyed, but it was obvious he was happy. "Okay, show us the dresses."

"With the red shoes, I thought I should stay more reserved in the dress color with black or steel grey."

"Well, sure." Drew rolled his eyes.

I pulled out both dresses. The grey, almost silvery one was strapless with a slight sweetheart-shaped neckline, while the black dress had a *v* neckline with thicker shoulder straps. They both hit at the upper calf and were fitted through the waist.

"I like both—tough choice," Andy said, examining both.

"We have to choose one because I'm returning the other. I only have room for one dress and the shoes on my credit card. Drew, give me a guy's opinion."

He looked up from the paper. "I don't know. They're both fine."

"We are not looking for *fiiine*." I drew out the word for emphasis.

"I think you're going to have to try them on." Andy picked up the shoes to put them back in the box.

"I'll have to do it tomorrow because I have to get ready for Josh's office party right now." I grabbed the bags and headed toward my room.

"You are becoming the regular escort. Maybe it could help offset the cost of your shoes," Drew called after me. I could hear Andy swat at him.

An hour and forty-five minutes later, I was opening the door for Josh. "Wow, you look great." He jokingly eyed me.

I was wearing a black slim-fitting blazer with black pants. I was hoping the cut of the jacket in front was stylish yet tasteful, and not to be perceived as slutty. I had hidden a safety pin to provide extra support to the button and secured it with fashion tape. I did not want Josh's colleagues to get an eyeful of anything.

"Watch it," I teased.

"Are you ready to go?"

"Sure, but do you want to come in for a glass of wine before we go? We don't want to get there too early, do we?"

"No, but with that outfit I want to make sure to get there with plenty of time to show you off."

"Just one glass and then we'll go. By the way, if you keep that up, you're going to have time for more than one glass."

"No, no please. I take it back. Please don't change." He shook his head. "You're impossible. I compliment you, and you threaten to change. If I had not complimented you, then you probably would have threatened to change too."

"I have to keep you on your toes. So, anything special about tonight?" I asked.

"No, just the usual suits we are trying to impress and make a deal."

"And I'm going because …"

"Because, as usual, we do not want it to appear that we are only concerned with business."

"Are these the same guys from the game?"

"Nope, a different set."

"How do you keep them straight? Don't they all start to run together?"

"It's my job to make sure they don't."

"I guess I should have asked this before, but is it just cocktails or dinner or both?"

"All you think about is food."

"Why do you think I go to these things with you?"

Josh feigned pain to the chest. "I thought it was my company."

"Just an added plus." I linked my arm through his.

We spent a couple of hours at the cocktail party. Wait staff passed around heavy hors d'oeuvres—the perfect dinner because I got to sample different things in small amounts. If I didn't like it, then there wasn't much to stuff in Josh's pocket. We mingled with his colleagues and clients. I helped to keep the conversation casual. Josh had a signal for me to jump into the conversation and steer it away from business topics. I teased him that he was saving the money conversations for later in the evening, after more alcohol flowed and the clients were too drunk to say no.

I woke up with my head pounding *thump, thump, thump*. I tried to open my eyes. As soon as they flickered open, I had to shut them to shield out the sun that was streaming into the room. I tried again. With the swirling of the fan above me, it took a minute to focus.

I looked around. That was not my chair. I looked down. Those were not my sheets, and this was most definitely not my bed. *Oh, shit. Oh, shit.* I sat up quickly, and the pain shot through me. I was holding a sheet to my chest and pulled it back to see I was wearing only my bra and underwear. *Oh, shit.*

"I thought I heard some movement." Josh walked in carrying a cup of coffee and a glass of water. "Here." He handed me the ice-cold glass. He leaned against his dresser, sipping his coffee.

My mouth seemed to be glued shut, and I couldn't arrange the words to articulate the questions now forming in my mind.

I couldn't help but notice his lack of clothing as well—pajama bottoms, no shirt.

"So, how are you feeling?"

"Groggy." I set down the glass and began to rub my eyes with the heels of my hands. "What happened?"

"I think the shots did you in." He was grinning. He was obviously enjoying this a little.

"Shots?" It was starting to come back to me. Josh and I had gone to a bar with some of his colleagues after the party. One of his coworkers ordered rounds for the group. They just kept coming. "I will never be able to smell tequila again." I gulped down the water. "Limes and salt may be out too."

"You were a champ last night. I don't think I've ever seen you drink that much."

I scooted up toward the top of the bed in order to lean against the wall. "So, um, what happened after the bar? I mean, did we … ?" I leaned my head back and stared at the ceiling.

He shook his head. "No, I took the couch."

"But how did I … ?" I cleared my throat. "What happened to my clothes?"

"That was all you." Josh raised his hands. "You were hot, so you said." He chuckled.

"Oh, no." I buried my head in my hands. Flashes were coming back to me—stripping off my top, then my pants. I seem to recall a shoe flying across the room. "Did I take off my clothes in front of you? And I get how ridiculous that question is, given that you have seen it all before. But, I must have looked absurd."

"Well, taking your pants off while your shoes were still on was impressive. I was the total gentleman, though. I covered my eyes and only looked quickly just to make sure you were standing upright."

"You let me take your bed."

"I don't know if *let* would be the right word. You stumbled in here, and by the time I came in you were passed out. Dead weight. There was no moving you. You also chose to pass out at a diagonal so I couldn't even take the other half of the bed."

"I passed out and stole your bed." I could feel my face flushing.

He smiled. "Don't worry about it." He tossed me an old T-shirt.

I wriggled into it, trying to keep the sheet tucked around me.

Later that afternoon, Andy and I met Beth for some boutique shopping. Andy knew Drew was hanging out with Jason, Beth's boyfriend, so she asked her to join us. Andy wanted to look for dresses that she might be able to wear to wedding showers or parties. She had complained that she didn't have anything cute enough to wear to Drew's law firm cocktail parties or to her upcoming bridal showers, now that she was a fiancée. I was just shopping in general, not needing an excuse to look for new clothes.

When we parked, we could see Beth in the store, milling around toward the front. "No offense, but you smell like alcohol." Andy said as she beeped the alarm on her car.

"I know. I can still taste it too. I showered and washed my hair twice. I brushed my teeth three times."

Beth saw us enter the store and waved us over to where she was standing. After greeting us, she went back to sifting through the rack of clothes in front of her.

"So what were Drew and Jason doing today?" I was looking through some dresses and holding them up for Andy to look at. She was either nodding or wrinkling her nose to indicate her approval or disapproval. Left on her own, I knew she would only pick out very conservative dresses to try on, so I was pulling clothes that were outside of her normal look to make her try. I had informed her of my plan, offering the point that she would be trying stuff on already as my rationale.

"I think they were going to meet up with Josh and some other guys to play basketball at the gym." Beth was handing some clothes to the salesperson to take back to the changing room. She turned back toward me and asked, "I know you probably hate people asking you this, but I have been dying to know why you and Josh aren't dating. What's the deal?" Beth looked a bit sheepish.

"We're friends," I replied.

She tried again. "No, I want the full story. All I get from Jason is that you two used to date."

Andy smiled. I was sure she was thinking about the conversation we had the other night, where I was lamenting everyone sticking their nose into our relationship. I hurriedly went through our history. As I did, Beth moved closer to where we were standing.

"We were friends in college. If I wasn't dating anyone and I had a sorority mixer, I'd take him. And if he wasn't dating anyone and he had a fraternity mixer, he's take me. That's it, though. We were just friends. And then about six months after we graduated, he looked at me funny and I looked at him funny and we kissed." I knew my response was grossly oversimplifying our history.

"And ... ?" Andy interjected. She knew the whole story and was not going to let me off that easily.

A look of guilt crossed my face. "Okay, and we slept together. But we figured we were friends of the opposite sex, drunk, and attracted to one another—no harm no foul. And then nothing, we went back to being friends. Then a couple months later, we kissed, just kissed. And that kept happening. So Josh asked me out and we began dating."

"They began calling what they were doing actually dating, but they were dating long before that," Andy clarified.

"So we were together for a few years, and now we're not." I waved it off.

"That's it?" Beth was wide-eyed, looking for more of an explanation than I was going to give.

"That's all she'll say," Andy replied for me.

"I guess that explains why you are always accompanying him to his work events." Beth was looking at a top and holding it up to herself in front of a mirror.

"What do you mean?" I looked at her.

"It's been part of your history. From what you were saying, you basically started that in college, and that was almost ten years ago."

"I guess that's true."

"With that amount of time, that's a hard habit to break," she teased.

I went back to looking through the racks of clothes. "Andy, what exactly are you looking for?"

"I don't know really. I think a couple of dresses. I just feel like my wardrobe has gotten so monochromatic lately. I am either wearing black or grey or khaki. There is nothing cute in it for when I go out or for an upcoming shower or when I go with Drew to his firm's cocktail parties. Not that I'm looking for pink, even if it is black. Maybe a dress with pockets."

We were able to get Andy into a dressing room to try on about twenty dresses, skirts, and tops. I tried on a few things but was more focused on Andy. We walked out of the store, Andy with two dresses, Beth with a top, and me empty-handed. That didn't happen too often, but I was thinking about my shopping excursion the day before, and knew I already had to return one of the dresses.

Chapter 6

I looked at the clock. It was 7:15. I still had my eye makeup left to go and then to slip into my dress. Earlier, Andy and I decided the strapless dress would be the perfect accessory to the red heels. And with that decision, a smoky effect was now required for my eyes.

At 7:30 there was no sign of Oakie and no call. I poured a glass of wine and sat at the kitchen table. Buddy was looking at me quizzically. "I hate waiting," I sighed. "I'm not patient." Buddy turned his head.

At 7:50 the buzzer went off to my apartment.

"It's Luke."

I buzzed him in. *Be nice, be nice,* I repeated to myself.

Luke knocked at the door a few seconds later.

Buddy started to growl at him from behind me. I was trying to stand between him and Luke, blocking the opening in the door.

Luke looked visibly nervous. *He's harmless, but you're late so you can sweat it.* "Are you ready?"

"I am." *I was ready twenty minutes ago when you said you would be here.* I grabbed my clutch, wrap, and keys, knelt down to say good-bye to Buddy, and then walked through the doorway. As I fumbled to lock the door, Luke stood there. *Don't offer to hold anything.*

"We're meeting some friends of mine for drinks first," Oakie said once we were in the car.

"Sounds good." He drove out of the parking lot and turned in the direction of downtown. I noticed he had golf clubs thrown in the back of his car.

"How was your day?" I asked, trying to fill the silence.

"Good. I played in a charity golf event. It ran long." He motioned to the clubs.

"How did you play?"

"Mostly bogey golf with a few pars here and there."

"I try to play when I get a chance. I had gotten my handicap down, but since I haven't been playing as frequently, it's started to creep back up."

"How long have you been playing?"

"Oh, I guess I started in high-school. I seemed to have a lot of time on my hands, or the days were just longer. My friends and I would go out to the driving range and hit balls."

"Do you play from the girls' tee?"

"You mean the front tees? I used to, but I've been playing back. I find that it usually helps when I am playing with men from my firm or clients' firms that they see I can hold my own."

I could feel the clamminess in my hands as we walked down the hall to his friend's place. It sometimes seemed ironic that I had chosen a job where I constantly met new people. I knew the anticipation was always the worst part. After the first conversation my nerves usually calmed. Tonight, I tried to discreetly use my wrap to wipe the dampness from my palms before I had to shake anyone's hand.

Luke knocked on the door and his friend Chase answered. "Hey, welcome." He quickly pumped Luke's hand and then shook mine. "You must be Kate. I'm Chase Michaels. I'm so glad you could make it. You look beautiful." His energy was immediately apparent. The room was full of people who were talking and laughing loudly. I suspected that Chase had set the mood.

"Thank you."

"Let me introduce you to everyone." He stuck out his arm for me to take and led me into the rest of the loft. Luke followed behind us.

"How do you and Luke know each other?" Chase asked.

"We don't, really. Our mothers play on the same tennis team, and we've run into each other a couple times at the club," I replied.

"Do you want something to drink? We have wine, red and white. And just about any kind of liquor you could think of."

"I would love a glass of chardonnay," I replied.

"No problem. Luke?"

"Jack and coke."

"Make yourself comfortable, and I'll be right back with your drinks. I apologize in advance for my hosting. My wife's flight was canceled this morning due to weather. She's visiting some friends in New York, and a later flight wouldn't get her here in time. So she's making a weekend of it, and I'm on my own."

"You're doing great," I assured him.

"He's really nice," I said to Luke once Chase had left us.

Luke pulled me off to the side. "I know this may be a little awkward, but would you mind just saying we know each other through friends of friends? Meeting through our mothers sounds a little adolescent, don't you think?"

"Actually, I think lying about how we know or don't know each other is adolescent." I could tell my blunt response surprised him. "You are thirty. Please tell me that your friends are not going to tease you because of how you meet someone." I could hear a voice inside telling me I should lay off a little.

"They're going to give me a hard time for having to get my mother to set me up with a date." I could see a genuine plea in his eyes.

And what about me? I'm here too. I took a deep breath. "Okay." This night was off to a rocky start, so what would being vague matter?

We rejoined the group, standing next to each other. Chase brought back our drinks. Luke was talking to some others but had not introduced me. Chase tapped my arm. "Have you had a chance to check out the place? We just moved in last month."

"It's beautiful. I love the kitchen—the dark wood cabinets, stainless appliances, and granite countertops. The built-in wine refrigerator in the island is a nice touch."

"That's my favorite. I hope you don't mind, but I'll probably be your third wheel tonight."

"No, not at all."

After thirty minutes of small talk, Chase caught everyone's attention. "Let's head out." He was shepherding everyone toward the door.

I was reaching for my wrap. "Here, let me." Chase took my wrap and draped it across my shoulders. Luke was completely oblivious to the gesture.

"Do you know how to get to the Museum of Natural Science?" Luke asked once we were back in his car.

"I know how to get to the museum district, but I'm not sure which one is the Natural Science. Can we follow someone?"

"They were parked on the other side of the building. I don't think we can catch them."

"Can we call someone?"

"We'll drive in the direction of the district, and if we can't find it, we'll call someone."

After a few wrong turns we arrived at the museum. A valet was waiting to open my door and help me out of the car, where a red carpet lined the steps to the museum. Even though it was misting, the walkway had been covered, preventing the arriving guests in black-tie attire from having to carry umbrellas or run in heels. The cocktail hour was still going strong when we entered, and people were mingling among the dinosaur bones.

"Let's make our way to the bar. What would you like to drink?" Oakie asked.

"A chardonnay."

"Hey, Mike." He grabbed some guy's shoulder to get his attention.

"Hey." They shook hands. He turned to me, waiting a bit awkwardly.

"I'm Kate." I extended my hand.

"Mike, and this is my wife, Sarah." He motioned to the woman standing to his right. She had been eyeing one of the dinosaurs nearby, but turned upon hearing her name. She smiled and took my hand for more of a squeeze than a shake.

"Nice to meet you both." I smiled.

"I was just on my way to the bar to get a couple of drinks."

"I'll go with you," Mike chimed in.

"I love your shoes." Sarah moved closer as they moved away. "I think I saw them in *InStyle*." She smiled.

"I am a bit of a shoe-aholic." I was twisting my ankle.

"Me, too, but I try to hide it from Mike."

Mike and Oakie returned with our drinks. "Should we try to find our table?" Mike asked. "I think it's downstairs."

We made our way single file through the crowd, down the stairs, and into a private room, where five large tables had been set up. This was only one area in the museum set up for the benefit. Small groups of tables were set up throughout the rest of the museum for dinner as well. We were the closest set of tables to the dance floor. Nearby, a few members of the band were playing background music.

Oakie held out my chair for me. He then took the seat next to me. "I probably should have asked before we sat down, but are you okay with your drink?"

"I am. Thank you." Then we both sat in silence for a moment. "So this is a bit of a weird first date for me. I feel like I know you because I have been hearing about you, but at the same time I don't know much about you."

"I know what you mean."

"So what do you do?"

"I dabble in commercial real estate. I just got into it actually fairly recently."

"Are you enjoying it?" I angled my chair so that I was more directly facing him.

"I am. It's the first time that I have really been interested in what I am doing. Before this, I was working at my father's company, but mixing family and business was not working for us."

"And now?"

"And now, I am enjoying work." He laughed a little before continuing. "Honestly, I feel like I can relax in the presence of my father again. And what about you? What is it that you do? I think the last I heard you were finishing a graduate degree." He raised his glass to take a drink.

As we were talking the rest of our table started filling with people— mostly people from Chase's place, Mike and Sarah, and then a couple I had not met.

"Well, I finished business school and started working at a marketing consulting firm a couple of years ago."

"If you'll excuse me for a minute." Oakie pushed his seat back from the table.

"Sure." I was a little startled by his abrupt departure.

"Have you been introduced to everyone at the table?" Chase took the seat to the other side of me. "Do you mind if I throw your wrap over the chair?" He pointed to the one to his other side. "I don't want people to think it's empty."

I chuckled. "Sure." I handed it to him. He took it and draped it over the back of the chair. "I think I've met everyone, with the exception of the couple directly across from us." I tried to be discreet so they would not overhear.

He nodded. "I will introduce you when there is a break in the conversation."

Oakie returned, only to excuse himself a few minutes later. He had been to the restroom three times in the fifteen minutes since we sat down.

When he returned the last time, he leaned in and quietly said in my ear, "My stomach is bothering me."

"I'm sorry." Then I tried to make it light. "You know, it's okay if you're having a bad time. Just say so."

"Actually, I'm having a blast, but can you excuse me again?" With that he got up to go to the bathroom yet again.

I turned to Chase. "I believe he isn't feeling well, but then again, maybe it's the company." I gave a wry smile.

"I can say with certainty that is not the case." Chase squeezed my shoulder.

It was sometimes odd to me that there were people whom I had never met and would probably never see again but could like and feel comfortable with so quickly. Chase was one of those people. "Thanks." I smiled.

Oakie returned to the table but did not sit. He leaned down to talk to me.

"Are you okay?" I looked up at him.

He grimaced, not really responding.

"It is all right if you need to leave."

"Are you sure? I'm sorry, but I just don't feel well." He genuinely looked pale. "You could stay if you're having a good time."

Your friends are nice enough, I am dressed up, and I would like to dance later. "Are you sure?" I asked. *Would it be rude?*

Chase and Oakie were talking quietly while the rest of the table had turned their attention to us. "I'm not sure he can drive himself home," Chase said to me.

I looked over at Oakie, who was turning paler by the second. "Of course I'll drive him home."

We made our excuses to the rest of the table and quickly weaved our way through the exhibits in the museum. We rushed down the stairs outside, and Oakie handed me the ticket with some money. I took it from him and walked a little ahead of him to get to the valet. "If you could hurry, I would really appreciate it," I said, handing him the ticket.

I felt like I was hitting every bump in the road on the drive to his house. I glanced over toward him. "I'm sorry."

"It's okay." He was hunched over and looked pained even in responding to me.

We arrived at his house in about ten minutes. "I'll call you tomorrow." He hopped out of the car.

"You have to. I have your car."

"I would have anyways." And with that, he shut the door and ducked through the garage to enter his house.

Buddy jumped down from the bed and sniffed under the door. He whimpered when Andy lightly rapped on the door. "Is Oakie still here?" Andy whispered as she cracked the door open.

I was lying in bed skimming the latest *People* magazine. "What?" I responded in a normal volume.

"I saw his car was still here when I got back from the gym. So where is he?" she said a little louder.

"At home I assume. I drove myself home in his car last night." I closed the magazine. "I bought a new dress and pair of shoes to be at the benefit for a total of thirty minutes. Not that I'm complaining about the shoes—at least I can wear those again. But I would like to have spent a little more time in the dress."

"What happened?"

"You can stop whispering. Nothing happened. He got sick and we had to leave."

"Well, that sucks. Have you heard from him this morning?"

"Nope, not yet." Buddy had rolled over so I could pet his stomach, and I obliged.

"I did meet a guy though."

"Really?" Andy plopped onto the bed, pulling her legs underneath her. "At least it wasn't a total waste then."

"Not like that. He was just someone I clicked with as a friend." Andy was eyeing me suspiciously. "Stop it. He's married. I'll probably never see him again, but he would completely mesh well with our group of friends. He was just a nice, likeable guy, and it felt like we were picking up a conversation where we just left off, rather than meeting for the first time."

"You're hopeless."

I was getting ready to leave for the airport. The clock read 5:30. No call from Luke. "How do you get the no call when you have the guy's car?" I muttered to myself. You would think that would pretty much guarantee a phone call the next day. I grabbed my bag and dragged it into the living room.

"I left a message on his cell phone saying if he wanted his car that I left his keys with you," I said to Andy. "I gave him your cell phone number as a backup to our number. Let me know if he calls you." I paused. "Do you think I was a horrible date?"

"Well, you haven't had much practice, and you can be on the direct side," she mused. "All that time your mothers have been trying to set you up, and he turns out to be a complete loser." She shook her head.

"I'm sure his mother does not think so."

"Have you told your mom what happened yet?"

"No, I wanted to see if he called today before I told her I would never let her set me up with anyone ever again. I need to have all of the

55

ammunition I can possibly have, painting the worst possible picture so she will not be tempted to set me up, for a while at least." I smiled.

"I should think this will do it."

"I left his keys on top of my dresser. If he comes here, make sure you are between him and Buddy. He didn't like Oakie, which should have told me something." Buddy had curled up on the couch next to Andy.

"He does seem to be a better judge than you."

"Have a good night. I'll be back Wednesday."

"Have a good trip. Tell the pilot to fly safe."

By the time I got to the hotel in Chicago it was 10:00. I had a message waiting from Ben telling me to meet him in the lobby at 6:30 the next morning. I checked my cell phone. No messages. *Seriously. I didn't want to go out with him again, but no follow-up call about his car or even to apologize. Seriously.*

Chapter 7

At nine o'clock we took a break from our meeting. We had already been in their offices for two hours that morning. Everyone in the room had dispersed, some to get coffee, some to go back to their offices. I was tired and envious of the coffee drinkers. I was in desperate need of an energy buzz and had been cold all morning. I grabbed my cell phone from my bag to step out and check messages. I had three missed calls. I dialed my number. The first two were from the office with questions, and the last was from Andy.

"Hey, it's me. I hope you're having a good day. I knew you would be curious, so I thought I would call and let you know that I have not heard from Oakie. When I left, his car was still parked in our garage. I'll let you know if anything changes. Can I just say what a jerk? Unless he is sick to the point of being in the hospital, then I am a horrible person." I smiled at Andy's waffling over the possibility of a worthy excuse.

Ben was walking toward me. I quickly snapped my phone shut.

"I think it's going well in there." He gestured back toward the conference room, and in doing so accidentally grazed my arm, sending a shock of electricity and causing me to jump. "I want you to lead them through the next part of the proposal. Do you feel comfortable doing that?"

"Sure." *Not really, given my familiarity with the project only goes back as far as Wednesday.*

Sensing my hesitancy, he added, "And don't worry. I'll jump in if I think there is anything that needs to be added."

"If everyone could please turn to page twenty-two in their binder, we can get started." There was a flipping of pages around the room. "I know the goal is for a culture of high customer service, and you want that yesterday. But the first step to making that happen is to define what it means in your organization. I know this may seem common sense or obvious, but we need to put your own company definition to what customer service is. I've put together a high-level description of the plan for how to define it—talking to customers, employees, and stakeholders. On the next page, you will see some examples of responses from employees at various organizations when asked what it means to them. And you can see just how different it can be depending on what company you are talking about. For example, at a hospital, the customers, specifically patients, want accurate and reliable service, whereas at a fast-food restaurant, customers want efficient and quick service."

During the cab ride back, Ben and I were pretty quiet, making idle comments here or there about the meeting. I kept replaying the presentation I made and one of the questions that I had from the client. It was such a crucial piece of background that I didn't have. Ben had jumped in to save me. I couldn't imagine that it escaped his attention. I was mentally flipping through all of the information I had read and then I thought about Simon's help. I couldn't blame Simon, but I was sure it was not an unintentional oversight.

The cab pulled up to the hotel, and I could feel my phone vibrating in the pocket of my jacket.

I debated for a split second. "Mom, I'm just getting back to the hotel. Can I call you back in a few minutes?" I spoke in a hushed voice, trying to avoid my pet peeve.

"Are you going to call back? You often forget sweetie."

"I promise. Less than ten minutes." I snapped shut the phone.

"We're done for the day. You could have taken the call," Ben said as he was pulling cash out of his wallet. "I'll need a receipt, please."

"It could have been a very lengthy call, and I didn't want to subject you and Chicago to my conversation." I still needed to tell my mother about the horrible date she set me up with, and I couldn't bear to have that discussion in front of Ben.

"Right. Then I appreciate that." He smiled at me.

I couldn't help but feel a slight flip in my stomach, and I hoped my cheeks were not flushing.

We both walked into the revolving door at the same time, getting stuck in the same partition. I could feel his breath on my neck. What must have been no more than five seconds felt like minutes. I tried to be graceful when it abruptly forced me forward and into the lobby.

"Is there anything that we need to discuss before tomorrow?" I glanced toward Ben as we moved across the lobby to the elevator.

"I would like to run through a few things, but I need a break from this. Why don't we meet in the lobby"—he checked his watch—"around eight? I think we will only need thirty minutes or so. If you need to get a hold of me before then, call my room."

He stopped and turned back. "Actually, I want to check at the front desk for any messages."

"I'll see you in a bit then." I shifted my bag and the papers I was carrying to my other arm and hit the elevator button.

The next day passed quickly, and Ben and I got back to the hotel about 6:30. We made small talk through the lobby and in the elevator. Just as the door was opening to my floor, he asked, "Do you want to meet for dinner?"

I nodded my head. "I've really been craving some pizza being in Chicago and all."

"That's fine. I want to look through e-mail and change. Why don't we meet down in the lobby in an hour?" He was punching numbers into his phone.

"Okay, see you then." I smiled as I got off the elevator on my floor.

I was in the lobby before Ben. I hated being the first to arrive, but within a minute the elevator opened and he got off. Seeing him in jeans and a pullover sweater was different. He was definitely sexy. But it wasn't just his clothes—he had a different vibe to him. He seemed relaxed.

"You ready?" he asked, running his hand through his hair.

I felt like I was staring, but his whole demeanor had changed. "Yeah, let's go."

"I looked online and found a great little pizza place. I called down to the front desk and they said it was more of a hole in the wall but really good. I thought we could go there."

"That sounds good." I was pleased he had taken the time to look for a place while we had gone to our rooms.

One of the bellmen hailed a cab for us. I was shifting my feet back and forth trying to stay warm in the chilled air while we waited. It was unseasonably chilly, and I had not packed appropriately. My light sweater was doing nothing to warm me. A cab pulled up to the curb. Ben waited for me to get inside.

"Thanks." He handed a bill to the bellman.

"Have a good evening, sir." He tipped his hat.

"Did you remember to call your mother back?" Ben turned his attention to me.

I couldn't tell if he was mocking me or genuinely interested. "Yes, I did."

"I gather you are close to your family?"

"Yes, we are. What about you?"

"Not really. My folks live out in Arizona. I see them usually once a year, at Christmas or Thanksgiving."

"My mom would never let that happen. And, I have to admit, I would miss not talking or seeing them frequently."

"Do they live in Houston?"

"They used to live in the city but have joined the masses in moving out to suburbia." I was watching the buildings pass by. "I probably see them twice a month, sometimes more depending on what's going on."

"What about any sisters or brothers?"

"I have a younger sister. She just graduated from college. What about you?"

"An only child."

"Somehow that doesn't surprise me."

"Why not?"

"It seems like you are used to being the center of attention." The words came out before I completely thought them through. "I'm so sorry. I didn't mean for that to sound like it did. I just meant that you seem to thrive on having clients, even our office, focused on what you are saying." I realized I was not making it sound any better. "You seem very at ease in those situations. I find myself wishing sometimes I felt that way."

"Somehow you have managed to turn an unpleasant remark into a compliment." Ben chuckled. "I don't think you give yourself credit. When you want it, people's focus goes to you."

The restaurant was a hole in the wall just as Ben described. I never would have noticed it were we not looking for it. The atmosphere was very casual. The tables had red-and-white checkered table cloths. A murmuring of voices deep in conversation held in the air with the smell of dough and cheese. We were led to a booth, where the waitress handed us menus. "Can I get you anything to drink?"

"I'll take whatever light beer you have on tap," Ben replied.

She looked at me. "The same."

"Oh, and two waters please," Ben added.

"Sure thing." She turned on her heel and headed toward the bar. She was back in a matter of minutes. "You two ready to order?"

Ben looked at me. "I think we'll need a few more minutes." She smiled at him and nodded. "What looks good to you?" He looked up from his menu at me.

"I'm torn between the toppings of sun-dried tomatoes with chicken and meat lovers'."

"Both of those sound good to me. We could get a large with half and half."

The waitress returned with our waters. I took the lemon out of mine and set it on the napkin. Ben picked it up. "Not a fan?" I shook my head, and he squeezed the lemon into his water, shielding it with his hand.

"Are you married?" I asked, a little surprised by my own directness. *Andy was right. I can be too direct.*

He choked a little on the beer he had just taken a drink of. "No, I'm divorced. Why do you ask?"

I don't think I had ever seen him lose his poise. "My roommate was telling me I can be too blunt. Just tell me to mind my own business."

"You're fine."

"I was just curious. I'd heard some rumors around the office and thought I would just ask."

"Rumors? What are the rumors?" He looked at me curiously.

"There just seems to be some confusion as to whether or not you are still married, if you left your wife or if she left you, why you left, if you are divorced, how long has it been—that sort of thing."

He gave a short laugh. "Oh, just the small details. So what are some of the guesses?"

"I don't know. I try not to listen to the office chatter." I looked down, playing with my glass.

"No, no, I don't think so." He was smiling. "You started this. Tell me."

The waitress briefly interrupted our conversation as she placed the pizza on a stand in front of us. Ben waited to take a piece until I had served myself.

"Well ..." Ben wasn't dropping the topic.

I could feel my cheeks flushing for the second time today. *Why did I open my mouth?* "The general consensus is that you are divorced. But there seems to be confusion as to when exactly. Most people agree within the past year. And the reasons why are all over the place." I hoped to leave it at that.

"Lay it on me."

I hesitated trying to think of how to best respond. I started tentatively, "I think most of them are the standard reasons you would expect for a divorce. Someone cheated. I believe *workaholic* was mentioned."

"And which reason are you buying into?" Ben's expression turned more serious as he stared at his beer. His concentration seemed fixed on whether he was going to finish it.

"My guess is that there is a little truth to all of it, but a lot of inaccuracy in the details and context of how it all played out," I said slowly. "Look, I'm sorry for bringing this up. It is none of my business. I was truly curious, but that is no reason for me to have asked."

"You're right." The waitress stopped by the table and Ben ordered another drink, looking at me to see if I needed another. I shook my head, trying to determine if he was upset. "There is a little truth to all the rumors. I'm not sure whether I was working long hours to avoid going home or whether I was just trying to get ahead at work. It was before I was a partner, and you have to put in long hours to get noticed. I was doing just that, and it was straining the marriage. I probably took the easy way out and spent more and more time at the office. And we just became distant to each other. And that led to some of the other things that people have speculated about."

I was taken back by his honesty.

"I'm not sure why I just told you that, except you are probably the first person to ask me directly. Enough of that. My turn to pry." His tone turned lighter. "Tell me about the guy I saw you eating with in the conference room."

"Josh?" He nodded. "He is one of my best friends. "He and Andy, my roommate, are very good about checking in on me. They know how late I've been staying at the office. They just want to make sure I don't forget what they look like, and vice versa."

"A guy roommate. A guy best friend. I bet it is tough to date you." Ben tilted his head back to finish the rest of his beer.

"It may be tough to date me, but not for those reasons. *Andy* is short for *Andrea*."

"How long have you two been roommates?"

We had finished eating our pizza, but I was still picking at the cheese from one of the pieces left.

"We roomed together our first semester in college, both majored in marketing, and have lived together even since. It is going to be a shock when she moves out. I have become very accustomed to seeing her at the end of the day, talking about what's going on, talking about work, talking about nothing in particular ..."

"Why is she moving out?"

"She's getting married in June, so shortly before or after she will move out. It will just mean we have to make more of an effort to stay up-to-date on each other's lives." I let my last sentence hang for a minute. "Enough of that. What about you? Have a house? An apartment? Live alone or with a roommate?"

"I live in an apartment inside the Loop. At my age, I don't think I could have a roommate."

"At your age. How old are you?"

"I'm forty-one. And you?"

"Don't you know never to ask a woman about her age?"

"I thought it only applied to women over thirty. And you aren't—I'm pretty safe here."

"Fair enough. Twenty-eight." I could feel myself wanting to flirt with Ben, but not in a just-to-pass-the-time kind of way. I wasn't ready to go back to the hotel, but I couldn't think of a way to lengthen the night any longer. So when the waitress returned with the receipt, Ben stood to leave and I followed.

"Ladies first." Ben held the door open for me.

"I was told to respect my elders." I smiled innocently.

"I'll be the bigger person and let that one go." He walked ahead and slid across the back seat of the cab.

"That must come with age."

He looked over at me with a bemused expression. "Kate, you surprised me tonight."

When I got back to my room, I checked my cell phone for messages. Andy had called at 9:15. "Hey, I just wanted to let you know that Oakie stopped by to pick up his car tonight. He called earlier this evening to see if it would be all right if he came by to get it. He didn't come in. Just said hello, I handed him his keys, and he said thanks. Can you believe that was the entire interaction? I thought about asking if he was feeling better, but didn't want him to think that we had even given him the importance of having a detailed conversation about him. Let me know if he called you. I'm completely curious. Talk to you later."

Andy was my only message. I couldn't believe Oakie didn't call. Even though I didn't want to go out with him again, my pride was stinging.

Chapter 8

"So how was Chicago?" Simon was hovering at the entrance to my office.

I looked up from my computer screen. "I think it went well. I'm in the middle of some things right now, but when I have a few minutes, I'll fill you in." I sat back in my chair and wiped my nose for what felt like the hundredth time that day. My cold had come on fast. We had flown in from Chicago that morning. We were ahead of schedule in our meetings, so we caught an earlier flight. When we departed I was fine, but by the time we landed my nose was running and my ears were hurting from the pressure that had yet to release. I was drinking a lot of water, hoping that the swallowing would help them finally pop. I had resorted to using my finger to try to shake the pressure out, but that didn't help either. Ben and I had taken separate cars to the airport, and I could tell he was somewhat relieved not to share the same confined air with me on the thirty-minute drive from the airport to the office.

"Don't worry about it. I'll talk to Ben." Simon's voice interrupted my thoughts. He began to turn and leave.

"Actually, Ben asked me to catch you up."

Simon stopped short. He shifted his glasses on his face. "Okay, let me know when you have a few minutes, then."

"Will do, and by the way, thanks again for your help last week." I squelched the sarcasm so that the tone he heard was sincere.

"No problem." He was already walking away as he called out over his shoulder.

I sneezed three times in a row and blew into a tissue, which, after picking up the box, I realized was the last one. I chucked the box and the tissue at the trash can. It rimmed the edge and then fell out.

"I'd pick that up, but I'm not sure I want to come within five feet of it. What are you doing here?" Ben was standing at the threshold of the door.

"You might want to stay back." I held my hand up. "This is an infected environment."

"Again, what are you doing here?"

"I think it's called busting my ass for a promotion, which means putting in the time for billable hours." My voice sounded weird since I couldn't breathe through my nose, and the sarcasm wasn't fitting. I had the unattractive necessity of keeping my mouth open just to get some air.

"I hope it wasn't something you picked up in Chicago. Then I might be getting it too."

"Thanks for the sympathy." I pulled out a new box of Kleenex, pulling the plastic off the box and taking the first one out to wipe my nose, which was running again.

"You know, you could go home and get better and then work more next week."

"There aren't enough hours in the day for that. I appreciate the concern, but I'll be fine."

"Clearly not the type to like being doted on when you're sick."

"No, I am. But not when I'm in a suit at the office. I prefer it when I'm in pajamas at home in bed and from my mom."

"There you go bursting my bubble. I was hoping you might say from me."

My head was swimming, and I wasn't sure if Ben was flirting with me or if his grin was masking his humor over the mess I was.

Ben disappeared and left me in my fog, which must have lasted for a couple of hours. The next thing I knew a guy delivering food was tapping on my door, "Kate Hayden."

"Yes." I looked up from some materials I had been reviewing from graphics.

"I have your order." He set a bag down on my desk.

"I didn't order anything."

He looked at the order slip again. "I have your name here. It's an order for chicken noodle soup. It's already been paid for. I just need your signature, indicating you received it."

I picked up the pen he handed me and signed the receipt. "Thank you." As he handed me the receipt, I noticed a card was attached. It read, "It may not be as good as your mom's cooking or being in pajamas, but it is one thing that makes me feel better when I am sick." I felt my cheeks color. I attributed my reaction to Ben's gesture rather than my cold.

I went home and fell asleep at six o'clock. I didn't wake up until the next morning at six and felt like a new person.

"You looked like death yesterday. How is it you're already better?" Andy was standing in the kitchen, tapping the granite countertop while waiting for the coffee to brew.

"It's amazing what twelve hours of sleep can do to heal a body." I poured some orange juice in a glass and took some vitamin C pills. "Just to ward off any lingering germs," I said as I popped them into my mouth.

"Are you going into work today?" She turned around, leaning her back against the counter.

"It must have been a twenty-four-hour thing. I feel fine. There's no reason not to." I finished the last of my juice and rinsed the remnants out before setting it in the dishwasher. "See you later tonight. Have a good day."

"See ya." Andy went back to watching the coffee.

"You know, a watched pot ..."

"I know, I know." She waved her hand at me. "It's the only thing I can do, though, until I have my coffee and wake up."

I buzzed around the office with my energy level back to normal, and toward the end of the day, I began my business development phone calls. I dreaded making calls when I knew they were unwanted by the receiver. I plugged away with each one though, spending only a few minutes with the person to check in and remind the company I was ready and waiting if they wanted to make a move. After my fourth call, I hung up the phone and jumped up from my chair, not quite certain what to do. I was so excited I had to tell someone. I picked up the phone to call Andy and changed my mind. I knew Ben would still be in the office, so I took off down the hall in the direction of his office. I slowed my steps as I got nearer. The light was still on, shining into the hall. The rest of the office was pretty dark. With my calls to the West Coast, I knew it had kept me longer than most of the others.

"Hey." I knocked softly on his door.

Ben turned around from his computer. He was just about to say something, but I hurried on. "I got it! I landed my first client!"

"That's great!" He stood up, and we had the awkward moment of wondering what to do next.

I stepped forward, fighting off any hesitation, and hugged him. It seemed to last an extra moment; I took in the way he smelled—his cologne, shampoo.

I pulled my head back, not letting go, and looked up at him. Then I kissed him, and he kissed me back. Then, just as suddenly as it started, we broke apart.

"Well," I stammered for words that just weren't coming.

He cleared his throat. "Congratulations." Then, as if searching for something of a normal exchange, "You'll need to tell Bill first thing in the morning. He will want to hear all of the details—about the project, I mean."

"Okay, then. Have a good night." I bumped into the door as I backed out of his office. "Oh, and thanks for the soup yesterday."

Ben ran his hand back and forth through his hair, disheveling it. "You're welcome. Looks like it did its job." He looked as taken aback as I was. "See you tomorrow." The words seemed to catch in his throat and he stumbled back into his chair.

Ohmygod. Ohmygod. Just act cool and get to your office before you flip out.

Within seconds, I packed up my belongings and made a run for the elevator, hoping to avoid running into Ben. I anxiously waited for the elevator to ascend the thirty-three floors and hopped on as soon as the doors opened. The doors remained open with no signs of closing, so I futilely hit the door close button a few times, trying to hurry it along. They finally closed, shielding me from any further embarrassment for the night.

I walked through the door and threw my stuff on the table before heading straight to the kitchen. "Do you want to hear the good news or the gossipy news first?" I opened up the refrigerator and pulled out a bottle of wine to pour myself a glass before joining Andy on the couch. I could hear her pause the TiVo.

"Always a tough call. Let's go with the good news first," Andy called out from the living room.

I sat down on the couch, squeezing myself in next to Buddy. "They accepted my proposal. The contract is going through their purchasing department, meaning I have my first true client."

"This calls for a toast!" Andy picked up her glass. "To the junior consultant on her way to quickly becoming a senior consultant."

"It's not a sure thing, but it definitely helps." I knew this next promotion was not going to be easy. They generally promoted only one junior to the senior level in a year, and Simon was in the running too.

"So when did it happen?"

"Late this afternoon. I called my point of contact, just to check in. She said she was glad that I called. They had just signed the papers and were going with our firm."

"Kate, that is so great. I am excited for you. Does this mean you might get to leave work earlier?"

"Assuming they let me take lead, it probably means I'll be working longer hours." I swirled my wine. "Are you ready for the gossipy news?"

"Of course."

"We kissed."

"Who kissed?"

"I guess I should say I kissed him." I prolonged answering her question.

"Who?" She shoved me with her foot.

"Ben." I recalled the scene in his office, going through every detail. Andy remained silent. "Say something," I prodded.

"Okay, Kate, I have to say this. You know I fully support you no matter what. However you handle this, I will be behind you. But," she paused, "are you sure this is the best time to start something with someone who is above you? This is just such a crucial time for you."

I sat silently for a moment, taking in her words. "I know that."

"Do you, though? You know how it would look if it ever got out." She set down the remote and turned toward me.

"It would look like I was trying to sleep my way up," I replied without meeting her eyes.

"It's different for a woman. I know he's not technically your boss. But he has more tenure and more seniority than you. Aren't you always saying Simon is looking for something?" She looked at me expectantly. I knew she wanted me to say I would put an end to it right here. I just couldn't bring myself to say it though. "Promise me you will be careful."

"I will." I replayed the day in my head—my call with my new client, my kiss with Ben, my conversation with Andy. I knew she was right that I needed to be careful. But I also felt the ball was in motion.

Andy and I were sprawled out on the couches by the time Josh stopped by. "How's broccoli?" He lifted my legs and plopped onto the couch, leaving my feet to rest in his lap. "So what unbelievably unrealistic romantic comedy did you watch tonight?"

"Ha-ha," I said dryly. "You know romantic comedies get a bad rap. The biggest complaints by critics seem to center on the short time period that it takes for the couple to fall in love and a lack of realism. There are real-life situations that are far more absurd." I nudged his hand with my toe.

"I'll bite. What are your real-life examples?" He obliged by picking up my foot and rubbing it.

"Remember Dave? He said he was falling in love with me after two weeks."

"And we, you included, thought he was crazy." Josh used his knuckle to kneed out a knot in the arch of my foot.

"Only because I didn't feel the same way, and I caught him looking through my caller ID."

"There was Britney's marriage …" Andy laughed, knowing this was not an example to help our case.

"Really? You're going to rely on celebrity lifestyles, which are so realistic?" Josh raised his eyebrows, making his skepticism obvious.

"There was the real-life runaway bride."

"Another crazy," Josh rebuffed.

"I'm sure there …" I trailed off, trying to think of someone else.

"You're having to look to emotionally volatile people. You're proving my point. It takes time to build—" Josh was smiling as he shook his head at me and Andy.

I cut him off. "No, my point is that there are far more absurd things in real life. You are discounting what you don't know." Then I tried another example. "At work, there is a woman who met and fell in love with her husband online."

"That's not the norm." Josh was unmoved by my contention that romantic comedies could be less absurd than real-life.

"No, the norm for us would be two jaded people meet, spend a few months playing games, feeling each other out for the will we or won't we commit. Is that what you were referring to with building?" My tone was full of sarcasm.

"Whoa! Did I touch a nerve?" Josh put his hands up.

"No," I said poutily.

"You know she is holding out for her own chase scene," Andy interjected into the conversation.

"The what?" Josh asked, looking confused.

"The chase scene. It's the scene where one of the characters in the movie realizes they love the other one, but they're never close by. So they have to run after the other one," Andy explained.

"Andy, you're funny," I said. "I know those don't happen in real life."

"Do you?" She looked at me quizzically.

"Well, I measure my reality by your and Drew's relationship. Did Drew chase you before he proposed?"

"I may have made him chase me a bit, but not in the full-out sprint through an airport or anything." She smiled.

"Just because I still somewhat naively believe in the happily ever after doesn't mean you have to make fun of me."

"Just giving you a hard time. Oh, come on." Josh tickled the bottom of my foot.

"Stop." I twisted my foot out of his grip.

"Hey, guys." Drew came in and joined Andy on her couch. "What's going on?"

"Just discussing the value of romantic comedies," I replied.

"Or lack thereof." Josh rolled his eyes.

"Well, I'm just in time then."

"You want to talk about movies?" Andy looked at him skeptically.

"No, *Sportscenter* is on." He snatched the remote from Andy, who futilely grabbed at it before he tossed it to Josh.

"I'm sorry, I think I'm confused. Whose apartment is this?" Andy nudged Drew with her foot.

"See, that's why you shouldn't operate heavy machinery. You get so easily confused." Drew kissed his hand and reached it to Andy's forehead. Andy moved out of his reach.

"There's a reason why there's an engagement period." Andy eyed Drew. "So you can determine if the guy is an ass."

Drew motioned for Josh to give him the remote, and he held it out to Andy. Instead of letting her have it, he pulled her toward him. "I was just kidding. Clearly, I was not funny. I'm sorry."

"Wow. You have him trained," I said.

"Who should take offense now?" Drew asked, not letting go of Andy.

"I was just making an observation."

We settled in to watch television. Andy and Drew were cuddled on one couch, and Josh and I had settled comfortably into the other. Buddy had nuzzled his way in between us and was softly snoring.

"Have you decided what you're getting me for Christmas?" Josh asked.

"Who said I was getting you anything?" I retorted.

"I guess I should take those designer shoes I got you back then?"

"Like I believe you would buy shoes for me."

"You don't know."

"Yeah, I do know, after about the hundredth lecture, I think it's a safe bet."

"Okay, you're right."

"Are you staying here or going to your dad's?" I asked.

"Both. I'm staying here for the actual day, and then flying out for a couple of days to hang with my dad and the new wife. Then I'm back here for New Year's. Do you want to come with?"

"Where?"

"To my dad's."

I deflected his question, turning to Drew and Andy. "What are you guys doing for the holidays?"

"Spending it with his family. We've begun the alternation between our families. And since Thanksgiving was with mine, Christmas is with his."

"Come on, you know your looking forward to the snow." Drew tugged at Andy's sleeve.

"I am. I think I still need to get some warmer clothes though."

"My mom will have some stuff you can borrow."

"Please tell me you can tell the difference in sizes. I'm not asking for discrimination between a two and four or a six and eight, but when there's six inches between two people in height, surely you notice."

"What? I didn't say pants. I was thinking about a sweater or something."

While Andy and Drew went back and forth, Josh asked, "Are you ignoring my question?"

"No."

"I think it would be fun—a couple of days away to relax, play golf."

"I'm tempted. I'm just not sure if I could get off work."

"That's your blanket excuse."

"What does that mean?"

"It means when you're eighty, are you going to look back and think I wished I worked more, or I wished I spent more time with my friends?"

I knew he was right, but I didn't answer him. And I knew Josh wouldn't ask again. If I wanted to go, then I would have to bring it up.

Chapter 9

*A*t the weekly morning staff meeting, we were all gathered in the large conference room. I was seated toward the middle of the conference table. People were still standing, milling by the coffee and bagels in the back of the room. Simon took the seat to my right. We exchanged brief "Good mornings," then proceeded to pay more attention to our BlackBerrys than each other. Others were starting to find a chair when Ben entered the room, followed closely by Bill. I tried discreetly to follow Ben with my eyes. Bill went to the front of the table, commanding everyone's attention with his presence alone, and I redirected my attention to him.

"Good morning, everyone. I want to welcome a couple of guests we have with us." He gestured to two individuals in the back of the room from our Atlanta office. He then continued to run through some updates with major clients. "I would also like to announce a new client that we have recently signed thanks to Kate Hayden. Please congratulate her when you have an opportunity, as this is a company where we have been trying to get our foot in the door for a while now. To be honest, I had written off the possibility of acquiring New Marcman department stores, but it goes to remind us what persistence and," he chuckled, "what gumption can do." I shifted uncomfortably in my seat, but held a closed-mouth smile. Simon was in my immediate line of sight, and I saw his face furrow at the announcement for a brief moment before plastering a smirk in its place. After a few more announcements, Bill closed the meeting, and everyone dispersed back to their offices. I got a few pats on the back as I left the room.

"Based on Bill's instructions, I was thinking a celebratory dinner is in order," Ben said, walking into my office. "Is tonight too short on notice?"

I clicked my pen a couple of times. "I could probably make it work," I responded, trying not to sound too eager.

"Eight o'clock?"

"Sure." I could feel myself holding my breath.

"I'll send you an e-mail with where." He paused for a second to look at me, his face breaking into a sexy grin.

The rest of the day went by in a blur. I worked on a report, responded to e-mails, and had a conference call, but my mind kept wandering back to dinner tonight with Ben. At 5:30 I gave up on work for the day. Just as the elevator doors were closing, a briefcase made them bounce back open. Ben followed the briefcase. I was in the back of the elevator, but I caught Ben's eyes. It was subtle, but the hint of a grin was there. As we descended, more and more people got on the elevator. Ben repositioned himself next to me. I was holding the back railing and Ben's hand was next to mine. His pinky began to trace mine. I was starting to feel my breath quicken, and just like that we reached the lobby, and Ben was out in front of me. I felt stuck in place, not able to move.

"Are you getting off?" A man was holding the door back for me, waiting for me to exit before him.

"Yes, thank you." I managed to release my hand from the bar.

As I was driving home, I mentally made a list of things I needed to do before dinner. Run. Shower. Shave legs. Pick out outfit.

"Hey, Buddy." He bounded at me as I walked through the door. "How was your day?" I asked, rubbing his ears. "Tonight will have to be a quick run." I began to change, trying to plug in my laptop at the same time. I had an e-mail notification. It was from Ben, with the subject line: "Tonight." Then the text of his e-mail: "Reservations at Damian's in my name. See you soon."

"Okay, get your leash." Buddy trotted into the hall and pulled his leash down from the table. He dragged it back to me. "Good boy." I knelt down to clip on his leash and then squatted to tie my shoes. "Let's go."

We ran about a mile of our usual route. Buddy was keeping a good pace, and he wanted to keep going. "Not tonight." I tugged on him to turn around. As I was getting closer to home, I could see Andy and Josh in the street. They seemed to be in the middle of a serious conversation. I waved to them, but they didn't appear to notice. By the time we approached, they had already disappeared. I would have to remember to ask Andy what they were talking about.

After my shower, I slipped into some black slacks, a pair I would never wear to work because they hugged my body a little more closely than I would want my coworkers to see. I was ready to cross that line with Ben tonight, from coworkers to something else. I put on a black silk camisole and grabbed a sweater in case it was cool in the restaurant and because I still felt the need to be a bit conservative. I stepped into my red heels and put on my large silver hoop earrings. I stood in front of my full-length mirror. "Well, here we go." Buddy's ears perked up. "I'm sorry, boy. They won't allow you in the restaurant."

"Andy, are you here?" I called down the hall. Not hearing anything, I jotted a quick note. "Gone to dinner. Probably be late. See you tomorrow."

Buddy followed me into the kitchen and sprawled out on the floor to cool down from his run. I refilled his water bowl and added food to his other bowl. He got up as I was scooping the last of it into his bowl. "See you later." I patted his head as I set down his bowl.

Ben was waiting in the bar when I arrived. He stood when I walked over to where he was seated. I hesitated, not knowing whether to shake hands or ... Sensing my uncertainty, he leaned in and kissed my cheek.

"Our table is ready." He placed his hand on the small of my back and guided me toward the host stand. I didn't have to fight my usual reaction to this gesture. "Ben Covney. We have an eight o'clock reservation." He smiled at the hostess.

"Yes, sir. If you'll follow me." She led us through a door upstairs to a private dining area. In the room, only one table was set. She pulled a chair out for me to sit and placed a menu before me. I smoothed the napkin in my lap while looking around the empty room and noting the waiter standing by to tend to us.

I waited to say anything until she was out of earshot. "What is this?" I tried to whisper so our waiter wouldn't hear.

"I wanted us to have some privacy. I thought it might make things more comfortable." Ben was opening the wine list that had been left on the table.

"Well, you definitely achieved the former. I'm not sure about the latter." My stomach seemed to do constant flips when I was around him.

"Do you like red or white wine?"

"I generally drink white."

He motioned for the waiter to come over and ordered a wine I had not heard of before. "If you don't like it, then we can always order by the glass."

The waiter returned, presenting the bottle to Ben. He nodded and waited for him to pour a taste of the wine. He took a sip. "It's good." The waiter filled both our glasses, then Ben directed his attention to me. "Here's to landing your first big client."

I raised my glass to his. "Thanks for doing this. It's more than I was expecting."

"I hope you mean that in a good way." His eyes seemed to chuckle as he spoke.

"I do." I set my glass down and cleared my throat. "We haven't really said anything about the other night."

"You're right. I was hoping to broach the subject tonight, but before we do, would you find it terribly objectionable if I asked you to dance?" He placed his napkin on the table.

It felt a bit cheesy and romantic at the same time. I pushed back my chair. "Maybe you should ask me."

Ben motioned to the waiter to give us some privacy. He stood up and held out his hand to me. It felt so warm when my fingers slid into his. He slid his arm around my back and pulled me into him. I could smell his cologne. It was something I had come to appreciate over the past couple of weeks. I had noticed myself getting a tingling sensation every time I smelled it lately. Tonight was no different.

"Does everyone so willingly do as you ask?" My voice came out softer than I intended.

"Are you referring to anyone in particular?"

"The waiter disappeared so readily. I agreed to your request to dance."

"I wouldn't dare to speak for you, but I think the waiter is rather agreeable, given I rented the entire room for the night. He only has to wait on one table for the evening. Not a bad gig, I would think compared, to his usual nights."

"Uh-huh." I was half listening to his response. I found myself more focused on the way his breath was hitting my neck. And how every impulse in my body was telling me to kiss him. I couldn't, though. I had kissed him already and was not sure that this gesture tonight was more than a congratulatory dinner.

It was almost as if he instinctively knew my question. Ben's fingers began to trace up the spine of my back. My body felt every touch and was aching for more. He dropped my hand and began to trace my neck with his finger. My breath caught in my throat. His finger traced my chin and then my lips. Ever so gently, he pressed his lips to mine. It was so soft. He pulled me into him, and the kissing became more passionate. His tongue gently opened my mouth and his hand ran through my hair. I ran my hand up his chest and could feel his heart beating. Our collective breath had become rapid. His hands moved to my hips and he pushed me back. Smiling, he said, "Now that we have talked about the other night, I think we can enjoy our dinner, don't you?"

I laughed. "We seem to be on the same page, but don't you think there may be a few other issues to talk about?"

He started to pull me back.

"Not that kind of discussion." I said and walked back to the table and sat down.

The waiter reappeared to take our order. Within minutes our appetizers were served. The rest of our food followed, choreographed in presentation and timing.

"Kate, obviously we will need to be discreet. I'm a partner in the firm, and this kind of relationship with a junior member would be frowned upon. That being said, given my position, I would completely understand if you wanted to leave it with a few kisses and nothing more. We could return to business as usual."

I didn't know whether to feel comforted or insulted. "You could easily return to business as usual?" I let the insulted me win out.

Ben picked up my hand and kissed my palm. "I didn't say I would be happy about it. I just said I would understand. I would be lying if I knew where this was headed. I mean, we haven't even gotten through one date and we've already derailed." He continued, "You have avoided me at work since our kiss, frustrating any attempt I have made at conversation. I guess I should not be surprised that you might turn out to be the most exasperating woman I have ever known."

"I'll take that as a compliment." Trying to sound nonchalant, I added, "Why don't we see where tonight leads?"

"Just so long as you agree to not ignore me in the office anymore. I think that might catch people's attention rather quickly."

"I would hardly say I could ignore you. That would imply you did not catch my attention." I took a bite of my pasta. "Things have changed quickly since our trip to Chicago. Before then I wasn't even sure I registered on your radar."

"You definitely registered. I think I was avoiding you to some extent. You're beautiful, and I would be lying if I didn't admit to hoping we would end up here, where I don't have to imagine any more what your lips taste like."

I felt myself flush. "I'm not sure what will be more distracting in meetings—the imagination or the knowledge."

"I'm looking forward to finding out." He poured the last of the wine into our glasses.

Ben walked me to my car after we left the restaurant. The parking lot was empty except for our two cars.

"I'm glad we did this." I brushed the curl that had fallen across his forehead.

"Me too," he murmured as he stepped in closer to kiss me. Our lips seemed to find each other with familiarity this time. He began to kiss my neck. "Can I convince you to come back to my place?"

"I think we should take things a bit slower."

"I can take things very slowly."

"Even slower than that. What would you have to imagine if we jumped into bed tonight?"

"I'm pretty sure it would only increase the number of fantasies I'll be having about you. But I can and will wait." He gently kissed my cheek. "I do look forward to seeing you tomorrow, Ms. Hayden."

I unlocked my car and got inside. "Thank you for dinner, Mr. Covney."

He paused for a moment and then shut my door. I watched until his shadow had disappeared into his car. *This was a good night.*

Ben was called away to one of our other offices to help with a project. I didn't see or hear from him. Not talking to or seeing him made it seem like our date had been more a figment of my imagination than reality.

On Saturday, I went up to the office to review some of the marketing materials our graphics department had finished the day before. I walked by Ben's office on my way to my own, just as I did every day—although prior to the Chicago trip and our first date, it had held no significance. When I passed his door, a jacket on a coat rack caught my attention. It had not been there the day before, which meant Ben was back and he had been to the office—and he had not called.

Andy had left with Drew to visit his parents for the holidays. I was driving out to my parents' house in the morning for Christmas Eve and Christmas Day, but tonight it was just Buddy and me in the apartment. "Let's see if Josh is still home." We walked up the thirty-three steps it took to get from our floor to his. Music was drifting out of the apartment next door to his. I banged on his door so that he would be able to hear me if he was home.

"Hey there."

"Hey. Mind if we come in?"

"Not at all." He opened the door wider so we could pass by him.

"What are you up to?"

"Packing. Want to do it for me?"

"As much fun as that sounds, I think I'll pass."

"Then you can come watch me."

"Okay."

He led the way back to his room, and Buddy obediently followed. I picked up a photo album and flopped onto the bed. Buddy sat next to it, waiting for an invitation. "Go ahead," Josh motioned.

Buddy looked to me, "Up." I patted my leg. "Do you have any cards?"

"I do, but I can't really play until I finish."

"I can play solitaire. What time is your flight tomorrow?"

"10:05. When are you heading out to your parents'?"

"As soon as I get up and throw my stuff together. I promised I would help cook."

"Your mother does know you don't cook, right?"

"I can follow instructions."

"I'm not sure I have ever seen you do something like that." He threw a couple more golf shirts in his bag. "I'm done. I'll finish the rest in the morning."

"Cards?" I asked as I pulled myself off the bed. Buddy waited to make sure we were leaving the room before he got down from the bed.

"Sure, let's go find 'em."

We sat on the floor next to the coffee table, and Josh dealt the hand to play gin rummy. He flipped the TV to ESPN Classic, which was showing a college bowl game from 1976.

"We weren't invited," I commented on the music that was thumping through the wall.

"Did you want to be?"

"Not if this music is any indication of them. It's horrible."

"How can you tell? All I can make out is base. It could be the best music in the world and sound horrible."

"I guess you weren't planning on sleeping tonight." I slammed down the last of my cards with a run.

"I planned to give them until 12:30 before I started to complain. Worst-case scenario, I'll crash at your place in Andy's room."

"I'm glad to know that's worst case." I feigned a hurt expression.

"So sensitive," he mocked.

"I have to tell you this makes me feel old. We're sitting in here playing cards while there's a party going on next door."

"We go out plenty if that is how you are judging age. I have to admit, it's nice to sit at home and not have to scream to be heard." I raised my eyebrows. "I'm just talking loudly. This isn't screaming. *This is screaming!*" Josh leaned toward me for added emphasis.

I covered my ears. "You can stop. I get the point." I set down the cards I had just shuffled. "This is ridiculous. Let's go to my apartment, where we can talk without raising our voices." I stood up and dragged him to his feet.

The next morning I woke up to an empty apartment. Upon inspection of Andy's room, it didn't look like Josh had slept in her bed. The bed was nicely made, even more so than when Andy had left. I walked down the hall from Andy's room to the kitchen and picked up the note that rested against the cookie jar. *I took Buddy outside and fed him before I left. Have a great Christmas and see you soon.*

"No wonder you're not bouncing around like a crazy man." Buddy's ears perked up, but he didn't move from his spot on the floor. "Are you ready to go to your grandparents' house?" His tail started wagging, but he still didn't move. "You are a lazy sack of bones."

I showered, got dressed, and threw some clothes in a bag. I checked my e-mail, but still had nothing from Ben. It was worse knowing he was back in town and not calling or e-mailing. It took three loads to get everything to the car with my stuff, Buddy's stuff, and the presents for my family. Buddy ran up and down the stairs leading the way each time.

Chapter 10

Christmas passed uneventfully. Caroline and I both stayed in our old bedrooms. Shawn stayed in the guest bedroom, although I had a suspicion that Caroline snuck in there after everyone was asleep. We ate, played board games, and watched old movies. Most of the people in my office took the whole week off, so I stayed an extra day before going back into work on Wednesday. I was probably one of three people in the office. It was almost too quiet. It was hard to brainstorm marketing ideas when there was no team in the office to talk with. Instead of working on new ideas, I wrote up some of the executive summaries for our clients that I had been putting off, talking about the market research and our proposal for their new slogan. I spent the rest of my week similarly, going in to a quiet office. I left early on Friday to shop for an outfit for New Year's Eve. The mall was extremely busy with people trying to capitalize on the after-holiday sales. I stuck with my purpose and parked near the store I was intending to look in and avoided crowds as much as possible. I found a top that I could wear, bought it, and exited the store as quickly as I could. When I got back home, I started leisurely getting ready for the night's festivities. I turned on the stereo, connected my iPod shuffle, and played a mix of songs that put me in the mood to go out.

The doorbell rang. I grabbed for my robe and threw it on before opening the door to the apartment. "Hey."

"Do you answer the door like that for everyone?" Josh looked me over.

"Well, since you were gone for Christmas, I didn't get to give you your gift. And here it is," I said, putting my hand on the tie of my robe. His eyes widened. "I'm kidding. I'm kidding." I pulled my robe around me tighter. "I looked through the peephole and saw it was you. Do you want to come in?"

"That's okay. I just wanted to give you an update on the plans for tonight." He wiped his forehead with the back of his hand. He was shaking out his legs post-run. "Tonight people are getting to Jason's about eight, and then we have a car picking us up at nine to take us to the bar."

"I doubt I'll make it by eight, but I'll definitely be there before nine." I winked.

"I can come by on my way out if you want. We could go together. No sense in both of us having our cars there."

"You just want to make sure I get there on time." I thought about it for a minute. "No, I want my car. I'll drive over. I promise to be there before nine, but you know I have to make an entrance."

True to my word, I got to Jason's at 8:50. Josh just shook his head when he saw me walk in. "That's the reaction I get? No, 'you look nice or anything'?" I walked over to where he was standing.

"You do look nice. But you were almost all dressed up with nowhere to go. We were just about to lock up and go downstairs to wait on the car."

I looked at my watch. "I still had ten minutes. It takes time to put this together."

"And it was time well spent." Jason walked up and kissed my cheek.

"See, that is the kind of reaction I was expecting from you," I said pointedly to Josh.

"Great, way to encourage her."

Jason slapped Josh on the back. "I've been with Beth long enough to know you don't say a word about how long it takes for a woman to get ready."

I chatted with Jason off and on the whole night. He had been a year ahead of Josh in college. They had run into each other a couple years back and transitioned from college acquaintances to friends. About ten minutes before midnight I ducked into the restroom to call Ben. No answer. I tried one more time. Nothing. I came back out, and they were already handing out champagne. I worked my way back to the group.

"Can you believe we're ringing in another new year together?" Josh asked. He handed me a glass of champagne and then slipped his arm around my waist. "Are you having a good time?"

"Definitely."

The countdown had started, and when it ended, I just stood there. Josh and I had kissed a hundred times at least, undoubtedly most of which had been when we were dating. Why did this feel awkward?

"Well," he smiled and leaned in slightly.

I turned at the last moment and we miss-kissed. We tried again, but we were pulled away by the group. Everyone started going around and wishing 'Happy New Year' to each other and cheersing.

My phone vibrated and I flipped it open before seeing who called.

"Happy New Year!" Andy sang across the line.

I was happy to hear from her, but my stomach fell a little, hoping that it had been Ben. "You too!" I yelled into the phone. "How's the party?" I could barely hear over the noise on my end and hers.

"It's great. I'll tell you all about it when I get back."

"Okay, see you tomorrow." I snapped shut my phone, feeling Jason reappear beside me.

"You know he's in love with you, right?" Jason whispered in my ear.

"What are you talking about?" I whirled around to face him.

"He might never act on it, but he's gone."

"I think you're mistaken." I could feel the annoyance at yet another person butting into Josh's and my friendship.

"Look, Kate, I don't want to get in the middle of things, but go easy on him. He really cares."

"Which implies that I don't?" I replied coolly, not attempting to mask my irritation.

"That's not what I meant." He sighed.

"Hey, we're heading down the street to Sky Bar," Josh said, barely looking me in the eye.

Jason had started to talk to some other people behind me.

"What's wrong?"

He looked at me blankly.

"Five minutes ago you were fine." I was screaming to be heard over the noise.

"I'm fine now."

We all grabbed our jackets and left the bar. Downtown was a madhouse, with streets filled with people and cars. Josh managed to get quite a bit in front of me. I weaved in and out of people but didn't catch him until we reached Sky Bar. I grabbed Josh's arm and held him back while everyone else went in.

"What's going on?" I could tell he was trying to decide what to say.

"You've been hitting on him all night."

"Who? Jason?"

He shrugged his shoulders.

"We've been talking." I was irritated. I knew it was because I couldn't reach Ben, not because of Josh, but I added fuel to the fire. "So what if I had been?"

"He said you've been coming on to him all night and it's making him uncomfortable."

"Are you serious? He's with Beth. She's out of town, so I was talking to him, keeping him company, nothing more. You should know me better." I threw up my hands. It was my turn to stare blankly at him. I raised my voice louder than necessary. "Look, I don't want to deal with this drama. It's late. You're drunk, and I'm feeling the alcohol." I could feel my head getting fuzzy. "I'm going to grab a cab." I turned on my heels and left.

I did not turn around to see his reaction. *Okay, good, stick to your high ground. Okay, maybe this wasn't such a good idea. I have no cash. Will cabs take credit cards? It's not that far. I can just walk. Where am I?* I turned around, surveying the street signs. I needed to figure out which way my office was. I turned to start in one direction, then turned back around. Street signs were starting to look familiar. I could see my office building in the distance. There were lots of people on the street, so I was feeling safe.

Jason's apartment was just a few blocks beyond my office building. As I passed my building, it occurred to me I would be walking under the freeway to get to his apartment. Maybe this wasn't so smart. I could call someone, but who? Everyone I know was out of town or out on the town. They wouldn't hear a cell phone, and even if they did it would take them forever to get here. I decided to walk fast. *If I keep to myself, I'll be fine.* I walked quickly, pulling my jacket close around me, as if it would protect me. I jumped about two feet when I noticed someone wrapped in a blanket sleeping. I could now see Jason's apartment building. When I turned the corner, my mouth dropped open. The gate to the parking lot was closed. The one time the freakin' gate worked! And no cars were coming or going. I looked at the fence and noticed a ledge off to the side. I hoisted myself up and started climbing the fence. Looking at my new Jimmy Choo half-calf black boots, I knew I had probably ruined them from my misadventure. I was straddling the top of the fence. There was no ledge on the other side, meaning I would have to jump if I wanted my car.

Stiletto heels were not the shoes for this, which made me wonder why female action stars are always fighting in heels. I jumped down, landing with a bit of a thud. *Happy freakin' New Year!* There's nothing like a thirty-minute walk through downtown at one in the morning and scaling a gate to sober a person.

An hour later, while I was at home and in bed, my cell phone rang.

"What happened to you?" Jason asked.

"I went home." I rolled over to see the time. It was 2:15.

"Josh seemed pretty upset when he came into the bar."

"I guess I was tired—all the unwanted hitting on you wore me out."

"What are you talking about?"

"Nothing. It doesn't matter." I shifted in bed, to which Buddy sighed to let me know I was bothering him.

"I didn't think you were hitting on me. If anything, I thought you were taking pity on me since Beth was out of town. Besides, if I thought you were, do you think I would be calling you?"

"Fair enough. So why are you calling me?"

"You left suddenly, and I just wanted to make sure you were all right."

"I'm fine. I know you're just being his friend, but he is my best friend. So thanks, but I think I have this under control."

"I'm being your friend too. We all care about both of you."

I hung up the phone, but couldn't help thinking about Josh. We hadn't been upset or yelled at each other in such a long time. I picked up the phone and scrolled to his name, but I couldn't bring myself to hit the send button.

At 10:30 the next morning, my stubbornness faded, and I picked up the phone and dialed.

"We can either let this fester, or you can go with me to the dog park so we can move past our funk. My vote and Buddy's, in case you were wondering, is for the dog park."

"Are you buying me a greasy lunch?"

"Are you that hungover?"

"I didn't leave at 12:30 like someone."

"Okay, okay, I'll buy. How long until you're ready?"

"I'll just throw on a hat and meet you at your car in a few minutes."

When I walked up, Josh was leaning against my car. "How is it that I am waiting on you?" he asked.

"You know how vain Buddy can be before we go to the park. Besides, some of us have to try to look good," I joked. I decided to push past any awkward stuff and give him a big bear hug. He felt stiff at first, but I held on until he gave in. Buddy jumped up and tried to join in the hug.

"You two know I'm a sucker for the group hug." He patted my butt as we broke apart.

"Hey, watch it there." I jumped away, feigning offense.

"Buddy doesn't seem to mind."

"You're comparing me to a dog. I appreciate that."

"In my book you can't rank much higher than Buddy."

"I do have the best dog." I opened the door and Buddy bounded into the back seat. "What are you hungry for?"

"I'd be fine driving through somewhere. Then we can eat at the park. What's in the bag?" he pointed to the back seat.

"A blanket, towels, and tennis balls. With the lake, I'm pretty sure we'll have a wet dog by the end of our outing."

When we arrived at the park, Josh grabbed one end of the blanket from me and we spread it out on the grass. Buddy was bouncing around, eager to be taken off leash. I grabbed our food and sat down on the blanket. Josh sat down next to me and leaned over to let Buddy off his leash. He tore off toward the water, leaping in without a thought. He ran back toward us, waiting until he reached us to shake off the water. "Thanks, boy." I laughed as I wiped off the water. Josh reached into the bag and pulled out a ball to throw toward the water. Buddy took off after it.

"Look, about last night ... ," I started.

"I never really got that movie."

"Seriously, I'm sorry. I should not have left like that. I don't like fighting with you."

"It has been a while since that's happened." He threw the ball again for Buddy. "Look, I think it was blown out of proportion. I'm sorry for my reaction. Can we just move past it? Let it go?"

"That's fine by me so long as we are really all right." I lay on my back, looking up at the sky. There were no clouds, and it was high sixties. When the wind blew, I got chills, but it was a beautiful day.

"We're fine."

"Fine?"

"I meant good. I know you don't like fine." Josh leaned on his elbow. Buddy was panting but rapidly wagging his tail. "I was surprised you didn't call last night." He tossed the ball again for Buddy. "I almost called you, but figured you would be asleep." I thought back to almost calling him. "So how long did it take you to get a cab?"

"I didn't have any cash, so I didn't get one."

"How did you get home?"

"I walked."

"You walked?" he repeated.

"Yep."

"Are you crazy? What were you thinking? Do you know what could have happened to you?"

"Clearly, I made it home safely."

"Kate." He took a deep breath. "I'm going to focus on the fact that you are all right, but please do not do that again ... even if we are yelling at each other, please."

"I know it was stupid. I won't do it again."

"You should have called me." He shook his head.

"To do what?"

"To knock some sense into you." In a more serious tone, he added, "You can always call me."

After a few minutes of silence, Josh asked, "Are you interested in Jason?"

"No, and like I said last night, he is with Beth. I would never mess with that. I was just *talking* to him. I don't think he read anything into it." I rolled over on my side to face him, propping my head up on my hand.

"I don't think he did either. What about someone else?"

"No one in particular." *Ben. I'm completely into Ben, but am afraid to talk about it just yet.* "What about you? You haven't mentioned anyone in a while."

"To be honest with you, I think I've gotten used to relying on you as my stand-in." He looked over at me. "And I mean that in the best possible way."

"Stand-in, huh?"

"I just mean I haven't really been looking for anyone. I mean, who is the last person I dated seriously? You. We broke up two years ago, and I still take you to all of my work functions. Don't get me wrong, you're a great date." He pushed some hair back behind my ear, "But …"

"But it is probably time for you to get back out there. I wasn't the best girlfriend, ya know. It'll be easy to fill my shoes." I knocked the tip of his baseball hat down.

"That's true."

"Heeey." I jabbed his shoulder. "You don't have to agree so readily."

"I thought you liked that about me. But in all seriousness"—he drew a breath—"it probably depends on the shoes we're talking about."

I smiled at his knock on my shoes. "Does this mean I'm not going to see you as much?"

"You're not getting rid of me that easily. You work late so much you probably won't even notice when I'm dating someone."

"I doubt that. She'll probably have something to say about you spending time with your ex-girlfriend."

"Anyone who dates me will have to know you are my best friend, and that's just how it is. I do think we are getting a little ahead of ourselves here, though. I haven't even gone out with the future girlfriend yet."

"It's still good to hear. I don't know what I would do without you."
I leaned over and kissed him on the cheek. I thought back to last night,
wondering why kissing him on the lips had affected me so much.

"Well, you don't even need to think about it." His words reassured
me. I felt a wave of guilt pass over me. I knew it wasn't fair to rely so
heavily on Josh. I couldn't deny that I was accustomed to leaning on
him. I rested my head on his shoulder, and Buddy finally lay down next
to us, resting and drying off from his game of fetch and swim.

Chapter 11

$\mathcal{I}$ was standing in front of my closet mirror, no closer to being dressed to go out than I was thirty minutes earlier. My room was now a mess, with jeans, black pants, and various tops thrown on my bed and chair. "Ugh! I absolutely hate this."

"Are you talking to anyone in particular?" Andy overhead me as she was walking past my room.

"I hate going out with people from work for the pure reason of deciding what to wear. I feel like I have to maintain a certain degree of professionalism. I just don't feel comfortable enough to wear what I would wear out with you guys. And since I'm meeting you and Josh later, I have to consider that also."

Andy rolled her eyes "I'm sure whatever you end up choosing will be fine." She was used to my overdramatization about my clothing dilemmas.

"You're not factoring in Ben," I wanted to say, but didn't want to start that conversation again.

I selected a strapless top with a sweater that could be taken off after dinner, but would cover the fitted nature of the top with some dark jeans.

"I'll see you around ten. I'll give you a call when I leave the restaurant."

"Okay. Have fun. It looks suitable for work people and Ben, by the way." Andy was leaning against my door frame.

She read me easily. I bent down to shake Buddy's paw. "I'll see you later tonight."

I got out of my car to see Ben pulling into the parking lot. An internal debate began about whether or not I should wait for him. I decided not to and headed toward the front of the restaurant when I heard his voice call out. "You not going to wait?" It was the first bit of conversation we had engaged in since our date.

"I thought I would just see you inside," I said casually.

He jogged over to where I was standing, glanced around, and then kissed me on the cheek. "I'm sorry we haven't had much of a chance to see each other lately."

You mean since our date. "Happy New Year." It stung a little that he didn't acknowledge that he hadn't returned my call.

"You too."

"Were you out of town?"

"I was. I've been meaning to tell you something since I got back."

"What was that?"

"I missed seeing you."

"We should go inside." I turned to walk toward the front door of the restaurant, but Ben caught my hand.

"Can I see you later tonight?" He squeezed before letting go.

"You really are going to have to start asking me further in advance. I have plans after dinner already."

"What about Sunday night?"

"Maybe. Let's talk about it later."

Most of the others had already arrived when Ben and I walked into the restaurant. They were seated at a table near the back. "By the way, you look great tonight. I just wanted you to know I noticed," he said.

There were three seats open. It looked like Simon had not gotten there yet either. Ben sat down before I could, taking the seat at one end of the table and leaving the seat on either side of him open. I was still standing when I heard, "Hey Simon," uttered from those at the table.

He sat down next to Ben. "Kate, are you waiting for someone to pull your seat out for you?" Simon asked.

"No." I quickly sat down. "I wouldn't presume that you were offering."

"I have to get some new furniture for my apartment but have no real interest in decorating it," Ben announced to the group.

"Why don't you hire a decorator?" Simon asked.

"There is this leather chair-and-a-half at Pottery Barn that I've been eying for the past six months, but I have nowhere to put it in my apartment," I remarked to no one in particular.

"I know just the one you are talking about," Olivia chimed in. "I can't stand it. Is it trying to be a couch or a chair? What is it?" Olivia was another senior consultant in the firm. She had this annoying tendency to oppose anything anyone ever said. At times I kept a running tally to see how many statements she would counter in one meeting.

"I don't think it's trying to be either one. I think it would be more in line with a loveseat if you had to liken it to some other furniture. It gives you more room than a chair, and it makes you sit close to someone if you want to. It also works if you have a smaller space where a couch won't fit," I replied.

"You've really put some thought into this. Maybe you could pitch your ideas to their marketing department," Simon observed.

I smiled.

"You know, if you both have some time, you could send me your ideas. I would not object." Ben looked between me and Olivia.

"I don't want to speak for Kate, but I think I'll pass."

"I would have to agree with Olivia. Somehow that seems outside of the typical job description, even considering other duties as assigned."

"Maybe I can have HR take a look at broadening the language. I would never dream of asking you to do anything outside of the scope of your job."

I felt his finger on my thigh. He was tracing figure eights. I coughed and raised my napkin to my mouth, then placed it back in my lap, leaving my hand there. I discreetly tried to push his hand away. I could not bear the thought that anyone would see.

"Excuse me." I pushed back my chair from the table and made my way toward the restroom. When I went inside, I inhaled deeply and let out the breath slowly. Since I was in there, I looked in the mirror, reapplied my lip gloss, and ran a quick brush through my hair.

Ben was leaning against the wall when I exited the bathroom. "I think the pony tail is underrated." He smiled.

"Well, then, I guess this is the second time you're disappointed."

"You look beautiful regardless of whether your hair is up or down."

"What are you doing?" I glanced down the hall in the direction of the dining area.

"Are you upset with me?"

Yes, I am. It's been almost three weeks since our date, and I haven't seen or talked to you. Instead, I said, "I don't want to take a chance that anyone would see us or find out what ..." I raised my fingers to my lips. I started again, "Look, I'm not interested in some affair or just sex. If that is the idea you have, then it needs to stop."

"Where is this coming from? I think you're sexy as hell, but that is not all that I'm interested in. But you are inches away from me, and I can't help it. I want to touch you. Even right now, but I won't. I can show restraint." He ran his hand through his hair.

It was a move of his that I couldn't get enough of. "You are charming, I'll give you that."

"I'll save it for when we are alone, which will be Sunday, right?"

"I'll try to make it work. Now let me go back to the table or people are going to start to wonder what happened to both of us."

I sat down at the table, and Ben returned a few moments after me. No one seemed to notice our absence or return. The table was engaged in a "who has the worst client" conversation. Olivia had just finished talking about the low talker with bad breath, forcing her to hold her breath and lean in to be able to hear him. Ben, the sole partner at the dinner, picked up the bill and charged it to the company, saying he could explain it as team bonding. I said my good-byes without lingering with Ben. I went to the other extreme and barely made eye contact, which may have inadvertently drawn attention.

I walked into the bar and stood on my tiptoes trying to see Andy or Josh. When I spotted them, I weaved between people and tables to where they were sitting.

"How was dinner?" Andy asked, while motioning the waitress to our table.

"It was fine." I threw my sweater on the empty chair the group had commandeered.

"What was it for anyway?" She took a sip of her martini and directed her attention back to me.

"Team-building, I guess. A chance to get everyone out of the office environment, relate to each other on a personal level. What some might refer to as psychosocial babble." I turned to the waitress. "Could I have vodka Sprite, please?"

"Was your whole firm there?"

"Yeah, right. One partner, a few SeCos and associates. And I am sure you can guess what other JuCo was there."

"How is Simon?" Andy rolled her eyes as she said his name.

"Snarky as usual."

"And Ben? Was he there?" I could see her pulling an innocent look out of the corner of my eye, even though she avoided eye contact.

"Uh-huh." I handed my credit card to the waitress to start a tab.

"Who's Ben?" Josh, silent until now, took this moment to pipe in.

"A guy from work."

"One that Kate is having a dangerously stupid flirtation with," Andy helpfully added to the conversation.

"I am not," I said pointedly to her. Then I continued to Josh, "He came into the conference room when we were in there eating. It's been a while now."

"Oh, him, I remember."

"You met him?" Andy asked excitedly. "What was he like?"

"I don't think I'm the best judge. I can't do the girly analysis that you all do in the level of detail."

"That's okay. Give it a shot. I just need a mental picture from an unbiased third party," Andy pleaded, grabbing Josh's arm for emphasis.

"He seemed to be all business." Josh looked bored with the direction of the conversation.

"I guess Kate is the exception then." Andy seemed pleased at uncovering the slightest detail.

"Where's Drew?" I tried to move the conversation off the topic of Ben.

"He's playing a game of pool. Speaking of, I think I'll go find him." Andy got up from the table.

"So have I missed anything tonight?" I asked.

"No, not really." He moved to the chair next to me. "Do you want to people watch?"

"Do you even have to ask?"

"Okay, you go first."

"I pick those two over there. See them in the corner booth?" I motioned in their direction with my head, not wanting to point. "Let's hear it."

"Well, we have Suzie and Timmy. They've known each other since first grade. He's been working as an undercover detective for the last two years and had to fake a marriage as part of the facade. Suzie's heart was broken, but she remained friends with him, hiding her pain.

"That's kind of sad."

"Well, tonight he's going to tell her the truth. He's working up liquid courage to tell her he's not really married."

I laughed. "I guess that's better than he's a lying, cheating husband who doesn't even bother taking off his ring when picking up another woman."

"Okay, my turn." Josh picked out another couple. This time I provided the backstory. We spent the rest of the night cozied up at the table trading off the storytelling. The backgrounds we detailed became more outlandish as the drinks continued flowing. By the end of the night we were barely able to get through them, we were laughing so hard.

Ben called a few times that Sunday. I was home but trying to hold out. By the fourth call, I answered and mildly protested about being able to see him. I let him talk me into going to his apartment that night.

Ben opened the door to let me into his apartment. I took in his surroundings, noting the sparseness—the lack of furniture or pictures on display. "Wow, no offense, but I see the need for some new furniture, any furniture, really."

"Yeah, well. I'm probably not the poster child they are looking for when people talk about the benefits to divorce. Would you like something to drink?"

"I wouldn't mind some water."

"Nothing stronger?"

"No, I would like to keep my wits about me."

"And I think it is so much fun when you don't." He handed me the glass of water on his way over to the couch. He sat down, crossing his legs and placing his arm on the back of the couch.

I sat down on the ottoman so I had the vantage of facing him. "How was your day?"

He set down his own drink, uncrossed his legs, and reached out to pull the ottoman closer. My knees were in between his legs. "Good." With the back of his fingers, he began to slowly rub my arm. "And how was your day?"

Before I could respond, he leaned in to kiss me. The kiss continued. I felt out of breath but did not want to stop. He pulled me from the ottoman, and we clumsily made it to his bedroom. "Are you sure we should do this? Now every time we are in a meeting together, I'll know you have seen me without my clothes."

"I know. That's something I look forward to." And almost as if he were prolonging the moment, Ben took his time taking off every piece of my clothing.

I couldn't help feeling slightly self-conscious and reached for the light switch. He stopped my arm. "No, I want to see you." He held my face in his hands, holding my gaze. "I want to see you," he said again in a whisper. And I fell into him.

⌒

I woke up and looked at the empty bed next to me. The clock read 3:15. I pulled the sheet up around my chest. "Ben," I called out. A T-shirt of his was thrown over a chair. I struggled keeping the sheet around me while I reached for his shirt to put on. I walked into the living room and saw Ben dozing in a chair with the TV playing. "Ben," I said quietly, touching his arm. "What are you doing out here?"

He stretched his arms and neck. "You fell asleep, but I wasn't quite tired so I came out here to watch some TV. What time is it?"

"After three," I said through a yawn. "I should probably get going."

"Are you okay to drive?"

"I'm a little tired, but it's not that far. Besides, you'll probably sleep better in your bed rather than this chair." I tugged at the bottom of the t-shirt.

"Come here." He pulled me to sit in his lap. "This shirt looks good on you. You don't have to leave right now, ya know." His hand was moving up my thigh.

"I thought you were tired."

"I was, but then you woke me up looking all sexy in one of my old shirts. It just made me realize I haven't had enough yet."

"Are you hoping to get your fill in one night?"

His hand stopped. "I didn't mean that." He stood up. "Do you want some coffee?"

"No, thanks, I don't drink it." I propped myself on the edge of the chair. "Were you watching this?"

He stopped to look at the television screen. "No, I don't even know what it is." He was running his hand through his hair. "I think I'll make some for myself."

"I love this movie." I picked up the remote to turn up the volume and sank onto the couch. "So where did you get this couch, anyway? It looks like it has seen better days."

"It was what I had back in my single days before marriage, you know, when I was in my twenties. It had been in storage for a while. I pulled it out after the divorce," he called from the kitchen.

"That old, huh? If that's the case, I don't know that it's safe to sit on."

"Funny. I had it sterilized. You can rest easy." He sat down on the opposite side of the couch, stretching out his legs. He reached down and grabbed my ankles to pull the rest of my body onto the couch. He shifted on his side and held my feet to his chest. "Turn it up."

Chapter 12

$\mathcal{J}$t had been a full week since Ben and I first slept together. I had been to his apartment three times since Sunday night. We seemed to be getting along pretty well, and I noticed I was waking up excited to get to work. Even though for the most part we weren't working on projects together, we still bumped into each other and were in staff meetings together. I had to hide the smile that wanted to creep onto my face when I saw him. I even found myself taking the long way past his office to get to the break room.

It was late Sunday afternoon and I was sitting across from Andy. We had secured our regular table at Taco Macho and were waiting for Josh to arrive. Often he would say he was no longer engaging in this demasculinizing activity, and just to show us he always came a few minutes late.

"I know they are made out of rubber and often called a 'rubber,' but I just hate the way they smell." I offered this random observation as a conversational topic.

"Is that your excuse for your lack of a sex life? How long has it been? I'm not sure you could even claim to know what a condom smells like.

And besides that, have they changed the content in *US* and *In Touch* magazines?"

I wasn't ready to tell her about Ben and this past week, so I shrugged off her questions. And to my relief, Josh was walking toward us. "We were just starting to think you bailed." I winked at Andy.

"Nah, I want to get my fill of celebrity gossip so I can impress my date tonight."

When we first started our afternoon of margs, chips, and salsa with gossip magazines, we had used this argument to get Josh to come. It had become his security blanket.

"Who is the lucky girl tonight?"

"No one special."

"Josh, you're horrible. Tell me you're kidding," Andy pleaded.

"I am kidding. You're just so easy to get riled up."

"I hate that you're right."

"How did you meet this one?" I interjected.

"Let me guess," Andy piped up. "At the gym." She then gave Josh a look.

"So what if I did? What is that look for?"

"You are just too predictable."

"And what about you?" He looked to me.

"What? How did this get turned around on me?" I put my hand to my chest.

"How is my dating strategy so much worse than yours?"

"What are you saying?" I cocked my head to the side.

"How long does it take for you to be yourself with a guy?" Josh questioned me.

"You do have a point," Andy said, then turned to me. "We spend all this time trying to get a guy, even to the extent of altering our behavior." She paused, then added, "The better part of it is that once we get the guy with our altered behavior, we revert to ourselves and then proceed to spend our energy trying to alter his."

"Did you do that with Drew?"

"The truth comes out. So that's how you work us?" Josh looked as if he'd had a breakthrough moment in understanding women.

Andy ignored Josh's question. "No, but we knew each other already. It was too late."

"I could see that when we were younger, like with you and Billy Bob," I smirked.

Andy picked up a chip and broke off a tiny piece of it. "His name was not Billy Bob and you know it." She sheepishly added, "It was Thorton."

"But I think we do that less as we get older."

"So, for example, you don't think if a guy now wanted to be casual you would fake it and act like it was no big deal? Or, you wouldn't keep a relationship undercover because that was what the guy wanted?"

I eyed her innocent expression. "Okay, I see your point. Maybe it can apply to all ages."

"Well, great. So how long until I get to see the real side of a person I date?" Josh looked exasperated.

I was relieved when Josh turned to his dating life. With Andy's comments, I realized I was not as coy as I thought I had been.

A few hours later, I was flipping through the TV channels trying to find something to catch my interest.

"So when are you going to talk to me about him?" Andy plopped down on the couch.

"Him who?"

"The him who you've been spending almost every night with this week before sneaking back into the apartment in the early morning hours."

I could feel a look of guilt flashing over my face. "Did I wake you up?" I postponed my answer.

"No, but Buddy only sleeps with me when you're not here, and lately he's been curled up at my feet."

"Traitor." I tugged on Buddy's ear. "I guess I know you don't exactly approve of the relationship." I felt sheepish just saying it.

"I don't know whether to be mad at you or just disappointed. Since when do we not talk about someone we are seeing, regardless of how the other person feels? Before Drew, how many guys did I date that you disapproved of? Should I start naming guys?"

"I know, I just … It somehow feels different this time. I just don't feel I could handle your not approving."

"Why do you think that?"

"I'm a little bit scared of how all of this could end up. I mean, not only could I fall for the guy and get hurt, but I could also mess up my job and what I have been working for. With all that, I don't want to add a friend's disapproval to the list."

"If you're feeling so uneasy about it, doesn't that tell you something?"

"Yeah, to be careful, which I'm trying to be."

"By taking things slow and spending every night over there."

I looked at her. "Andy, this is exactly what I wanted to avoid."

"Kate, I'm not going to hold back what I think. Our friendship has been based on our honesty with each other. If I think you're making a mistake, I'm going to tell you." She paused, shifting her legs underneath her. "I know our friendship is strong enough to get through it. And even though I may not approve, you can still talk to me." Her voice had become a little shaky with emotion. She cleared her throat. "What I'm trying to say is that I've voiced my feelings. You know where I stand and have known me long enough to know that once I've said my peace, I'll move on."

I was having trouble meeting her eyes, hating how uncomfortable conversations like this made me. "Fair enough." I forced myself to look at Andy and smile. I patted the couch next to me so Buddy would get up there.

"Well, I'm moving on, but now you have to let me by talking to me about it." She nudged my knee. "So it seems as though things are moving along." Andy forged ahead with the conversation.

"They are." I pulled the pillow from behind my back into my lap and fiddled with the corner. "He's different than anyone I've dated before. I can't really predict where things are headed or what he's thinking. It's kind of exciting."

"What do you mean?"

"One minute we're watching TV; the next he's carrying me into his bedroom. At the office, he'll sneak a knowing smile in my direction, and then the next minute it's as though he doesn't know I'm in the room." I bit my lip.

"And you like not knowing which one you're going to get?"

"It's not that. I like trying to figure him out. I like that it is not so easy or obvious."

"I think it's what some people would call the thrill of the chase. I'm not surprised. You have dated some guys that just seem to roll over." As if on cue, Buddy rolled over to have his stomach rubbed. We both giggled and indulged him.

I worked at a client's office the next day. Ben sent me an e-mail asking me to meet him downtown after work. We weren't meeting until seven, so I had time to go back to my office. I called Andy to let her know I would be late and ask her to feed and walk Buddy for me. As I set down the receiver, Simon stuck his head in my office.

"What are you doing back here?" He sat down into the chair across from my desk.

"I had a few things I needed since I wasn't in the office all day."

Ben must have seen my light on. He came around the corner and stopped abruptly, changing his demeanor when he saw Simon sitting in my office. He hesitated with whether to back up without saying anything. Simon, sensing someone's presence, turned around. "Hey, Ben." Ben eased into office chitchat with him. After a few minutes, I cut them off. "Guys, I would love listen to you two go on about the matchup in the Super Bowl. Really, I would, but unfortunately I need to get going." They both scrambled out of my office, and I collected my things to leave.

⁓

"What took you so long?" Ben was waiting in the lobby of One Oil Plaza downtown. It was deserted, causing my words to echo across the room.

"Well, I had to get my car out of our parking garage, then drive a few blocks and find another garage, and walk over here. Oh, and there was the little detail of making sure Simon wasn't still around." When I got closer to him, I quickly kissed him. "So why am I meeting you here?"

"You'll see." He held out his hand for me to take. "Why did you move your car?"

I let my hand slip into his and we ascended the forty-eight floors in the elevator. "With Simon still there, I didn't think it was a good idea for both of our cars to still be there without either of us in the office." He nodded.

The top floor housed a restaurant that overlooked downtown Houston. When the elevator doors opened, we heard jazz music being played by a band. Other than the musicians, however, there were no other diners in the room. "Tell me you didn't rent out another restaurant."

"Okay, I didn't rent out another restaurant."

"And a band?"

"I didn't want to dance to muzak this time. I thought dancing to a real, live band would be nice."

"Ben, please do not take this as a complaint, but a simple dinner would be okay with me." I was flattered by his extravagant gesture, but I was also recognizing that it would be nice to grab a casual dinner together with other patrons.

"We don't have the luxury of a simple dinner. And you're welcome."

Ben pulled me into the restaurant, which was filled with empty tables. One was set up with candles and a bottle of wine already chilling in a bucket. We drank the wine, drifted onto the dance floor, and then back to eat one of the courses. By the end of the night, I had forgotten my initial displeasure and saw the benefit to being the only people in the restaurant.

Chapter 13

Andy and I had decided to watch the Super Bowl game at our apartment. The guys had complained about not having a big screen, but we were able to win them over by highlighting our free alcohol and no lines at the bar or bathroom. Drew countered that the bathroom was really a pro for us, since as guys they managed to avoid lines in the bathroom.

"When are we going to meet this guy?" Shawn asked. He and Caroline arrived just in time to watch the game. They made themselves comfortable on the couch and started picking at the chips and hot sauce that were out.

"Andy said you've been seeing a lot of him." Caroline looked up at me.

"If it becomes serious, you'll meet him soon enough," I responded, ignoring Caroline's comment. Meeting Ben seemed to be the topic of conversation lately. "So what's new with you two? How's the center?"

"It's good. I mean, it can be hard hearing some of the horrible things people go through. But at the end of the day, even though I'm tired and drained, I feel like I'm helping."

"Don't let her kid you. She's loving it," Shawn chimed in.

She straightened up, positioning herself on the edge of the couch. "So, I've been wanting to talk to you."

"Yeah, what's up?"

"Well, Shawn and I have been talking about moving in together."

"Guys, that's great. Where are you thinking you'll live?"

"There are some apartments pretty close to the medical center that we've been looking at," Shawn replied, but didn't expand on his response when he saw Caroline's face.

"I wanted to get your perspective on what you think mom and dad will say."

"Caroline," I smiled, "you two are out of college. You have a job and Shawn's in med school." I gestured in his direction. "You've been dating for years now. I think it's a given that they'll be happy. Besides, you always have the card you can pull on them."

"What card?"

"The one about them living together before they were married."

"What? They did not!"

"Oh, yes they did. How did you not know that?"

"I don't know. How do you know that?"

"I guess I just ask our parents questions about themselves. I must be the better daughter."

"You should talk to her," Andy said. "Tell her how you feel."

"Why would I do that? Do I or we have any indication that she would respond with, 'I've been waiting for you to say something?' It was just a few weeks ago where we talked about how we were avoiding dating and using each other as stand-ins. And then you yourself said just the other night that she may be having a thing with this guy Ben. If I say something, it will just become weird between the two of us as friends—and the rest of us, for that matter." Josh took a swig of his beer.

"You have to man up. Either act on it or move on, but you have to stop this. You gotta stop riding the pine," Andrew said, while rocking the kitchen chair back and forth.

"Drew," Andy said in a forced whisper, "could you show some sensitivity?"

"You are showing enough sensitivity for both of us. He needs to hear a guy's perspective." Andrew looked a bit sheepish, knowing he would hear more from her later.

"I'm not saying he should sit around and wistfully hope for something to happen. I mean, who knows what this Ben thing is, if it's anything at all? But you are reducing this to something inconsequential." She grabbed one end of the chair, forcing all legs to hit the floor.

"And you are making more out of this than you should." Drew released his hold on the chair and slid into it, forcing Andy to fall into his lap.

"Hey," Josh piped in, "I appreciate the concern for both sides, but really, this is something I have to figure out."

"We know you have to do this on your own terms, but"—Andy looked at Drew for emphasis—"we both don't want you to wait until it's too late and you can't do anything about it."

I walked into the kitchen, where Andy, Drew, and Josh were sitting around the table. "Are you going to watch the game? I thought guys actually cared about this sort of thing." I looked around at the three of them and then stopped short when I saw Josh's face. "Are you okay? What's wrong?"

At my question, Andy hopped up and grabbed Drew's arm to pull him out of the kitchen. I sat down across from Josh, waiting to hear what was going on.

"Kate, I've been wanting—"

My phone started vibrating. I glanced at the screen and saw Ben's number flashing across it. "Can you hold that thought just one second? I have to take this." I stood up and walked out of the room. "I'll be right back," I mouthed to Josh.

"Hi." Ben's voice came over the line.

"Hey." I smiled into the phone. I was excited to hear from him. With his traveling for business, I hadn't talked to him in a few days.

"What are you up to?"

"Andy and I have some friends over to watch the game. Aren't you watching?"

"Yeah, I was thinking I might head down to the hotel bar in a little bit. Or I might stay in and order room service."

"Sounds like a lively Super Bowl party. Would you mind terribly if I gave you a call back after the game?"

"Sure, that's fine. I'll talk to you then."

I snapped my phone shut and went back into the kitchen.

Josh had just finished blending some margaritas. "Want one?" He was handing me the one he just poured.

"Sure. Sorry about that." I motioned to my phone. "What were you saying before?"

"Nothing, it was nothing." Josh smiled.

"Are you sure?" I put my hand on his arm.

"Yeah, it was no big deal." Josh filled a couple more glasses, balancing them before taking them into the living room.

"Who wants one?" he set them onto the coffee table, taking one for himself and sitting in one of the arm chairs. Drew was sitting in the other one, while Andy had sprawled out on the floor.

I grabbed a big pillow and propped it against the chair in front of Josh. Almost before I had a chance to get situated, he was up from the chair. "Where are you going? The game's already started."

"I'll be back in a minute," he answered over his shoulder.

"Do you know what is going on with him?" I looked over at Andy and Drew to read their expressions.

"No," they said in unison.

When Josh came back to the apartment, he grabbed a chair from the kitchen and pulled it into the living room.

"I think the chair over here is more comfortable," I said, "or even the other couch, for that matter."

"I'm good." His tone was detached.

"Okay then." I looked at Andy or Drew, but neither seemed to notice.

After the game, Josh and I moved around the apartment picking up glasses and plates in silence. I finally broke it by saying, "I could go back to my high school days, wait for you to leave, and then beg Andy to tell me what you were talking about in the kitchen … but I'll be mature and leave that alone. I'll even be more mature and ask you directly if something is up."

"Was there are a question in there? All I heard was some healthy self-esteem." He gave a wry smile.

"Are you being distant?"

"Kate, we talked about this. Things can't be the same."

"Yeah, I get that, but right now it doesn't feel much like us. It just feels like one day we're good and the next we're not."

"And I thought you liked roller coasters. We're in a valley right now. It's just awkward, but we'll get there."

"Well, I don't accept that. If we don't talk and barely acknowledge each other, then we won't get back to being us."

"We haven't stopped being *us*." He rolled his eyes as he used air quotes. "Don't be so dramatic."

I set down the pile I was collecting. "Tomorrow we are going to lunch, and the day after that too."

"You are going to get away from work two days in a row." He raised his eyebrows in skepticism.

"And I will get away the day after that if we still haven't gotten Stella's groove back. It's important to me."

"And what about me?"

"Don't care. I was taught persistence pays off, so I will just bug you until you cave."

"So what they say in grade school is true—you ignore a girl and she'll come running? So simple, and yet the last thing I thought of."

"That's because you're not so simpleminded, like some people say. And what can I say? I have trouble focusing on more than one thing at a time, so the one that makes the most noise—or, in your case, the least—is the one that gets my attention."

"Who are the *they* and *some*? I want to be referenced so casually like them." Josh grabbed a trash bag and snapped it open for me to toss my trash in. "By the way, I'm not sure you're logic is sound, but I suppose I will make time to go to lunch with you tomorrow."

Chapter 14

Bill summoned Simon and me to his office to meet with him at 8:30. When I arrived, his assistant nodded at me to take a seat. She was softly talking into her headset while typing on her keyboard. Simon was already waiting, so I took the seat next to him. We exchanged a few words, trying to ignore our obvious discomfort. Bill occasionally met with each of us individually, but we had never been called to meet with him together.

Angie placed her earpiece on her desk. "You can go in now." She motioned us to the door.

I tapped on the door as I walked through it. "Good morning."

"Good morning, Kate, Simon." Bill turned from his computer and walked around his desk to join us around his small, circular conference table. I was thankful that he didn't reach for my hand, as I could feel its clamminess.

"I apologize in advance for my abruptness. I only have a few minutes, so I will get right to it. Next week we have some of our colleagues from our East Coast offices visiting. They'll be observing for a couple of days. I would like for them to get an idea of the clients and projects we've been working on. I would like each of you to take one of your clients and walk us through your pitch for a new product or a special event, whatever you think will give us the best overview of what you've been working on." He was twirling a pen in his hand as he spoke. "I was thinking we would set aside time at the next staff meeting—about twenty minutes a piece. Sound okay?"

Simon and I were both silently nodding along.

"Great! Well, as I said, I have to get going. I do appreciate you both doing this."

We all pushed back our chairs. Bill returned to his desk to pick up his briefcase, and Simon and I exited the office.

"Like we had any choice," Simon muttered under his breath.

I smiled but offered nothing more in response.

I wandered into Ben's office. I was carrying a decoy document with me to add purpose to my visit.

"Am I seeing you tonight?" I asked as I sat down in the chair across from his desk.

"I don't know yet. I have a lot of work that I still need to finish." He stopped typing on his keyboard and looked up at me. "If we do, it will have to be much later."

"How late?"

"Kate, I don't know yet."

"I was just asking for a time frame." I felt like I had been reprimanded.

He let out a sigh. "I have work that will keep me busy until midnight. I know that's late. If I think it can be any earlier, I'll call you."

"Okay." I stood up to leave.

"Is there a time after which I shouldn't call?" He asked without taking his eyes off his computer.

I paused for a moment. "Well, I do want to see you, but I'm not a huge fan of trekking across the city after midnight."

"Really?" He leaned back in his chair. "Then what's with the going out with your friends? You're out much later than that."

"Funny. It's different. I'm meeting up or going out with a group of people." *It also doesn't feel like a booty call.* "I'm also out by that time, not leaving to go out."

"And New Year's Eve?"

"Very different. It was a matter of principle." I added more quietly, "And stupidity."

"I see."

"I'll talk to you later." I walked out of his office, almost bumping into Simon. "Sorry, I didn't see you there." I jumped a bit.

"That's okay. Are you done in Ben's office?" He asked as he walked around me.

"Yep."

I hoped he hadn't overheard our interaction.

Simon tapped on Ben's door.

"Back so soon?"

"I'm sorry?" Simon responded.

"Oh, Simon, come in."

I moved away from the doorway.

I packed up some work to take with me, getting home relatively early. Even though I knew he wouldn't call until much later, I kept checking my phone for a missed call. I tried to concentrate on the computer in front of me. By midnight he had not called, and I was exhausted. I turned off the light and patted the bed for Buddy. He hopped up and then promptly curled up into a ball next to my legs.

I woke up before my alarm went off and reached over to my cell phone. I flipped it open; no missed calls. *He didn't call.* I swung my legs out of bed and slowly walked over to my computer. Leaning over my chair, I clicked the send/receive button to update my e-mail. There was one message from Ben.

Sorry I didn't call last night. I didn't finish working until two and knew that was too late to call. Maybe tonight.

That's it. No call, just a lame, two-line e-mail.

I tried to let yesterday slide and stayed upbeat as I approached Ben's office late in the day. "So how was your day?" I leaned up against his desk.

"Not bad, not good." He stood up and stretched. He then walked over to his doorway and looked up and down the hall.

"What are you doing?"

"Looking to see who else is around."

"We're it." I picked up a paper weight off his desk and shifted it back and forth between my hands.

He walked back around to his desk and sat down. He rolled his chair closer to where I had positioned myself. "So how was your day?" He placed his hands on my thighs. I was wearing a skirt, so his hands were warm with just my tights between him and my skin. He started inching his hands higher.

"What are you doing?"

"Improving my day."

"We're not going to do that here." I pushed his hands away and moved around to the other side of his desk.

"No one else is here."

"You know as well as I do that people come and go at night. The excitement is not worth the risk—my risk—of being caught." I softened my reproach. "I would be happy to continue this back at one of our places."

"I wish I could. I need to stay." He pushed his chair back in front of his computer. He looked back over his shoulder, eying my skirt. "Are you sure I can't convince you to stay for a few minutes?"

"A few minutes sounds tempting." I rolled my eyes at him. "Call me later." I left his office, returning to mine to grab my bag. Fifteen minutes later I was in my apartment sitting in the kitchen, flipping through the newspaper.

"Hey, I'm going to grab some pizza with Drew. Wanna come with?" Andy was throwing her wallet, phone, and keys in her purse.

I checked my cell phone for the hundredth time that evening.

"Do you really want to be that available?"

"I know. I know." I set it on the table.

"You shouldn't refuse to do things because you're afraid he'll call. Otherwise, you may sit around doing nothing all of the time."

"Point taken. Let me grab a sweater." I looked at my phone and left it sitting on the table.

Drew drove the three of us to the restaurant. I let the two of them carry the conversation, only half listening while the street signs passed in front of me. We went to a pizza place located in midtown, which was really just on the outskirts of downtown. They had the heat lamps on the patio, so we grabbed a table outside. We had a pitcher of beer with our pizza. When we finished, we walked across the street to shoot a few games of pool. Josh was there when we arrived.

"Hey, guys." He waved us over. He and Jason had commandeered some bar stools close to the table for us to sit and watch.

"I'm not very good at watching. Can we play teams?" I picked up a cue stick off the wall.

"We have an odd number," Jason observed. "Besides, I'm kicking Josh's ass right now."

"You can still do that if we play teams, as long as you're not on the same team. And, a person on the losing team can rotate out," I offered.

"Sounds good to me." Drew picked up another cue and rolled it on the table to check that it wasn't warped.

"I would actually be okay with watching." Andy took a seat on one of the stools.

"Nope, you don't get off that easy. You'll have to rotate in." Drew kissed Andy on the forehead.

"Okay, fine. But I'll let you guys play the first game."

"Since I was winning I pick first, and that would be Drew." Jason racked up the balls.

"That's fine by us. We have perfected the pool partnership." Josh picked up his beer. "Are you ready to kick some ass?" he asked me.

"I'm always ready, and these two should be easy."

"Already talking smack. Is there any money on these games? I would love to take some off of these two jokers."

"And I was just playing for the pure thrill of competition." I pulled a quarter out of my pocket. "Quarter a game?" I set it on the side of the table.

"No one could ever call Kate cheap." Josh ponied up some change.

"I would just feel bad taking money from these two. I mean, Andy and Drew have this big wedding coming up and they're house hunting. They're already bleeding cash."

"Don't remind me." Drew set his quarter down.

Jason ended up leaving after a few games to see Beth. She was getting back in town from a business trip. Andy was tired of playing, so Drew was sitting with her. It was just Josh and me left at the table.

"Okay, you have to show me how to jump the ball," I told him. "I don't know why, but I can't do it consistently. It seems like every other time, I send it off the table if I try to do it."

"Let me show you." He placed a ball and demonstrated how to jump it.

I sent the first one flying off the table. "Crap!" My hand flew to my mouth.

"Line it up," Josh instructed. I positioned the ball and lined up my stick. Then Josh stood behind me, taking my hands on either side. "I'll guide you through it a few times so you can get the feel." He took me through it a couple of times, and by the third one he let go and I did it myself. I stood up. "Thanks. You better be careful, though. You may be arming the student to surpass the teacher."

"I'm not too worried. Do you want to play another game?"

"One more." I chalked the tip of my cue.

Chapter 15

At the staff meeting, Bill ran through a few updates, then turned it over to Simon. My mouth felt dry, and the water I was drinking was having no affect on moistening it. I knew my presentation backward and forward and could do it in my sleep, but giving it in front of my coworkers, who were just waiting to critique me, was a little unnerving. I was paying attention to Simon only peripherally, but my focus narrowed in when I noticed the dead silence in the room. He began clearing his throat and shifting his glasses, obviously searching for his train of thought. He flipped open his portfolio. Quickly skimming through his notes, he picked up with his pitch.

He made it through the rest of his presentation. Bill opened the floor up for questions. Ben spoke up from the back of the room, tossing Simon, what I perceived to be, an easy question. Simon, though, looked as if the question caught him off guard and actually asked one of his team members to field it, to my surprise.

There were only a few questions after that, so Bill turned it over to me. I took my place in front of the room. I sailed through my presentation, trying to plug in the contributions of my team members without shamelessly overdoing it. I also hit the lines I had rehearsed to appear off-the-cuff, which registered the appropriate level of chuckling in the room. There were more questions from the people in the room, including our colleagues from the East Coast, when I opened it up at the end of the presentation. Ben asked a question, which I noted was substantially more difficult. The discussion wound down, and Bill wrapped up the meeting, thanking both Simon and me for our presentations.

An instant message alert went off on my computer.

"Can you sneak away for lunch?" Andy typed.

"Yeah, but it will have to be quick. Meet you in thirty."

"Usual," she replied.

We worked within a few blocks of each other. Sky bridges connected the buildings, so we usually met in the middle when we grabbed lunch together, typically at the same place and, if possible, the same table next to the window that overlooked the foot traffic below.

"So how did your presentation go this morning?" Andy asked.

"I think it went well." I replayed the meeting for her, after looking around to make sure no one from my office was nearby. "Tell me it was my imagination that Ben's line of questioning directed at me was substantially more difficult."

"Would you have wanted your question to be easier?"

I considered what she asked. "No, not at all. I'm not saying I should not have gotten that question. But I do think getting questions that are on the same level of difficulty is only fair."

"I think you need to give credit to people in the room. I'm sure they noticed the difference in the questions, just as you did. Just let your work speak for itself and don't sweat the other stuff."

I nodded and played with my food for a few seconds before switching gears. "So I've been seeing him for three months now." I could tell she was suppressing a look of skepticism as I broached this topic.

"I know this is going to sound paranoid, but in thirteen weekends I have not seen him once. I take that back … I have seen him late on a Sunday night." I was chewing on my straw. "And I know this will sound weird, but when I call him, it always goes to voice mail. I never actually reach him. And, if he does call me on the weekend, it's not until Sunday either." I took a deep breath. "It's like I'm the weekday girlfriend, which means …" I drew it out, "… there could be a weekend girlfriend, for all I know."

"Are you two only seeing each other?" she asked cautiously.

"No. I don't know. Maybe. We haven't talked about it."

"Maybe you should."

"Yeah, that always goes well. You know how we all love talking about the relationship. Do you and Drew?"

"Actually, with the wedding, I think it might be all we talk about. But seriously, I'm sure you are not the weekday girlfriend. Other things have come up, right?"

I nodded.

"You said he's been working out of town a lot and staying weekends rather than flying home. Maybe you should just casually bring it to his attention."

"I know, I know. I completely see myself being neurotic. Okay, enough. So what's new with the wedding plans?"

"Nothing. Everything. I had no idea how many details there were to deal with. I have appointments every day after work with photographers and videographers. Vegas looks better and better. Actually, if it weren't for Andrew really wanting a church wedding, we'd be headed there. If I could get him there, maybe I could …" She trailed off in thought.

"But then you wouldn't get to wear your dress. It will all come together, and before you know it all of the details will be taken care of and you can sit back and relax until the big day gets here. Is there anything I can help with?" I took a forkful of my salad and dunked it into the dressing.

Her eyes brightened. "Speaking of dresses, I think I found a dress." She twirled a fry in her fingers. "Can you go with me Saturday? I want to try it on one more time, and I want your opinion."

"Absolutely, but I have to tell you that you suck. Not many brides-to-be are stuffing fries in their mouths."

She stuck another handful of fries in her mouth.

"Oh, we need to nail down a shower date."

"I think we're pretty open." She pulled out her BlackBerry to bring up her calendar. "I don't want it too far before the wedding."

"Well, give me a couple dates for the two months prior."

"We have the family shower, some run-throughs. Okay, here's one." She scrolled some more. "And another. I'm e-mailing them to you right now."

"Great. Do you have a preference for couples or just girls?"

"Drew's stuck going to the family shower. I think I'll let him off the hook."

"Just girls it is. I'll talk to Caroline and Beth. I know they wanted to host too."

"None of the cheesy games, though." She threw her BlackBerry back in her bag. "On an entirely different subject, have you thought about what you're getting Josh for his birthday?"

"I have. I've alternated between getting him some golf lessons, a new driver, or tickets to the Astros. His company gets so many tickets to games, though, that I'm leaning away from that. What do you think?"

"I think my gift is going to pale in comparison. Drew and I were just going to get him a golf shirt or something."

"He'll like a shirt, and you know he'll wear it."

"Now, I just need to make sure we give him our gift before yours," Andy teased.

"I think I'll get him the driver."

"How do you even know which one to get him?"

"He's talked enough about what he's been wanting. It's a no-brainer. I think it's been drilled into my head."

"Was he dropping hints?"

"I don't think so. I think he was just talking wistfully."

Friday night I was running extremely late for Josh's surprise birthday party. Jason and I had arranged everything, and I was supposed to have been there thirty minutes ago with the catered food I was picking up on my way to his place. I had foolishly turned Andy down when she offered to help me with the cake. Instead of buying one from a bakery, I was baking a cake from scratch. As I surveyed the mess in the kitchen, the time on the stove caught my attention. I wiped my forehead with the back of my hand, smearing flour across it. The cake still had twenty minutes left in the oven, so I showered and dressed in the meantime. Thankfully, I had already laid out what I would be wearing or I would have been even later. When I took the cake out of the oven, I burned my finger on the side of the pan. Sticking it in my mouth was the only remedy I had time for. I broke multiple traffic laws between my apartment, the restaurant, and Jason's apartment.

"Hey, I'm here. Sorry I'm late." I fell into Jason's place with my arms full of bags. "There's more in my car. I'm double-parked downstairs."

"I'm glad you weren't in charge of the drinks. We would have had some upset guests on our hands. I'll text Rachel to let her know they can head over now. She's supposed to hit the buzzer on their way into the building." Rachel was a girl Josh had gone on a few dates with, and she was dragging him around until we were ready for him to arrive.

I ran back downstairs and found a space to park. I grabbed the rest of the food out of my car and took the elevator back up. This time when I walked into the apartment, I looked to see who had shown up. Josh's father was there sans his new wife. It was the first time I had seen him since their wedding in Santa Fe. Josh's mom and her husband were across the room. I made a note to myself to talk to her later in the evening.

I ignored the guests for the time being in order to set up the food and frost the cake. I was just putting the finishing touches of icing and placing the candles around the cake when Josh's dad appeared by my side.

"Hey, Mr. R." I gave him a hug, turning my cheek for his quick peck.

"Well, hello, Kate. You look beautiful tonight."

"You look great. Congratulations on the recent nuptials. Married life must be treating you well."

"No complaints. Unfortunately, Liz is home sick with a head cold."

"Oh, I'm sorry to hear that."

"Thanks, but she'll be fine. I think she caught it on the flight back from the recycled air on the airplane."

"That will do it. At least it was on the back end of the honeymoon. How was Maui?"

The buzzer sounded in the apartment, abruptly cutting into the conversations that were filling the room. We all gathered into the kitchen, speaking in hushed voices. We could hear the door opening. "Surprise!" everyone yelled.

Josh laughed, and then said a few words of thanks to everyone. Josh's dad returned his attention to me after the initial frenzy died down. Josh was making his way through the room and crowd of people. "Who's Josh with? Have you met her?" he asked in a hushed tone.

"Only briefly. I think her name is Rachel. She seemed nice enough." I was twisting a cool paper towel around my finger to lessen the stinging I was feeling from the burn.

He paused, looking back and forth between Josh and me. "What ever happened with you two? Whenever I ask Josh, he gives pretty evasive answers." He smiled.

"I'm not sure that I can come up with a much better response, but it really came down to bad timing. I think we've managed to come out of it being better friends. And just think, this way I get to give you the scoop on the girls he brings home."

"Then you need to get to work because you haven't done your job with his date to this party."

"True, but you have to remember, this wasn't a planned date. She may be someone we'd never have met if it wasn't convenient to have her keep him out of our hair while we got ready."

"Well, it wouldn't upset me if you two decided to start dating again."

"I'll keep that in mind." I smiled.

"Either way, you two are welcome to come to our house in Santa Fe once it's finished. We can get in some golf and sun." His tone lightened as he extended the invitation.

"Sounds good to me. I'll let Josh know he can tag along with me."

Josh was making his way toward his dad, so I stepped back to let them talk for a minute. Right before we stopped seeing each, we had gone the longest without talking. I had bombarded him with phone calls, to which he finally responded by e-mail.

I'm not trying to teach you a lesson. It was more to teach me a lesson. I just don't think we should do this anymore. I am to the point of such frustration with you that I don't want to talk to you. I'm tired of trying and getting nothing in return. I think that if you at least showed some effort or interest, it would be different, but you don't. I know you're busy, and I understand that, but I think you are only calling me now because I'm not answering my phone. Like you only want to get in touch with me because you think something might be wrong, not because you really want to talk to me. I haven't seen you in almost two weeks. I have a hard time believing that in two weeks you couldn't see me once. It's just not important to you and that's not fair to me. I've seen you withdraw and gradually stop acting like you're interested. I think it's best if we just don't do this anymore.

When I had received the e-mail, I couldn't figure out whether I was upset because I was angry or sad. I did feel guilty, but at the same time I think I had a new respect for Josh because he called me out on my horrible behavior. I had withdrawn from him. Had it not been for him putting it out there, though, we probably wouldn't have been able to be friends afterward.

Josh's dad started talking to Jason, so I excused myself to go and talk to Josh's mom.

"Hi, Judy."

"Hi, Kate." She gave me a big hug, squeezing me tight before she released. "I'm so glad you're here."

"Hi, Richard." I gave a quick side hug to Josh's stepfather.

"Hey, kid. You look nice."

Judy had remarried about five years after she and Josh's dad had divorced. She and Richard had been married now for about two years. It had been hard on Josh at first. Even though he wanted his mother to be happy, he had been crushed when his parents divorced. He had forced himself to show his support with his mother's new marriage. He had walked her down the aisle, fighting back the little kid in him who had secretly hoped that his parents would reunite, a secret he only divulged after too much alcohol at the reception. Now, he was getting accustomed to the different sets of holiday dinners and the new spouses who stayed on separate sides of the room, although they had started to more civilly coexist when thrown into the same space.

"Thank you. How's the foot?" I looked down at Judy's brace.

"Oh, it's fine. This is the third time in three years I've done this. You would think I'd learn that the dishwasher always wins."

"Is this the same one or a new one?"

"It's a new one. I just don't seem to have much luck with them."

"We have a new arrangement. Only I deal directly with the dishwasher," Richard added.

"That sounds like a good arrangement. I hate unloading the dishwasher."

Drew and Andy joined us. "Hi Judy, Richard." Andy gave them both hugs. Drew shook Richard's hand and kissed Judy's cheek.

"Andy, Drew, it's so good to see you. I don't think we've seen you since the engagement. Congratulations."

"Thank you," they both said.

"Let me see the ring." Andy obliged and held out her hand. "It's beautiful," Judy gushed.

The party was starting to wind down, and I was trying to hold out and make sure Josh continued to have a good time. But I was sitting on the couch and failing my fight against the yawns. I got up, stretching my legs. "Hey, walk me out." I grabbed Josh's arm.

"You're leaving already?" He threw his arm over my shoulder.

"Already? It's almost two in the morning. I need my beauty sleep." We walked toward the elevator. "So, did you have a good time tonight?"

"I had a great time. Thanks for helping and being here tonight."

"Nowhere else I'd be."

"Did you have a chance to talk to Rachel?"

I could tell he was only asking to be polite. "Not really. She seems pretty quiet."

"What do you think about her?"

Well, she's twenty ... she can't even legally drink. I realize nine years is not a huge difference, but it is when you're working and she's still in school. I also realize I'm being hypocritical, as I am sure Ben's thirty- or forty-something-year-old girlfriends would say the same thing about me. That is, if they actually knew about me. "I've already told you. What matters more is what you think about her."

Just then the doors to the elevator opened. "Happy birthday. I'll talk to you tomorrow." I leaned in and gave him a quick peck at the same time he leaned forward to kiss my forehead. I ended up bumping my nose on his chin. "Ouch." I rubbed my nose and stepped back. "When did we become so awkward with this?"

He was rubbing his chin. "I'm not sure. We may be in need of how-to instructions for ending the night with a close friend of the opposite sex."

"I doubt something like that exists. We could go in halves on it."

"I came up with the idea."

"Okay, sixty-forty, but only because it's your birthday." The elevator door began to blare. "I'll see you tomorrow. You still look good for thirty." The doors slid closed.

My mind flashed back to his birthday five years before. "Now that was a good way to start the day and my birthday, for that matter." Josh kissed my stomach. I let my head fall back and my hair sprayed across the pillow. I reached out for my robe, wriggling myself out from under Josh. Andy and I had been living in a tiny apartment, a year out of college. My bed took up most of my room with a foot around it on either side. The good thing about it was I could reach anything without leaving my bed, and I was able to pull my robe off the closet door just by shifting closer to the edge of the bed. He had asked where I was going. "To get your present." He said that the morning had been present enough. "If I had known that, I could have saved some money." He stopped me from getting out of bed. "Wait. I need to tell you something." I sat back down. He tucked some hair back behind my ear and cupped my chin in his hand. "I love you." And I replied that I loved him too. We didn't leave the bed the rest of the day. His gift waited.

The elevators opened at the bottom of Jason's apartment building and I was brought back into the present. I forced back the memory, chalking it up to nostalgia. That was the problem with remaining friends with someone you had not only dated but had been in love with. Memories like that could just unexpectedly pop up.

Chapter 16

ndy's dress had finally come in, and we were sitting in the dressing room of Saks waiting for Mimi to bring it out. I was leaning my chair back against the wall. "I'm dehydrated. Do you have any water?"

"No, but they'll bring you some if you ask." Andy was sitting with her arm draped over the chair and her legs crossed. She was anxiously tapping her foot.

"It's just gorgeous," we could hear Mimi trill as she was bustling down the hall. "Here it is. Do you want me to help you get into it?"

"No, that's okay. I have Kate here to help." Andy stood up and did her best to force a smile in Mimi's direction.

"Okay, just call me once you have it on," Mimi said as she closed the door behind her.

I had already turned my attention to the dress. "Oh, Andy, your dress, it's amazing." It was strapless, more of an ivory color. It fitted her through the top with a drop waist and pearl detailing down the back of the bodice.

She smiled genuinely this time. "Okay, I can do most of it myself, but give me your arm for balance as I step into it."

It was most of the way on at this point, and I was moving around to look at Andy from the front.

"What do you think?"

"I think you will be a beautiful bride. Drew will love it."

"Thank you. I just cannot believe how quickly it is approaching. It seems like we just got engaged."

"Ready for me to zip you up so we can get the full effect?"

She nodded and I moved back behind her.

"I can't believe it. It fits perfectly through the hips, the waist." Just as I was saying this, the dress was getting harder to zip. "It's a little tighter here."

"Can you pull it together? What if I push it from the front?" Andy was trying to push to give extra material.

"I'll try, but I don't know," I said hesitantly. After a few more attempts, I added, "I don't think it's going up anymore."

"What's wrong with it?" Andy's voice had become panicky. She was trying to angle herself in the mirror to see the back of the dress.

"Why don't I get Mimi?"

I peeked my head out the door.

"Is she ready, dear?" Mimi asked.

"You could say that." I opened the door and Mimi entered. Andy was facing both of us.

"Oh, dear, you look beautiful," Mimi cooed.

"It doesn't fit," Andy said flatly.

"Let's see. Where?"

Andy pointed. "Here around my chest."

"Let me try to zip it up."

"We already tried."

"I'll just give it a go." Mimi started pulling tightly.

"I can't breathe." Andy's face was turning red.

"It's like, two inches. Even if you pull it, it's not going to zip up," I stated.

"Hmmm." Mimi's face had scrunched up, looking puzzled. "Are you about to start your period? Have you gained any weight since you were measured?"

Andy's eyes flashed with this remark and her voice went up. "No, I am not about to start, and I have not …"

I could tell Andy was starting to lose it, so I cut in "The dress fits perfectly everywhere else. If it was too small, I think it would be tight elsewhere. Could there be a mistake with the dress?"

"I really do not think so. The designer is very good. Maybe you wait a week and come back to see if you lose weight?"

Andy's eyes widened.

"Could we just remeasure her and the dress to be sure?" I asked.

Mimi took out her notes and her tape measure. "Let's have you take the dress off." She took a tape measure around Andy. "The hips." Then she checked her sheet with the original measurements. "Same. The waist. Same. The bust. Same. Hmmm. Now let me just measure the dress quickly. Could you hold it here?" She was motioning to us. "The hips and waist are according to their chart." She was moving the measuring tape around the different points of the dress. "The bust is not. It is one and a half inches smaller. That is peculiar. It just never happens."

"So what now?" Andy asked.

"Well, I will need to get on the phone to the designer. We will need to discuss whether this dress can be altered or if we need a new one altogether."

"How could they fix this one? How long will it take?"

"We can get this taken care of quickly, I think. It's Saturday, so I will not be able to call them until Tuesday when the designer is open. I will call first thing and then get in touch with you."

She headed toward the door.

"It will be okay. They will get you the dress in time, and it will fit perfectly," I comforted Andy.

She was tearing just a bit.

"You know, normally it is a good thing for your boobs to get bigger and everything else to stay the same." I winked.

She broke into a half smile, though still on the verge of tears.

"Have you started your period?" I asked in a horrible attempt at a French accent.

She started laughing.

"Would you like to come back next week after removing a rib and see if it fits then?" She started laughing uncontrollably. We both collapsed on the dressing room floor in a giggling fit. "I thought you might rip her head off."

"I was definitely contemplating it." We were still laughing.

"Are you okay in there?" Mimi asked through the door.

I covered my mouth, stifling any more laughter. "We're fine. We'll be right out."

Andy finished dressing and we collected our things.

"I'll call you Tuesday," Mimi called to us. We waved.

"Do you want to get a drink?"

Andy looked at her watch. "It's a little early. Never mind—it's five o'clock somewhere."

"I'll let Josh know."

I sent Josh a text: "dress f-up. starting early @ tm. u in?"

Twenty minutes later Josh was walking in the door to Taco Macho. "Hey. Sorry to hear about the dress." Josh squeezed Andy's shoulder. "But I'm glad we're starting earlier." He slid into a seat across from her.

"Why's that?"

"I just can't put this together in ten minutes," Josh motioned toward himself.

"Uh-huh." I didn't bother asking him to explain, instead waiting him out.

"I have early dinner plans tonight."

"Someone new or someone older?" I quipped.

"Who is it this time?" Andy asked.

"Betty, Barbara, Bonnie, who can remember?" he playfully responded.

"Okay, funny. Seriously." She swatted him playfully in the arm.

"Bridget."

"And you met her ... ?" Andy prompted.

"At the gym," Josh replied, stalling on the details.

I rolled my eyes discreetly at Andy. Josh's trend of late seemed to be continuing.

"Don't think I didn't see that. She's twenty-seven and a lawyer. How's that for breaking out? I need a margarita before you guys continue with the third degree. Usual?" Josh hopped up to grab drinks for us.

"So who hit on whom?" Andy asked when Josh got back to the table, helping herself to one of the drinks he was setting down.

"You may find this hard to believe, but I wasn't actually scoping her out. I broke into one of her sets on a weight machine, not realizing it."

"Uh-huh. Did you actually see her using the machine?" I asked.

"Well, no. Why?"

"I think you were getting scoped out. She used that as a line to meet you."

"Turned the tables on you. You're just some guy."

"Good for her." Andy took a sip from her margarita.

Chapter 17

I was taking a couple days off during my birthday. Ben had planned something, though he still wasn't telling me what. I was still scrambling to finish packing and was unsuccessful in fitting everything in my carry-on when I heard a knock at the door. Buddy began barking.

"Hey." Ben gave me a peck on the cheek as he walked through the doorway.

"Hey, you. I'm just about ready."

He eyed his watch, which was more than enough to convey his point.

"I know, I know. I'm hurrying," I said, rushing past him back to my bedroom. "So can I now know where we're going?" I called out from my closet.

"Uh-uh. There is no way I am telling you anything that could slow you down. Wherever I told you would cause you to rethink what you packed."

"Are you going to blindfold me at the airport? It might raise a few red flags from security."

"No, once we are in the car, I will tell you where we are going."

Ben was picking up pictures and looking at them. "Parents, I assume?" I glanced over at the frame he was holding and nodded.

I realized it was the first time he had been in my apartment and stopped packing. "Is it what you expected?"

"What?"

"My apartment."

"Don't stop. I don't know. I guess I hadn't really pictured it. No pun intended."

We got to the airport and had to push through a sea of people. It seemed I was going in the opposite direction of everyone else in the airport. I felt a little out of breath as I was trying to twist and turn with my luggage, trying to jump out of the way of people almost walking straight into me. I stopped for a second and looked over at Ben, who seemed to be effortlessly navigating the crowd. He saw me stop out of the corner of his eye. "What are you doing?"

I blew a piece of hair out of my face. "Trying to figure out why it seems that everyone expects me to get out of their way when we are walking in the same space. I mean, there is not even a pause to see who is going to adjust their path from anyone, and you seem to not even notice the crowd."

He ignored my comment. "Come on. We're this way." He gestured to the line for first-class passengers through security. A little guilt passed through me as we walked past all of the customers waiting in the coach line, but it was easily remedied after I remembered my feeling of a fish swimming upstream moments earlier. We continued on to the gate, skipping Ben's usual stop at the President's Club.

"Can I get something for you to drink?" the flight attendant asked as we took our seats. "We still have a few minutes before takeoff."

"No, thank you." I took my pillow and blanket and snuggled in for the three-hour flight. Ben had taken out his laptop in preparation to work once the *ding* signaling it was okay had sounded.

I woke up and saw a note next to me on the pillow. "Order room service for breakfast in bed. I will be back as soon as the meeting is over. –Ben"

Even though I had taken vacation days, he had planned the trip around his work. I had tried to not let my disappointment show when he told me. We were out of the office, spending three days together in Southern California. I was trying to look on the bright side.

I rolled over to look at the clock, which read 8:15. It felt good to sleep in. I stretched my legs out and arms over my head and let out a big yawn. Ben wouldn't be back for a couple of hours. I swung my legs out from under the blankets, forcing myself to get out of bed.

When we had gotten in last night it had been dark, so I hadn't seen much of the resort. I walked straight to the windows and pulled back the curtains. It was absolutely beautiful—the cloudless sky was blue, and the ocean was within walking distance. "I think I'll go for a run," I mumbled aloud to myself. I pulled out my laptop and let it power up while I changed clothes.

I opened my inbox and scrolled through my new e-mail. Thankfully there was nothing urgent. I snapped the computer shut and pulled my hair into a ponytail.

I ran down the sidewalk next to the ocean. After thirty minutes out, I turned around to head back to the hotel. When I got back to the room, I was happy to see the cleaning service had already turned the room. I threw the "Do Not Disturb" sign on the door. I wanted to be showered and dressed by the time Ben came back to the room.

After I was dressed, I clicked through the channels on the television, but nothing caught my interest. I looked at the clock; it was now 11:30. I was starting to get restless and hungry. I opened the sliding door and positioned the lounge chair toward the beach. If I was going to wait, I should at least enjoy the beautiful weather while doing so.

An hour later I heard the door shut.

"I was thinking you might lounge around in bed this morning, but that doesn't look to be the case."

I opened my eyes to see Ben standing over me. "Hey."

"Hey." He smiled and sat down on the edge of the lounge chair.

"It was so beautiful I couldn't stay inside."

"Did you order room service at least?"

"No, I went for a run. I wasn't sure when you would be back so I decided to wait. Have you eaten?" I pushed myself up in the chair.

"Not yet. Let me change and then we can go get something." He stood up and walked back into the room.

"Hurry, I'm starving," I called after him.

"Where did you run?" His voice was muffled as he pulled his shirt over his head.

"There's a walkway that parallels the beach, so I ran along that."

"How far?"

"I'm not sure. I ran about an hour. It was a slow run, so I would guess about five miles."

"After last night and then the run, you must be starving."

"The run did me in." I got up from the chair, closing the door to the balcony behind me. I kept my back to him to hide my smile.

"I guess I'll have to do a better job then." He scooped me up and threw me onto the bed.

"No, no, no," I laughed. "You were wonderful, great."

"Well, now I know you're just saying that because you're hungry." He pulled me up from the bed. "I will do a better job later."

"I look forward to it, but for now I need food." I slid into my wedge sandals.

Ben looked down at my shoe choice. "Are you going to be all right to walk around for a while in those?"

"These are comfortable. I'll be fine."

"I'm not sure I've ever seen you in flat shoes. I think I'd actually like to see your running shoes on."

"Maybe if you didn't leave me alone all morning, you would have had the chance." I grabbed his hand to pull him out of the room. "Do you have a key?"

"Yes. Do you?"

"No, that's why I asked you."

"You should carry one too."

"Aren't I going to be with you?" I stopped. "Unless you're planning on losing me."

"I might if you complain about your shoes being uncomfortable while we're out."

"If you keep this up, I am purposely not going to wear any of the flats or flip-flops I brought with me."

"That would show me." He pushed the down button at the elevator. "You are too much sometimes."

"Thank you."

When Ben returned later in the day, I was in the process of getting ready for dinner. I had closed myself in the bathroom, not wanting him to see me until I was ready so he would get the full effect.

"Kate, we're going to be late for our reservation."

I didn't respond but put the finishing touches on my eye makeup. I ran a brush through my hair once more and smoothed down my dress.

"Kate, are you ...," he trailed off as I opened the door. "That's some dress."

"Thank you. You clean up pretty well yourself." I grabbed my purse. "I'm ready to go."

"The restaurant is just along the beach. Do you think you are okay to walk?"

"I am. These aren't just for looks; they're for comfort too," I lied.

The walk was about five minutes down from our hotel. A breeze was blowing in from the ocean, causing me to shiver a couple of times.

"Reservation for Covney."

"Right this way." The hostess directed us to a table. "We have this one set up on the patio for you. Will it be okay?"

"I think so." He looked at me expectantly. I nodded in response.

We had spent two days in California, but dinner was the longest amount of time we spent together, outside of sleeping. I alternated between working in the room and soaking in the sun while he was in meetings— except for today, when I went shopping at some of the small boutiques nearby. I wanted to make the most of tonight since we were leaving tomorrow.

The conversation during dinner centered mostly on work and the meetings that Ben had been holding over the past couple of days. We had a popcorn risotto that melted in my mouth. It was such an odd combination that went surprisingly well together. I felt a little tipsy from the wine at dinner. I couldn't quite tell how many glasses I had because the waiter never let me finish a glass. As soon as I had less than a third in my glass, he poured more. It felt like a competition to finish before he refreshed it.

"Did you enjoy dinner?" Ben asked.

"I did." We were slowly swinging our hands back and forth as we walked down the hall.

"I still have a surprise for you."

"You do? What is it?"

"You'll have to wait and see."

"Then why did you bring it up?"

"To get you excited."

"I hate surprises. If I know I'm being surprised, I would rather just know."

"I'll remember that next time."

"What about this time?"

"You'll just have to suffer all of two minutes until we get back to the room." The walkway from the beach led into an open lobby. With the breeze from the ocean, it was quite cool. I was wishing I had packed a wrap while rubbing my arms to keep warm. As soon as we turned the corner to the hallway, I instantly warmed up. Ben put the key in the door and waited for the light to turn green.

When we entered the room, a bottle of champagne was chilling in a bucket of ice. Two glasses were set next to it with a card propped next to them. I walked toward the table and picked up the card. "Happy Birthday, Kate. Thank you for spending it with me. — Ben." In the chair next to the table was a beautifully wrapped box.

"Is this for me?"

"It is."

"Can I open it?" He nodded. I quickly tore the paper away and rested the top of the box on the chair. I placed the box on the table so that I could get rid of the tissue paper. Inside was black silk lingerie. I lifted it from the box. "Is this my surprise?"

"It is. Do you like?"

"Ummm." I pursed my lips. I kept my head down and nodded. I knew it was a little too strong, overcompensating, but hoped Ben didn't notice. "Thank you." I felt myself forcing a smile for him.

On Saturday, Josh and I drove to the country club, where we met Shawn and my dad for a round of golf. After that, we were going to my parents' house for a belated celebratory birthday lunch.

"Thanks for driving this morning."

"Sure, no problem." I glanced sideways at him. "It's easier to fit all the clubs into an SUV anyway."

"You've surprised me."

"Why's that?"

"Well, your birthday was a few days ago, and you haven't once asked me for your present."

"Delayed gratification."

"When have you once wanted to delay anything?"

"There's a first time for everything." I turned my blinker on as we approached the club.

"Well, I guess it's good that you're wanting to delay it."

"Why's that?"

"Because I don't have it with me. You'll have to wait until later when we get back."

"That's just wrong. Tease me about it, and you can't deliver."

"You can open it as soon as we get back to your apartment. I dropped it off before we left."

"I didn't see anything."

"That's because you were running around trying to get everything together. And I know you hate surprises. But I also know that if I had distracted you with the present then, we would have been late for our tee time."

We pulled into the club, which was located in the middle of the city. I always loved the club because it was an expanse of trees and greens for miles. Just two minutes before, we were driving through blocks of pavement and buildings of varying heights. Without zoning laws, Houston was a city where a business could be set up next to a house. It made for an eccentric city, which people often loved or hated, never staying on the fence. We settled into a parking spot in the midst of SUVs and Texas-sized trucks. The number of cars was directly proportional to the weather: the better the weather, the more cars. And today was no exception. The sky was cloudless. Unfortunately, it was also especially hot, with the humid air hanging around us.

My dad and Shawn were milling around the pro shop. "Hey, Dad," I called out.

My dad enveloped me in a hug. Then he pulled back and tipped my hat. "Good to see ya kid. And happy belated birthday." He gave me another hug.

"You act like you haven't seen me in years."

"I haven't seen you since you turned twenty-nine. You're mother has been weepy all week."

"It's not that big of a deal."

"It is when it means she's getting older too," he teased. "I think it's also because you're her firstborn."

We walked to our carts, which were already loaded with our clubs and water. "You guys ready?" Shawn asked.

"I'm ready. No warm-up for me. Then I waste my best shots," Dad replied.

"So what's new with you?" Josh asked as he drove the cart to the first hole.

I had yet to tell him about Ben, and for some reason, I couldn't bring myself to talk to him about it. "Nothing." I shook my head.

"Are you sure?" He glanced over at me, searching my face.

"Yeah, yeah. I'm just tired." I shook myself out of it. I needed to better conceal what I was thinking. "So, a dollar a hole?"

"That's too rich for my blood."

"It's not like I ever make you pay."

"I don't like being so far in debt to you."

"Maybe you should take some lessons," I said with a straight face.

"Oh, you are spitting in the face of the golf gods. You are going to be in the woods today."

"So, then, do you want to bet?"

"Hey, you two, are you out for a Sunday drive or here to play golf?" Dad called to us as he and Shawn puttered by in their cart.

"Your daughter's trying to take my money," Josh called back to him.

"Well, at least she moved on to someone else other than me."

"Hey, I take exception to that." I pulled a pouty face.

Houston had been getting so much rain lately that Josh and I spent most of the time trying to leave the cart in a good location between our shots, and then one or both of us running quickly to catch up. By the end of our round, we were all pretty sweaty and our clothes were sticking to us.

Because my mother told us we smelled, we ate lunch on the patio. She made ice cream in belated celebration of my birthday. Josh and

I sat on the swing enjoying the ice cream before it melted. A breeze finally picked up, and the combination finally cooled us down. We spent another hour or so on the patio with my parents, Shawn, and Caroline before my mother brought out a gift bag overflowing with decorative tissue paper and ribbons. "This is from all of us," she said as she handed me the bag. Inside were cards from my parents and Caroline, which I read before reaching further into the bag. I pushed aside the tissue paper to see a pink shoe box. "You didn't." I slid the box out from the bag, leaving the ribbon tying the handles in tact. I opened up the box and pulled out a pair of grey Jimmy Choo pumps with a delicate buckle near the toe. "Thank you. Thank you. Thank you." I held them up for all to admire.

"You're welcome, sweetie." My mom kissed my forehead.

"I will never understand, but I am happy that they seem to bring you so much joy," my dad said with a bemused expression.

Caroline and Shawn had to leave to meet up with his parents, so Josh and I took that as our cue to leave too.

When we got back to my apartment, I saw that Josh had left a small wrapped box on my dresser. I picked it up and brought it back into the living room. "Hmmm. Definitely not shoes."

"It could be a gift card that you could use to buy shoes."

"It's too heavy."

"I put a rock in it." Josh was sitting on the couch, so I sat down next to him. "Just open it already."

"Okay." I untied the ribbon, letting it fall into my lap. Then I tore the wrapping paper from the box. I set the lid to the side, held my hand open, and let the contents fall from the velvet bag.

It was a white gold bangle with a tiny locket.

"Josh, this is beautiful." I traced my finger on the locket.

"It opens."

I snapped it open, and there was a picture of Buddy from when he was a puppy.

"Oh, Josh. It's perfect."

"I've been wanting to give it to you for awhile now. Just thought your birthday finally seemed like the right time. It's not too cheesy?"

"No."

"The locket was actually my mom's."

"Josh, this is too nice. Are you sure?" I could feel my eyes tearing up.

"I want you to have it. So does my mom."

"Thank you." I set the bracelet down and moved closer to Josh to give him a hug. "Thank you so much. I love it."

"You're welcome."

I pulled back and picked up the bracelet. "Now, how does it look?" I showed it off on my wrist. With my other hand, I wiped the tear that had fallen onto my cheek. "Apparently, as I get older, I get more emotional." I shrugged off my sappiness.

Chapter 18

We were sitting in Ben's office at the end of the day. The rest of the office was deserted about a half hour earlier. I walked through the office, just to be sure, before sitting down in the chair across from Ben. I didn't want to be surprised with Simon or someone else lurking around.

I was starting in about us grabbing a bite to eat after work. I knew under usual circumstances I wouldn't see him until much later in the evening. But I felt like eating dinner at a decent hour with the man I was seeing. And then I felt like curling up in bed early, perhaps watching a movie with Buddy at my feet. I didn't include Ben in that scenario. Ben was the man to go out with. He didn't strike me as the man to cuddle in bed with.

That was okay with me, but it was also why dinner in a restaurant was important. It didn't seem like too much to ask for. Still, I knew my request wasn't quite so simple.

"I believe we both agreed that we should be discreet." The annoyance was painfully clear on Ben's face.

"We did agree, and we have been, are being, and will continue to be discreet. But being discreet does not preclude two coworkers from having dinner in a restaurant with people. Besides, if we were to run into anyone, it could be easily explained."

"Is such a mundane act really so important to you?"

"Actually, yes. It sounds perfect to me."

I could see he was caving. He hesitated for one second too long, and I knew he was giving in. "Well, then, if it's important, let's go." He pushed back his chair and started shutting down his computer. "Give me about ten minutes to get everything together. You can follow me to the restaurant."

The restaurant was not one that I had ever noticed or even heard of. The entrance was somewhat obstructed from view, so that if I had not been following Ben, I would have passed right by it. I tried to ignore the seediness I felt when we entered the restaurant. Even though Houston had been smoke-free for the last year, a layer of murky film hung in the air. There was a large bar area lined with booths to one side. The dining area was set up with individual booths turned away from the bar to add extra privacy. As I took in the diners, I noticed they were mostly couples. But something about them didn't look "couplely." These couples looked exactly like what I would envision of people who were engaged in some illicit entanglement. I suppressed my disappointment with his choice of venue and tried to focus on the fact that Ben and I were going to eat dinner in public.

We helped ourselves to a booth toward the back. I angled myself to have a view of the door. I couldn't resist my intrigue with the people walking into this place. I briefly thought of Josh and our game. He would have had a field day. It occurred to me that people may be looking at us and wondering about our story.

I reached out, placing my hand gently on his. Ben immediately withdrew it, and he began to run his hand back and forth through his hair, slightly disheveling it. The tension was showing in his face, and when he placed his hand back down on top of mine, I could feel it. He was pressing his thumb and middle finger into my hand. I could tell this gesture was meant to convey a point. "Kate," he drew a breath.

Before he continued, I pulled my hand out of his clutch. "Never mind. I get it." I waved it off.

He motioned the waitress over and ordered drinks for both of us.

"How was your day? Anything exciting happen?" I asked.

"Not really. Just working on a couple of proposals." He loosened his tie and unbuttoned the top button to his shirt. "How is your project going?"

"Pretty well. Olivia and I butt heads probably a little too often. I'm pulling against the reins she keeps trying to put on me."

"Sometimes finesse can work better than brute force."

"Is that how you think you operate?"

"Do you disagree?"

I ignored his baiting me. "I think it's a little weird. I brought in the client, and they feel comfortable with me. Can I help it that they come to me when they want updates or have questions?" I carried on without waiting for his response, "I think Olivia feels like I'm cutting her out."

"Are you?"

"No. And you know you would never direct a client to someone else. 'I'm sorry, you need to speak to so-and-so.'" I mimicked talking to a client. "I can't believe she would expect that of me either."

"Then what?"

I hesitated for a moment. I wanted to be careful with my choice of words. "Olivia has a reputation for being a micromanager," I finally said, feeling safe with that description. That was acceptable to say about a coworker without seeming harsh. With my comment, he smiled. "What?" I looked at him expectantly.

"Two people with AR. I see the problem."

"AR? Should I know what that is?"

"Anal retentive."

"I am not AR!" I looked at him in disbelief. "You've seen my office. It's a mess."

152

"That's a ruse. I've seen what you do if I nudge a pile of paper an inch."

"I don't care about the mess though. I don't want stuff moved because I don't want to lose my system. Even with the mess, I know exactly where everything is."

"And if someone moves something, you can't help but move it back. Quite a conundrum to be messy and AR, but it's the need for control in you. You control the mess."

"I feel like I should be lying on a couch." I smiled. The door to the restaurant opened and I watched a group file in.

Shit. I could only hope that she wouldn't see us. The size of the restaurant made me doubtful that I would be so lucky. And then, as I watched her survey the room, her face lit up as she saw me. I could see her say something to the people she was with, and now she was walking toward us. Ben saw my reaction and the smile that was seemingly frozen in place. He looked over his shoulder at who was holding my attention and turned back to me, "Who's that?" Two little words that normally wouldn't sound ominous suddenly did with his change in tone.

"My roommate, Andy." A look in his eyes, which I could only read as anger, flashed briefly before it disappeared. "I had no idea," I proffered, knowing that any explanation at this point would not make a difference.

"Shit." He echoed my earlier thought.

"Hey, what are you doing here?" Andy leaned down to give me a hug.

"Just catching a quick dinner. What about you?"

"One of my coworkers kept raving about this hole-in-the-wall around the corner from where he lived. He said it sometimes drew a sl—" She broke off mid-word before resuming, "a different crowd, but that the bruschetta and crab cakes were to die for. So a few of us from work came for drinks and appetizers." She was standing somewhat uneasily, as I had yet to introduce her and Ben to one another. She was glancing in his direction, and I could tell she was waiting for me to make a proper introduction.

153

"Andy, this is Ben. We are working on that project I was talking to you about." Her attention to what I was saying ended as soon as I uttered his name. The recognition on her face was obvious, though I hoped Ben missed it. "Ben, this is Andy, my roommate." I added the last part unnecessarily, because he knew and she knew that he knew. But I was uncomfortable, and talking seemed to be the only way I could attempt nonchalance with the two of them meeting. I knew I was failing miserably and wanted to sink into the booth.

"Nice to meet you." Andy extended her hand to Ben, who shook it, but said nothing in return.

An awkward silence fell over the three of us.

I couldn't help but think that if this were anyone else, I would have asked Andy to join us. I would have wanted her to get to know the guy, and then, when we were home, I would make her dissect him, giving me her full appraisal. I knew that wouldn't or couldn't happen tonight.

I looked apologetically at Andy. Ben stared at his drink. Andy searched my face to make sure I was all right before making an excuse to get back to the people she was with. "I told them I wouldn't be long, so I should get back," she finally said.

At the same time I was nodding for her to leave, I wanted to say something to prolong her from doing so, because I knew as soon as she left Ben's silence would be deafening.

"I'll see you later." Andy backed away from the table as I mouthed "sorry" to her.

After Andy left, the silence remained. Ben was slowly swirling the ice in his drink. It felt like we were in a standoff, willing the other to speak first.

I broke first. "It's not that big of a deal," I mumbled, not able to meet his eyes. "She already knows about us."

"What do you mean?" His question was barely above a whisper.

I clasped my hands together in my lap. I took a deep breath and looked up to match his gaze. "She's my roommate. She notices when I'm not home," I stated simply.

"Is this your idea of discreet? Telling everyone?"

"Everyone? You must know you're exaggerating. She's my best friend. She knows me. She knows when I'm keeping something from her."

"You're such a child." He shook his head with disgust.

The look on his face got under my skin, making it impossible for me to brush his remark aside. "Because I'm honest with people in my life?"

"Because you still have a roommate. Because you still hang out with a group of friends who are caught up in each others' lives, thriving on gossip. You're twenty-nine and you live like you're twenty-two."

"What do you know about my friends? Until tonight you had not met a single one of them. You have shown no interest in doing so. Do not judge me. Do not judge my life. And, do not judge my friends." My voice was becoming louder, and I knew it was attracting the attention of other diners. "You have decided that you want to be on the periphery of my life. Then stay there, but do not condemn what you know nothing about." He stared at me, so I continued my verbal attack. "When we talked about dinner tonight, this is the place that came to mind? This is how you see me?"

"What are you talking about?"

"This place is sleazy." I knew that was the word Andy was going to use when she stopped herself, because it was the word that came to my mind when Ben and I first walked into the place.

"Well, I'm sorry if this does not live up to your standards." His tone was sarcastic, without a trace of regret in it.

"You're being an ass tonight. Not only to me, but you were one to Andy as well. If you didn't want to do this, you should have just told me."

"I did. Remember? That is what I was saying in my office."

I balled up my napkin and threw it on the table. I stood up, grabbing my bag without saying another word, and made my exit.

I knew Andy was watching me leave, but I couldn't face her, not now. I knew what she would think, and I didn't have it in me to make any excuses for Ben's behavior and why I would tolerate it.

I was in bed, pretending to be asleep, when Andy returned home. I couldn't avoid her for long, but I could at least put off the discussion of Ben until tomorrow.

The next morning I left before Andy was up. I wouldn't be able to avoid Andy for much longer, but at least it gave me the rest of the day to get my thoughts together. Ben was working with Simon and a couple of the graphic artists, holed up in one of the conference rooms. I breathed a sigh of relief that I wouldn't have to deal with either one of them today. I could hear Andy's voice reminding me about why I shouldn't get involved with anyone at work: *You'll end up hiding in your office.*

Flowers arrived for me later that afternoon. The card simply read, "From an ass. You were right." I couldn't smile. I wasn't ready to forgive him. I was still too mad and too hurt from the night before. But I kept the card. I slid it into my pocket, knowing that I would want to look at it again when my resentment subsided.

I left the flowers at work and braced myself for Andy's interrogation when I walked in the apartment. She was sitting on the couch eating out of a box of cereal and watching the news. "I'm too tired to cook tonight."

I sat down next to her and held out my hand, cupping it as she poured some Cheerios. "He was having a bad day." I knew it was a lousy excuse, but it was all I could muster. Andy raised an eyebrow but didn't say anything in return.

I sat there waiting for her to bring it up, but she started talking about the caterer and his inability to return a call before the third message.

Chapter 19

"So I hear you and Andrea are the two I really have to get the stamp of approval from," Bridget began as she slid onto the barstool next to mine.

"Oh, that's not true. If Josh is happy, then Andy and I are too."

"In all sincerity, I know you two mean the world to him."

"We are a pretty close group, and we watch out for each other." I followed her gaze to where Josh and some of the guys were standing. They had positioned themselves into their having-a-good-time-but-still-watching-the-rest-of-the-bar stance. Sadly, their technique had not changed much in the eight years since college.

"This may sound out of the blue, but I'd love for us to go to lunch some time," Bridget continued.

Why? I caught myself from saying what I was thinking. "That sounds great." As the words came out of my mouth, I could hear the enthusiasm and was sure she could tell it was false.

"Really? Great. I'll get your number from Josh. Speaking of, I'm going to see what kind of trouble he's getting into." She slid off of the stool, and seconds later Andy slid into it. "So?" she asked, motioning to the bartender for another apple martini.

"There's something about her I just don't like."

"Yeah, I can see that. She's smart, pretty, successful. Josh really should raise his standards."

"I'm not saying she isn't those things. She just isn't a good fit for him." I was absently fiddling with my new bracelet.

"All you have to say to him is that you're interested." Andy eyed my wrist.

I stopped playing with it. "That's not it." I knew I sounded jealous. But that wasn't it. "I want him to be with someone who gets him."

"How do you know she doesn't?"

"Kate," Jason came up behind us. I swiveled on my stool to face him. "I want to introduce you to a friend of mine." I looked out of the corner of my eye to see if Andy looked like she was in on this. "This is Matt."

Matt stuck out his hand. "Hi, it's nice to meet you."

"Nice to meet you as well." I shook his hand.

"Matt is a huge Red Sox fan and follows baseball avidly. And Kate is a pretty avid follower herself." Jason lightly punched my arm.

"That's me." I smiled.

"If you'll excuse me, I need to grab Drew for a second." Andy pushed herself back from the bar.

"I'll go with you. I need to talk to Beth." Jason stepped back.

Very subtle, guys.

"Do you mind if I join you?" Matt asked.

"Not at all." I motioned to the stool Andy had just vacated.

"So, did you jump on the bandwagon, or were you a fan before they won a couple years back?" I asked.

"I grew up in Boston, so it's pretty much bred in me."

"Ummm. So how do you and Jason know each other?"

"Work. It looks like you're almost empty. Need another?" he gestured to my glass.

"Sure."

Matt motioned to the bartender, who brought us another round. I pulled out my credit card.

"Let me." Matt handed him money before I could object.

"Thank you." I finished the last of my drink. "How long have you been in Houston?"

"Not that long actually. It's been about a month since I transferred from our Boston office."

"How are you liking it?" I offered the next logical question. I knew I was phoning it in with my line of questioning, so I redirected my attention away from the TV and toward him. This guy could potentially become a regular with our friends. It couldn't hurt to be friendly, even though I knew Andy and Jason were obviously hoping for more.

"It's fine so far. I'm meeting some nice people, but it's strange being in a new place not really knowing anyone."

"I can only imagine. I've known most of these people going on ten years. Some less, but still quite a while. And my family lives close by."

"Well, if you're looking to expand the company you keep, maybe we could get a drink or dinner sometime."

I nodded, non-committal in my response. "Are you into other sports or just baseball?" I tried to redirect us back to a safe conversation topic.

I still hadn't talked to Ben about whether we were seeing other people, but I was not interested in Matt. I was hoping that not having the conversation meant that Ben wasn't interested in dating someone else, but I knew that was wishful thinking. Matt and I exchanged trivia regarding baseball for the next half hour.

Josh slid into the booth. "No reading aloud today. I cannot fill my head with any more of 'are they dating, will they get married, I know they had a baby but do you think they faked the pregnancy, is he really the father.'" His voice had gone up a falsetto in mockery of us.

"And to think I brought a guilty pleasure for you." I put down the *US* magazine I was reading. We were sitting across from one another in the back corner of the restaurant. The windows to the restaurant were open letting the sun illuminate the room rather than fluorescent lighting.

"What are you talking about?" He repositioned his baseball hat to face backward.

I lifted my sunglasses up and placed them on top of my head. "Let's see who they have on the cover this month. The new I'm-sluttier-than-usual-but-not-too-slutty girl." I was pulling the magazine out of my bag.

"Hand it over." He held out his hand.

"I don't know. You seem a little grouchy today and I'm not sure I want to reward that behavior." I was holding it out of his reach.

Andy walked up from behind and snatched it from my hand. Then she slid it across the table to Josh.

"You took away my fun." I moved over in the booth so she could squeeze in.

"I swear sometimes you two act like you are in grade school."

Josh thumbed through the magazine, not really looking at the pages. Then he set it aside.

"I saw the two of you talking to Bridget last night. Let me have it."

"Have what?" Andy picked up *US* and started to flip through it.

"I'm ready for you to dissect all of her problems and personality flaws."

"Do you think she has personality flaws?" I picked up the *In Touch* following Andy's lead. "That sounds more on you."

"Cut the crap." He put his hands over both our magazines and pushed them to the table.

"Whoa, a little testy. What's the big deal?"

"The big deal is I don't know how many hours I have listened to your wedding details. And you," he turned his attention to me, "how many crappy dates have we discussed? I should get ... really, I *deserve* your undivided attention on the topic of Bridget and your full catty analysis." He took a drink from the water in front of him. "It's the very least for putting up with the two of you and your 'can I get your perspective as a guy?'" His voice went up an octave again as he took on our whine.

"Well, this is different. You actually care whether we like the girl," Andy said with surprise in her voice.

"We don't sound like that," I muttered quietly.

"I get so much crap from the guys for spending so much time with you two. I always tell them I'm gaining insight to the female psyche. Well, you have to come through for me every once in a while."

"She's a lawyer, so maybe you can get a sugar mamma out of this." Josh winced at my remark. "Sorry. I'll be serious. I like that she has herself together," I tried again.

"She must be interested. The fact that she even is taking the time to be friendly with us. She has to know we are going to be her biggest critics," Andy added.

"Speaking of, being friends with her, I do have a favor to ask."

"Who was speaking of being friends? Does she not have any friends? You know that probably says something about her."

"Ease off." Josh's look silenced me. "I know she mentioned to you two about getting together for lunch. Would you take her up on it?" A look of confusion crossed Andy's face.

I jumped in. "How long have you been dating? Don't you think it's a little too soon for us to invest our time in getting to know her until you know that it's serious?"

"I think what Kate is trying to say not so eloquently is, where do you see this going?"

"I don't know yet, but I cannot believe you two. And Kate, what is with the attitude? I would think you'd be thrilled. You are always riding me about dating girls old enough to 'vote'. I am, and you can't even give her a chance." Josh got up, picking his empty glass from the table to refill his water.

Andy turned toward me. "She asked us to lunch? You forgot to mention that."

"Did I?" I picked up the magazine to avoid her stare.

"We have to show him some support. It's a good thing. He actually likes someone, which hasn't been the case for a long time." As if to make her point hit home, "He's been so hung up on you."

I was surprised by her tone. "Well, he's definitely not hung up on me now," I said quietly.

"Kate, you have to stop it. You can't have it both ways. You can't have your own relationship and be pouty when Josh finally gets one of his own. Do you really want him to sit home pining for you?" Andy was getting upset with me, which didn't happen too often.

"No." I swirled the ice in my drink. "I just don't want it to affect our friendship. I don't want it to change." She raised her eyebrows and opened her mouth to interject, but I stopped her. "I get that I am being selfish."

"Be a good friend and think about him."

Josh came back to the table.

I pulled out my cell phone. "So what's her number?"

"Are you going to call her right now?"

"No, but I will need it to call her later to schedule lunch."

He smiled for the first time since he had arrived.

Chapter 20

"Do you want anything to drink?" Ben said over his shoulder as he walked into the kitchen.

"No, I'm fine," I replied, not looking up from the computer screen in front of me.

He returned with two glasses of water and set one down on the end table next to me. "In case you change your mind."

"Thanks." I pushed a piece of hair that had fallen out of ponytail behind my ear.

"What are you working on so intently?" He sat down across the room. "You usually are fully focused on me when we're together."

I ignored the conceit in that statement and was slightly happy that he seemed a little perturbed by my inattention. *That has to mean something.* "The invitation and guest list for Andy's bridal shower."

"Sounds fun." His voice lacked any enthusiasm. "Do you want to get married?"

His question caught me off guard, but I decided to deflect with humor. "It's a little soon, don't ya think?"

He was flipping through TV channels. "I wasn't asking. I was curious if it was contagious."

"I don't think so. I don't think my feelings have changed on the subject." I was trying to act nonchalant but could feel myself feeling nervous. This was the most serious conversation about a relationship we'd broached, even if it wasn't directly about us.

"And those would be?"

"I am not in any rush, but some day I think I would like to be married."

"That sounded overwhelmingly certain."

"Shut up." I threw a pillow in his direction. "What about you?"

"I've been married. Now I'm into dating. I want to see what is out there."

Seriously? Well, that's good to know where I stand. I could feel my stomach turn. "I guess this is as good of a time as any to ask, does that mean you're dating other people?"

"Not actively."

"What does that mean?"

"If an opportunity presented itself, I wouldn't turn it down."

"Oh."

"Kate, I'm not in any position to get serious with someone. I thought we were having fun."

"We are."

The conversation with Ben struck a chord. I didn't feel like I was in any position to demand more. He made his feelings on the subject clear with just a few short statements. I wasn't sure if it was me or him, but over the next week we spent less time together. At work, I didn't make excuses to go into his office. It didn't seem to register with him, and on Friday, it was another weekend that I was finding myself Ben-less.

"Ugh." Andy threw another shirt on the floor.

I looked up from my laptop.

"I'm starting to understand your shopping frequency." She stared listlessly at her closet.

"Nothing fits right. This shirt is too short for those pants." She was pointing to clothes that were now strewn across her room. "How is it possible that my shirts are shorter?"

"See, I'm not an addict. I'm a victim." I went on to explain, "My theory is that from season to season designers slightly change the length of shirts and the height of where pants hit on the waist. So if you do not update your closet, then clothes from different seasons will not work together." She gave a small smile. "What's the deal? You've had dinner with Drew's parents a hundred times."

"I know, I know. I think as the wedding gets closer that my stress level is rising and spilling over and influencing things like this. I mean, you know how I care, or should say, don't care, about wearing the right thing. And look at me tonight!"

"Who is going to be there tonight?"

"That's the other thing. It was originally just our parents, who have met and gone to dinner together before. But now it has extended to our grandparents and some other extended family members. So what I thought was going to be a run-through of all the wedding details has turned into a meeting of extended families. And who knows how the grandparents will get along. Our families are very different—different cultures, different lifestyles. Is it too late to elope? Have I asked that before?"

"Just a few times. But that's okay." I picked up a shirt and held it in front of me in the mirror. "Different cultures? I'm not sure different parts of the U.S. qualify as different cultures."

"My grandparents didn't grow up in the States."

"But they have lived here for quite a while, and I think have pretty well adapted to American culture. I mean, your grandmother even follows celebrity gossip with us."

"Not the kind of culture that I think his family will be interested in talking about."

"Well, I hate to break it to you, but I do think it's too late to elope, given that you are only three months away from the wedding. Your parents might be a little upset if you ran off. But you know I'm always up for Vegas." I smiled empathetically at her.

"I'm sure it brings a different kind of stress, but ..." She trailed off.

"Tonight will be fine and Drew will be there. You know he'll be able to help smooth over any issues that may come up. And just think, in a few months you'll be lying on the beach with your new husband, miles away from all of this." It dawned on me that Andy was throwing clothes into a suitcase. "Wait. Why are you packing?"

"Because *someone* thought it would be a good idea for us to stay at the hotel. Kind of like a dry run for our wedding so we can make sure the guests get the level of service they should."

I could tell by the emphasis on *someone* that she meant Drew's mom.

"Drew and I even have separate rooms." She rolled her eyes.

"I'm sure they're adjoining."

"I'm sure she made sure that was not the case," she said sarcastically. "So anyway, what were you planning to do tonight?"

"I think I'll stay in."

"What? Why? Have you talked to Josh?"

"It's been a long week at work. I thought I'd stay in and watch a movie with Buddy. Josh is probably going out with Bridget anyway."

"How do you know?"

"Well, he hasn't called much lately, so I assume he's out with her."

"Have you called him?"

"No."

"Maybe he's waiting for you to call him." She let that sink in before asking, "Is Ben in town this weekend?"

"I don't think so."

"Where'd he go?"

"I really don't know. He was kind of vague, and I didn't really press him on it."

Andy just nodded, and I could tell by her silence and lack of eye contact she was trying to hide her disapproval.

After Andy left, I threw myself on the couch. I grabbed the phone, started to dial, and hung up. "Oh, this is ridiculous," I mumbled to myself. I completed dialing the number.

"Hello." Josh's voice came over the phone.

"Hey."

"Hey yourself. What are you up to?" His voice sounded completely comfortable. I loved that about talking to him.

"Nothing much. Thinking I would order in and cuddle on the couch with Buddy. What are you doing?"

"Just got back from a run, and now I'm waiting on a pizza to arrive."

"Is it all for you?"

"As far as I know. I probably have enough to share."

I thought I should be a little more direct. "Are you alone?"

"As far as I know."

"Cute."

"Thanks."

"Do you want to come down and watch a movie with me and Buddy?"

"And bring the pizza?"

"Obviously."

"What are you planning to watch?"

"Don't know yet, but I'll at least give you veto power," I said, knowing he was worried about what romantic comedy I might have in mind.

"Okay then. I'll hop in the shower and be down after the pizza gets here. It should be about fifteen minutes or so." As an afterthought, he asked, "Do you have any beer?"

"Yeah, I'm pretty sure Drew left some over here." I hauled myself off the couch to check. "Yep, a twelve-pack. I assume that's enough for you. See you in a few."

I sat staring at my phone. I flipped it open and hit the speed dial. It went straight to Ben's voice mail. I closed my phone, not bothering to leave a message. I knew he would call me when he wanted to talk. My leaving a message did not speed that up. Whenever I asked him if he got my message, he would respond that he did, not that he was sorry he didn't call back sooner.

I unlocked the door so that Josh could let himself in. Ten minutes later he was doing just that with pizza in hand. We sat down and pulled the coffee table up to the couch. I had already filled glasses of water for us. While we ate, we caught up on the events of the day.

The cardboard box to the pizza lay open with three slices left. "Do you want anymore?"

"I'm stuffed." I blew out my cheeks.

Josh picked it up and took it into the kitchen. He brought back two beers.

All three of us were now on the couch, and Buddy had rolled over onto his back.

"I'm not sure he's quite comfortable." I laughed and patted Buddy on the stomach. "Where's Bridget tonight?"

"Out, I assume." I didn't say anything, but my face must have conveyed my question. "We're going out tomorrow night. We," he cleared his throat, "I am not in a place to go out both weekend nights together."

"I see."

"Do you need anything?" Josh asked as he got up. Buddy let out a sigh to show his irritation with Josh's movement. "Sorry."

We both chuckled. "No, I'm good."

He returned with another beer. We settled in to watch the movie turning out the lights and stretching out on the couch directly in front of the TV. We agreed to watch *Knocked Up*, which had enough crudeness for a guy and enough romance for a girl.

I woke up with my head on Josh's chest. He was sleeping soundly. A couple hours must have passed. The screen was black since the DVD had stopped. His shirt smelled clean, a mix of his laundry detergent and him. Buddy had curled up against my legs so that my body was contorted between the two of them. I thought about moving to my bed, but my body felt so heavy that I gave in and fell back to sleep.

"Good morning." Josh gently tipped my nose with his finger.

"Morning." I sleepily rubbed my eyes. Buddy started to stretch and slowly get up from the couch. I lifted my head up, and Josh pulled his arm out and started stretching it. "Sorry, I hope you weren't uncomfortable."

"No, I was fine."

Buddy was letting out a slow whine. I sat up slowly, shifting my body to the other side of the couch.

"I'll take him." He stood up from the couch and slid on his flip-flops. "Come on, boy."

While they were downstairs, I ran into the bathroom to quickly brush my teeth and ran my fingers through my hair. I was back on the couch before they returned. A few minutes later, Buddy bounded back inside, jumping up and down with excitement. The sheer level made it seem as though he was never fed. Josh scooped the food into a bowl for Buddy, who at this point was shaking for it to be set down on the floor. I smiled as I watched, resting my chin on my knees, which I had pulled close to me. He looked up from watching Buddy. "Now that he'll live, I'm going to head back to my apartment and shower. What time did you want to leave?"

I looked at the clock. "Is a couple hours okay?"

"That works. See you then."

I took two water bottles out of the refrigerator and placed them on the counter next to the sunscreen. I started my search for my favorite baseball cap that I wanted to throw on. I was looking behind cushions on the couch when I heard a knock and then Josh's voice. "Hey."

"Hey," I said as I continued removing pillows.

"Looking for something?"

"Yeah, my red baseball hat." I saw him sit down out of the corner of my eye. "You could help me look."

"Why would I do that?"

"Because you're a—" I turned around to see my hat propped on his knee. "Where did you find it?"

"You left it at my place the other day. Thought you might want to wear it today."

"I'm that predictable, huh?"

"No, you just wear it a lot." He tossed it to me.

"Well, I don't want to get wrinkles."

"And here I thought it might be a preventative measure against skin cancer."

"Well, that too."

"Are you going to stop smiling?"

"What? Why?"

"That causes wrinkles too. I just wondered if you were going to become expressionless."

I swatted my hat at him. "I hope you at least find yourself funny."

"I do."

I put my hat on and pulled my hair threw it. I moved back into the kitchen and threw our items in my bag. "So it's just going to be us. Drew and Andy bailed. They couldn't get away from their families."

"You should have told me sooner. I would have bailed too." He held a serious face for all of twenty seconds before his face broke into a smile.

I ignored his comment. "I've been going back and forth about taking Buddy."

"Did you look online to see if they allowed dogs into the festival?"

"I did and they do. But I'm worried about the heat. It's awfully hot today, but I don't want to look at his sad eyes if we leave him."

"They allow reentrance, don't they? We can take him. If he gets too hot, we'll bring him home. It's not that far, and it's good for him to get out and not be cooped up in the apartment all day."

"Okay, then it's settled." I grabbed Buddy's water Thermos, filled it up, and added it to my bag. "His leash is by the door."

Fifteen minutes later we managed to find a parking spot downtown relatively close to the art festival.

"So what are you looking for?"

"Well, I'm just browsing really, but if I were to come across something abstract with colors I like that's not too large in size, but not so small"—I was motioning with my hands—"I wouldn't be opposed to buying it."

"So nothing specific."

"The definition of *abstract*."

"You're going to lug that around all day?" He raised his eyes in suspicion.

"Until it gets heavy, then you'll lug it," I said, as I threw the bag over my shoulder. "You get to hold onto the boy." We walked a couple of blocks to the entrance. "I'll get the tickets. You wait here."

"Sure thing. I think Buddy has a few things he'd like to sniff."

A few blocks had been cordoned off, and tents had been set up with the artists' works. Right at the front, just inside the entrance, were tents with food. My mouth was watering with the smell, and I saw Buddy was drooling just a bit.

"Do you mind wandering a bit?" I asked.

"Not at all."

"So are you looking for anything?"

"No, not really. You've seen my place. Do I look like I need anything else to fill my walls?" Josh was watching Buddy sniff the ground a few feet to our left. He was trying to keep the leash pretty short.

"Good point."

Josh's walls were filled mostly by pictures he had taken of scenery while on vacation. There were a few of us over the years as well. They were actually pretty good. He managed to take them at an angle that wasn't just the obvious. Even in the ones of friends he had caught us in a moment where we were completely unaware of the camera, like in a moment laughing at the beach. By now, no one even paid attention when he was snapping pictures. I had been begging him to let me have one for my wall, but he was too critical of himself to give one away.

"You know, you would save me the time of looking if you would give me one of yours or let me look through the images and see if there is one you could blow up for me."

"You want something nice for your wall. These are great. Mine are nowhere near these."

"You don't give yourself enough credit." We wandered a little bit more. "You know, I was thinking it would be nice to give Andy and Drew a book of pictures of them. It could be bound or something. Do you think we could look through your pictures for something like that?"

"Kate." He drew my name out.

"You know they would love it. Besides, I'm the maid of honor and you're the best man. We need to do something special. It could be a small, like five-by-seven book so it's not like we'd be blowing up the pictures." I did my best attempt to bat my eyes sweetly at him. "Please."

He sighed and shuffled his foot back and forth.

"Please."

"Okay."

Ben called Sunday night as usual to see how my weekend had been. I told him about the art festival. "It seems like you spent a lot of time with Josh this weekend," he commented when I finished telling him about my failed attempt at finding anything for the apartment.

"I'm surprised you would notice." I was simultaneously happy and bothered by his remark. I could feel my frustration rising to the surface about him making any remark about my weekend and who I spent it with, when once again he was not around.

"Are you trying to make me jealous?" Ben quipped.

"My hanging out with Josh has nothing to do with you." My attempt to push my disappointment in him aside was failing miserably.

"That's a little harsh." I could tell from his tone that I was grating on him.

"Maybe if you were ..." I changed my mind. "Look, I'm tired. I'll talk to you later." I didn't have the energy for one of our arguments thinly veiled as a light conversation.

Chapter 21

"How much do I really not want to go today? How much of a bitch am I?"

"Are these rhetorical questions?"

"I know I'm horrible, but it's the first Saturday in a while that I am not going into the office at any point. Do I really have to spend it with someone I don't know?"

"I think that is the point, sweetie. We're supposed to get to know her. You know it means a lot to Josh for us to go to lunch with her," Andy said.

"I know. I'm just bitter about my Saturday."

"Really? That's what you're going with?"

"What?"

"Come on." Andy looked at me earnestly.

"Come on what? What are you talking about?"

"I'm pretty sure that's not why you're bitter." She sat down on the edge of my bed.

"Please enlighten me."

"Could it be that you are a bit jealous?"

"Please don't start in on me and Josh again."

"I wasn't. I was going to say that could you be jealous that we are spending the day getting to know Josh's new girlfriend, and you wish it was us meeting Ben."

When we arrived at the restaurant, Bridget was already at the table. She stood as we approached. First she took Andy's hand and gave her a kiss on the cheek. Then she turned to me, taking my hand and kissing my cheek, making more sound than contact.

"I'm so glad we're doing this." She took her seat across from us.

"Uh-huh," I managed to get out.

Andy did better, "Us too."

"I hope you don't find me rude for going ahead and getting a table."

"No, not at all. This way we don't have to wait." Andy smiled.

"I know this is a bit awkward, but I really wanted to have a chance to talk, just us girls. It can be hard when we're out at a bar." She spoke fast and in a manner that made her seem a little nervous. "I haven't ever dated anyone whose best friends are girls. And one he used to date, for that matter."

I couldn't help but wish Josh hadn't shared that history with her. "You are straight to the point, aren't you?" I took the lemon out of my water, trying to not let any lemon juice squeeze in, and then took a sip.

"Probably the lawyer in me."

"And I thought lawyers were the exact opposite," I said wryly.

Andy pinched me under the table. "Did you have a chance to meet Drew the other night?"

"No, I don't think so. He's your fiancé, right?" She turned her attention to Andy, who nodded. "When are you two getting married?"

"June 14th. The day I can't wait for, but also dread." She smiled. "I mean, I couldn't be happier about the marriage, but all of the details and decisions that go along with it I think I could pass on."

"I think once it gets closer you'll change your mind. All of those details, the special touches, will make the difference," I chimed in.

"I agree, and just think, you'll have a honeymoon to relax on after the wedding," Bridget added.

"I know, and in relative terms, I know I don't really have much of a reason for a pity party."

"It's understandable. Even though it's such a wonderful event, it can be stressful. Where's the honeymoon?"

"We're going to Greece. Drew's family has a villa that we are staying in for a couple of weeks."

"That sounds amazing."

The waiter stopped by the table to take our order. We all selected salads.

"Kate, Josh mentioned you were working toward a promotion. How is that going for you?" Bridget turned toward me.

I hated talking about this with people I was close with, much less someone I barely knew. *She's just trying to be nice,* I reminded myself. "It's going fine as far as I can tell at this point. I just have to keep up my productivity, and I should be all right." I tried to sound light in my response.

"I'm sure that you'll get it. Josh talks about how hard you work, and if it's even half of what he says, you would have to be a shoe-in."

Aw, man! She is taking an active interest in me and through flattery no less. I smiled at her.

"She would never agree, but I will for her." Andy squeezed my shoulder.

"So Bridget, how long have you lived in Houston?" I asked, making a genuine effort.

"I moved here last year after finishing law school. I was up in Austin and took a job with a firm in Houston after graduation."

"Where are you from originally?"

"Savannah, Georgia. Texas was a bit of a transition, but I'm liking it."

"Is your family still in Georgia?"

"Yeah. My parents and two brothers and their families are all still there."

"Do you see them often?"

"Not as much as I would like."

The waiter returned with our salads and drinks. The interruption stopped the flow of conversation, and there was an uncomfortable silence; it was obvious we were all trying to come up with the next topic.

"So tell me about the weekend at the beach." Bridget stated.

I couldn't hide my expression of confusion, and Bridget must have noticed.

"I hope it's okay that he invited me."

"Absolutely, that's great," I said quickly, trying to regroup.

The brief exchange faltered, and Bridget looked down at her salad. She was moving it around as if she were searching for words rather than a tomato. It was obvious that she was as uncomfortable as I was, but I couldn't find any words of my own to make it any less awkward. Andy was watching the wordless conversation take place and ended its silence. She launched into a story about us in college that I had heard a hundred times. It was the most comforting thing she could have done at that moment.

The rest of the lunch passed quickly. We made small talk about the beach weekend and getting to know about each other's background. It felt a little like a first date from that standpoint. Andy and I told a story from our freshman year living together. We then each told the story about how we met Josh.

When Andy and I got back to the car, I pounced. "Did you know?"

"Know what?"

"That he was planning to take her to the beach."

"No, but he doesn't exactly have to run it by me." A bemused expression covered her face.

Chapter 22

On my drive to Ben's, I rehearsed asking him to the beach. It had been on my mind since Saturday's lunch with Bridget. As soon as I saw him at work, I wanted to pounce, but I knew we wouldn't have been able to talk about it, so I held off. I knew no one would care if I showed up alone, but I really didn't want to be the only single there. The end of the night with everyone pairing up to go to sleep wasn't thrilling.

I collapsed into the chair when I got to Ben's. He was finishing something on the computer, so I was idly watching TV. "Sorry about that. I just didn't want to lose my train of thought." He walked over and sat down on the couch. "How was your day?"

"Pretty good."

"Something you want to add?"

"What do you mean?"

"It looks like you're holding something back."

"Well, I've been meaning to ask you, and not to put any pressure on us ..." I paused, mustering my courage. I hated that I could still get nervous around him. "But, my friends and I take a trip once a year to the beach. It usually ends up being both singles and couples. And we have two beach houses close to each other." I wiped my palms on the side of my pants. "Anyway, I was wondering if you might want to go with me."

"Just jump in, huh?"

"I know we haven't had an opportunity to really get together with any of them. To be honest, other than Andy no one really knows of your existence." I laughed nervously.

"We're not exactly trying to broadcast." He sighed, "I don't know. It seems a bit much for us."

"I know where you stand, but if you're not dating anyone else and I'm not dating anyone else, is this really that big of a step? I mean, it would be nice for us to exist outside of this apartment."

He started to reply and then paused. He ran his hand through his hair. "Well, when is this trip?"

"The last weekend of the month."

"I'll have to look at my calendar. Can I get back to you?"

"Sure. At least it's not an immediate no."

"Well, it's not an immediate no." Ben's tone was teasing. He pulled me over to the couch to sit next to him. "Your hands are sweaty."

"I know." I wiped them again self-consciously.

"Have you eaten already?"

"It's ten o'clock. Of course I've eaten. If I ate now, it would go straight to my hips. Some of us have to worry about our girlish figure."

"Well, I haven't eaten yet, so I think I'll throw some pasta together."

"You'll have to ask me earlier if you want to eat dinner together."

I followed him into the kitchen and watched while he threw the pasta in the boiling water and pulled out garlic and butter for seasoning. "Do you have any milk?"

"I think so." He opened the refrigerator door.

"What about chocolate syrup?" I pushed myself off the counter and grabbed the carton of milk he was holding.

He rooted around in the back of one of the shelves. "It looks like I do." He handed it to me.

I poured the milk into a glass and then stirred in some of the chocolate as I squeezed the bottle.

"That doesn't seem like much chocolate. Are you sure you don't need more?" He critiqued my technique.

"I guess I'm more into milk than chocolate. I just like the hint of flavoring. I don't suppose you have a straw."

"If I do, it would be in the pantry." He pointed behind me.

I moved some stuff around on the shelves but didn't see anything and gave up. We moved back into the living room. He ate his pasta and fed me a couple of bites, even though I protested. "So how is the chocolate milk?"

"It's okay. I think it has a little too much chocolate actually."

"Really?" He shook his head.

"Yeah, why?"

"I added a little in it while you were looking for a straw."

I crinkled my nose. "Why would you do that?"

"I thought you might be wrong in your combination."

I left it alone but was bothered by the fact that he would add chocolate to my drink. I couldn't pinpoint what it was that bothered me about it. It seemed like a harmless enough gesture.

When Ben finished eating, he took his plate and my glass back to the kitchen. I could hear the rinsing of dishes and then the sound of him rooting through cabinets in the bathroom off the kitchen.

"Kate, what's this?" Ben called out.

"I can't see what you're referring to."

"The box of tampons under my sink."

"It's probably a box of tampons."

"Why is it under my sink?" He stood in the frame of the door, holding the box.

"I put it there."

"Why?"

I took a deep breath. "Because I hate having to carry tampons back and forth with me when I sleep over. I thought I could throw a box under the sink and it wouldn't be in your way. I didn't think it was a big deal."

"Then why didn't you say anything?"

"Like I said, I didn't think it would be a big deal."

"Well, what if I had a date over, and she looked under the sink to find it? Don't you think she would find it odd?"

"No, I think she might find it helpful if it was that time of the month. But wouldn't you find her nosy if she was going through your cabinets?"

"That's not the point."

"Well, are you dating someone else that she might stumble across them?"

"No, but the point is with this," he was waving the box in the air, "and with your question about the weekend at the beach … the point is that I might be." He blew out his breath, then shook his head. "Kate, we have had this conversation."

"I know. It was like an hour ago. Throw me the box." He tossed it to me, and I set it beside my bag.

"Now you're upset."

"I'm not upset. I just think you're overreacting. It was a matter of convenience, nothing more."

"So you weren't trying to stake your claim?"

"Don't you think I would be leaving something else behind, rather than feminine products, if that was the case?"

"We can't keep having this conversation."

"I agree," I said quietly.

The next day I was still feeling the sting from my tiff with Ben. I was not actively avoiding him, but I did take the long way through the office to get my lunch from the kitchen. I was sure my absence had not even registered on his radar.

An instant message popped up on my screen. "When are you leaving?"

"Don't know. It will probably be another hour or so."

"Well, I'm getting ready to get out of here. Am I eating alone?"

"How would I know that?"

"I love it when you're literal. Do you think you might want to eat dinner with me? It makes it hard to plan my evening when I know nothing of your plans."

"Funny."

"Hey, I'm asking earlier."

"That's true. Speaking of plans, did you look at your calendar for the last weekend of the month?"

"I did. Unfortunately, I won't be able to make it."

I couldn't think of a response to type that wouldn't make my disappointment obvious.

"Are you interested in dinner or not?" his message pinged.

I wasn't. I didn't really feel hungry. "I think I'll pass tonight. I need to get some work done. I'll probably order something to the office. Thanks for the offer, though."

"Okay then. Talk to you later."

Thirty minutes later Ben walked past my office and stuck his head in the door. "Last chance."

I shook my head.

"Okay, I'll talk to you later."

I wondered if I was punishing myself or him by not going.

I left the office about thirty minutes later. Instead of calling Ben to let him know that I could go to dinner, I decided that Josh and I needed to get to work on Andy and Drew's gift. He had finally caved in and started pulling all his pictures out for us to look through.

"You dressed up," Josh commented, looking up from the piles of pictures that he had spread out over the floor.

"I need to be comfortable." I was wearing my pajama pants and an oversized T-shirt. I closed the door behind me.

"Hey, Buddy." He nuzzled his head and tried to avoid being head-butted while he bounced around.

"I'm hoping he will do well with the pictures. I don't think you'll want his paw prints across them." I plopped down next to him on the floor.

"You have the best trained dog I know."

Buddy sniffed around the apartment and then paused in front of the couch.

"Go ahead." Josh motioned to him. Buddy then got up on the couch and laid down. "Like I was saying, you have the politest dog."

"He has the good qualities that I lack." I smirked. "You have a lot." I stated the obvious as I took in how many prints were covering the floor.

He pulled out his laptop and set it on the coffee table. "I have most of the pictures catalogued in this program. You can look through it to get an idea of the shots I have. Some are already in prints and others we will have to develop."

"How will it work if I want to have it in an album of some sort?"

"What are you thinking?" He was combing through the prints, pulling out any with Drew and Andy.

"I was thinking a sort of magazine style, where some are candid and others posed. Some pages would have multiple pictures on the same page. What do you think of that?"

"I think that could work." He set down the pictures and moved back to the laptop. He typed in a Web address. "Take a look through this site. It may be what you're thinking. We can upload the pictures into their program and monkey with the format and colors for the background. Once we have it completed, it takes about ten days, I think, to get the order."

"How do you know so much about this?"

"A hobby. What can I say?"

I looked through the site while he went back to the prints. We spent the next few hours picking out pictures and reminiscing about our friends over the past ten years.

Ben left a voice mail and sent e-mails, trying to find out if I would come over that night. By the time Josh and I finished, though, it was late and I crawled into bed without returning the messages. The next day I nonchalantly sent him an e-mail saying that I would be available tonight.

"Hello," I said into the phone while standing in my closet looking at the clothes I had already laid on the bed. I was trying to determine what I would wear to work the next day. Ben had asked me to spend the night, and I thought it would be easier to get ready there. But I was struggling with picking anything because my outfits were often dependent on my mood. I can't just wear a skirt. I have to be in a skirt-wearing mood.

"Hi, is Kate there?" the male voice asked.

"You got her."

"Oh, hey, this is Matt. I hope it's okay that I got your number from Jason. How are you?"

"Fine. And yourself?"

"Good, good. Well, I guess you're probably wondering why I'm calling."

Jason and Andy weren't exactly subtle with their objective. I didn't bring it up, though, since it had been a while since we first met, and I didn't want to be presumptuous with my assumption.

"Well," he paused, clearing his throat, "I was wondering if you might like to grab lunch with me one day this week."

"You know, I really did enjoy our conversation the other night. But I'm headed out of town on business for the rest of the week and it's just really hectic right now."

"Well, how about this weekend?"

"Like I said, I'm just really slammed right now," I tried again.

"I understand you're a busy woman." He laughed. "It doesn't have to be a big date thing."

"It's not—"

Matt hurriedly interrupted. "I just think you're really attractive." He cleared his throat and then asked, "Would you be up for sporting?"

"Excuse me? Am I supposed to know what that is?"

"It doesn't have to be—"

"I'm not sure I follow. What is sporting?"

"It just means we don't bother with the relationship aspect or dating, but if we're attracted to one another we could just get together for—"

"Stop." I cut him off, now understanding where the conversation was leading. Before I hung up, I let my curiosity win out over my indignation. "What would make you think it was okay to ask me that?"

"Nothing." He paused. "I just figured it couldn't hurt to ask."

"Well then," I was dumbfounded. "I need to get off the phone now." Not waiting for him to answer, I hung up, outraged. I'd have to remember to thank Jason the next time I saw him. In the meantime, I went to the person who was available. "Andy!" I yelled.

"What's wrong?" She peeked her head in my door.

I relayed my phone call with Matt to her. She listened while picking out clothes that I could wear tomorrow.

When I arrived at Ben's I was already in a foul mood. And I was still upset that he'd said no to the weekend beach trip. I was thwarting his attempts at conversation and getting physical. We sat watching reruns of sitcoms.

He broke the silence. "You've been a peach tonight."

"I'm in a bad mood."

"I noticed. What's wrong?"

"I guess I'm just not ..." *How can I put this? I don't want to complain.* "I guess I'm bummed that you can't come to the beach and that we haven't spent much time together lately." I hated that I felt like I was pushing for more.

"We're spending time now."

"I know, but it always seems like I come over after ten or so. And it just seems like we spend an hour or so in the bedroom and that's it."

"Do you need more time in the bedroom?" A grin spread on his face.

"That's not my issue. I feel claustrophobic."

"Why?" Ben looked skeptical.

"Because we never go outside this apartment. I know the beach is a whole weekend, but can't we go out to dinner or something?"

"We've gone out to dinner."

"I mean a normal dinner with other people actually dining in the restaurant at the same time."

"You know, most women would find such gestures romantic and be appreciative."

"I am."

"You don't sound it."

"I know this will sound trite, but if a tree falls in the forest and no one is around to see it, does it really fall? If we never exist outside of this apartment, do we really exist?"

"We can't go out in public and you know that." Ben was not hiding his annoyance with the topic of conversation.

"We can't or you won't?"

"Kate, you're being irrational."

"I'm voicing my frustration with you and us—that's not being irrational. I don't know how to be in this if it's not moving in some direction. It seems like every time I start to feel something real, you put up a tampon box—I mean, a barrier."

"I'm not putting up barriers, and it's not like I don't want to spend time with you." His smile quickly faded and was replaced with a wrinkle in his forehead.

"If you want to spend time with me, you would." Even though I was trying not to, the statement felt like I was whining, and I knew it came across that way.

"It's not that simple. When I have things I *need* to do, they are going to take priority over things I *want* to do. Nothing would have made me happier than having you over earlier tonight and you and me lounging around most of the day tomorrow, but I just can't do that. I have too much to do."

"I appreciate that. I work long hours too. But there has to be some balance."

"I agree. But bottom line, and where I think your concern lies, is that I am leaving town and then you are leaving town. In case you are wondering, this doesn't make me happy either. But I don't think things are going to change between us if we don't see each other for a week."

"I think that's the problem."

"What do you mean?"

"I want things to change."

"Are we going to continue to have this same conversation?"

Our conversation ended and we returned to watching TV in silence. An hour later I picked up my garment bag and carried it out to the car, not wanting to spend the night.

Andy and Drew were lying on the couch when I let myself into the apartment. She lifted her head from his chest. "What are you doing back?" she whispered so as to not wake Drew.

I walked to the other couch, laid my bag across the back of it, and sat down. "Not a good night."

"Did you get into a fight?"

"A fight would imply that he cares, and I'm not sure that he does."

"Well, what happened?" she prodded.

"I was complaining that we don't spend that much time together and that I only go over there after ten."

"There are times that Drew and I don't see each other until then."

187

"But that's just it. There are times. It's not all of the time. And you two had a period of courting where you went to dinner, movies … actual dates." I sighed.

"You don't seem happy, Kate." She looked at me with concern.

"I'm not at the moment."

"But just generally. This relationship doesn't seem to be making you happy." She was treading carefully. "And if it's not, then should you be staying in it?"

"It's not that easy. I can't help it. I've fallen for him."

"You may not be able to help how you feel, but if it's not working and you are not getting what you need, you can stop your own actions— what you are doing. It may suck at first, but it might be better in the long run."

"I agree," Drew cut in.

"Hey, I thought you were sleeping." Andy sat up.

"Just resting my eyes." He cracked one open. "And waiting to see if I got any gossip by pretending to be asleep."

Andy swatted him on the arm. "But seriously," she said to me, "are you sure you want to be with him or is it that you just want to be in a relationship?"

A smile crept across my face.

"What?" Andy asked.

"I'm such a hypocrite. I'm the person who was mentally lampooning these two girls at the airport." I recounted part of the conversation I overheard. "These girls were defining their whole lives by their relationship status. They were talking timetables for husbands and babies. And I swear, they couldn't have been more than seventeen."

"I don't think you can equate their conversation and your situation."

"Your clock's started ticking," Drew chimed in.

"Funny. Speaking of …" I looked at my watch. It was 11:30. "I'm going to call Josh. I'll see you later."

Josh was still awake and up for working some more on the pictures for Andy and Drew's book, so Buddy and I ducked out of the apartment and darted up the stairs to his place. I was in my pajamas again and didn't want to run into any neighbors. His door was unlocked, so I let myself in. "Hey, we're here."

"Hey," he replied, walking out of his bedroom. He had on a T-shirt and flannel pajama pants. "I knew you would be dressed for bed, so I figured I would as well." He held his hand out to shake Buddy's paw, so Buddy trotted over and stuck his paw into Josh's hand. "I didn't move anything from the other day, so we can pick up where we left off."

"Great." I grabbed a pillow from the couch and sat down on the floor in the middle of the pictures.

"Are you cold?"

I looked down at my tank top. "Yeah, a little."

He walked back into his bedroom and returned a moment later with a sweatshirt. "Let's do this then." He sat down next to me.

We started looking through the pictures, and Josh stopped on one that was a very unflattering angle of me. "I could blackmail you with this." He held a picture out of my reach.

"Josh!" I shoved him playfully and grabbed for the picture but missed, so I was caught off balance and fell against him. He caught my arm and grazed the side of my chest. I was surprised that I was aroused by his accidentally touching me. We both flushed, and I looked away. He was still holding my arm. I looked back at him and he tilted his head slightly and leaned in. We were stuck in that position for a second before we both broke away.

"I'm sorry," he said and cleared his throat.

"It's okay." I pushed myself off the floor. "It's getting late. I should probably go."

"You don't have to." He looked at me, and I could tell where this would lead if I stayed.

"Yes, I do."

"It's late. Let me walk you back downstairs."

"I have this big dog. I think he can protect me."

"He's more likely to hide behind you rather than get in someone's face."

"That's probably true. He is a big wuss."

Josh grabbed his keys and locked the door behind us. We walked down the stairs in silence with Buddy leading the way. When we got to my door, I turned to face him. "I'll see you later." I leaned in to give him a hug. He pulled me close into him. I took in the smell of him, and neither of us let go. We stood there, not saying a word. Without letting go, I looked up at him. He took his cheek and placed it next to mine. Our lips were so close and almost grazed each other but never met. I let my hand drop from around his neck and run down his chest to his waist. With our bodies so close, I could feel him respond.

"Kate, what are we doing?" he whispered.

"I don't know."

"I should probably go." He didn't make any movement away from me.

"You probably should." I finally broke our hold on one another and stepped back. "Good night." I could see his disappointment but didn't stop him from walking away.

Buddy and I entered the apartment, which was pitch-black. "Oww." I bumped into the table in the hallway and stopped to let my eyes adjust to the darkness.

"Why don't you turn on a light?"

"Holy crap!" I brought my hand to my chest. "Andy, you scared the crap out of me."

She laughed. She was holding a glass of water that she had just filled from the kitchen sink. "What have you been up to?" She flipped the switch to the light in the kitchen.

"Just hanging out at Josh's."

She eyed me. "Why do you look guilty?"

"I don't know what you're talking about."

"What's going on? Kate, I can tell when you are hiding something. You're pretty transparent."

"We almost kissed."

"Who?"

"Me and Josh."

"What? What happened? What about Bridget? What about Ben?"

"I don't know. I don't know. I don't know."

"We have got to stop having these conversations."

"What conversations?"

"The ones that involve you kissing the wrong guy."

"I thought you of all people wanted me to kiss Josh. And it was an *almost* kiss," I reminded her.

"Yeah, when you two were both not dating anyone. That would have been the perfect time. Now that he actually is out there and dating, not so much."

"I get that."

She set down her glass. "Let me just say one more thing out of love and concern for you both." She paused. "Unless you are into Josh and interested in something, you should back away or else it is not going to end well for either of you. And let me just say for the record, I think you two would be great together, and I am rooting for it, but it needs to be under the right circumstances." She gave me a hug and then grabbed her water before going back to her bedroom.

I turned to Buddy. "I think I might be losing it. I don't want Josh, then I want Ben, then out of nowhere I maybe want Josh, but what about Ben? Do you think maybe I'm just attracted to the drama? I'm starting to think it has more to do with me than either of them." Buddy wagged his tail. I patted my shoulders and bent over. Buddy jumped up and gave me a hug.

Chapter 23

I was riding to the beach with Drew and Andy. Drew had gotten to our apartment at 7:30 that morning, but Andy and I were still struggling to get our stuff together. It never ceased to amaze me how much stuff ended up going with us. Fortunately, it was Drew's parents' house, so a lot of the basics were already there, like towels and beach chairs. I finally threw the last of my stuff in my bag and grabbed my pillow for the car. Buddy had been excitedly going back and forth between Andy's room and my room all morning. As soon as he saw me grab his bag, he started bunny hopping.

I dozed on and off for the hour and half it took to get there. We were just unloading the last of it when Josh and Bridget pulled in. Beth and Jason, with Matt in tow, were walking over from next door.

"Hey, guys." Beth waved.

Josh did the formalities in introducing Bridget to the three of them.

"I didn't know he was coming," I whispered to Andy. "Did you say anything to Drew?"

"Not yet."

"This will be fun," I muttered under my breath.

We all trudged up the steps to the house.

"What's on the agenda outside of food?" Beth was surveying the food laid out on the counter.

"I think we have lunch, dinner, and munchies covered. Drew, did you remember the coal for the grill?" Andy looked up from unloading the groceries.

"It's already on the deck."

"More importantly, did you remember to bring the alcohol? I plan to be drinking my lunch," Matt chimed in.

Charming. I rolled my eyes at Andy, who turned to put something in the refrigerator to hide her smile. Buddy was nudging my hand for attention.

"I'm going to change and head down to the water with the boy." I walked toward the downstairs bedroom. Hesitating, I turned back to Bridget and Josh. "I threw my stuff in the room downstairs, but I'd be happy to switch if you would rather have it."

"No, we'll be fine upstairs," Josh answered.

"Thanks," Bridget smiled. "I think I'm going to change, too, and may join you on the beach if you don't mind, unless you need some help." She turned to Andy.

"I think we have it under control. I may blend some margaritas, but then I'll be down there myself."

Drew was loading the cooler when I came back out. Everyone else had scattered either to change or to the beach. I grabbed some tennis balls, a Frisbee, doggie Thermos, and Buddy's leash. He ran down the stairs and looked back as if to say, "Hurry up."

"I'm going to head down. I think Buddy might explode if he has to wait any longer."

"I think you're right. Matt tried to get him to go down with them, and Buddy started backing up."

"Good judge of character." I smiled.

"Andy told me what he said to you. I'll keep my eye out for you."

"I'll be fine." I looked back to the house and paused.

"I'll let them know that Buddy was itching to get to the water," Drew said.

"Thanks. See you in a little bit."

I managed to avoid Matt for almost the entire day and evening. Buddy had been a great way to avoid him without being blatantly rude. We were playing fetch, and any time Matt came close, I just threw the ball in the opposite direction. Buddy also prevented me from feeling like a fifth wheel when the couples settled in on the beach in the lounge chairs. I felt a tug when I saw the scene, but I'd made a pact with myself to not call Ben and just use the weekend to clear my head. Andy's comments were staying with me.

"Mind some company?" Josh jogged up next to me.

"Not at all." We walked along the water while Buddy splashed in and out. Josh took the ball from me and threw it for Buddy, who went tromping through the waves.

"Drew mentioned what happened with Matt. You okay?" Josh kept his attention on Buddy.

"It's fine. Does everyone know?"

"Probably everyone with the exception of Bridget. I didn't see the need to say anything."

"Hmmm."

"We're all just looking out for you."

"He's probably just all talk, no bite." I shielded my eyes to watch Buddy in the water. "I'm glad we have a minute alone."

"That sounds ominous." He stopped to pick up a shell.

I turned to face him. "So, the other night, what was that?"

He flipped the shell over in his hand before throwing it into the ocean. "Just two friends feeling sentimental. We were looking through old pictures, a lot of which were of us as a couple. It brought back some feelings."

"That's it?"

"That's it."

"So I haven't totally screwed up things between you and Bridget?" We had been walking for about thirty minutes, so we started back toward the group.

"You give yourself too much credit." His tone was serious, and the only hint of his teasing was the glint in his eyes. "Seriously, nothing happened."

"Well, then, what's the deal with you two?"

"It's casual. We're just seeing how things go. Letting it play out."

"And she's on the same page?" Before he could answer, Andy approached us.

"Hey," she waved. "Bridget was starting to feel like she was getting too much sun, so she went up to the house."

"I'll go check on her." Josh left us.

"Is she okay?" I turned to Andy.

"I think she was bothered by you and Josh going off by yourselves."

"It's not like you couldn't see us. What was I supposed to do? Tell him not to walk with me?"

She shrugged her shoulders. "Don't ask me. I'm just trying to keep the drama to a minimum."

"It seems to follow me." I dug my toes into the sand.

"Honey, I think you make it." She linked her arm with mine.

"Harsh."

"Come on. Let's go bug Drew." She pulled me over to where he was sitting in a beach chair.

That night we went to the Strand which housed our favorite bar. It had a huge deck that opened to the beach providing for a nice breeze off the ocean. And it usually had a pretty good band playing.

Beth and I had just gotten our drinks and were milling by the bar. "You've got to be kidding me," I murmured to no one in particular.

My beach strategy was not going to work in the bar and now I was cornered. Matt was heading straight for me.

"He's a good guy. He just made a mistake, and I think he wants to make it right with you," Beth whispered in my ear.

"I can't believe you want me to go out with him. What he asked me was degrading and not acceptable."

"Hey, how are you?" Matt asked. I saw Beth sliding back out of the conversation.

I stood stone-faced, evaluating my options for escape routes.

"Listen, I'm sorry about what I said when we talked the other day. I just thought we had a connection and wanted to act on it. Do you think—"

"Stop. Thank you for apologizing. I do appreciate that."

"I realize that I probably brought up the topic too soon. The timing wasn't right."

"It's just not going to happen. The timing for that would never be right with me." *It's not me, it's you.* "If you'll excuse me." At that I tried to sidestep him, but he caught my wrist. I looked down, caught off balance.

"Kate, can you just give me a chance to explain? I really think—"

"I really don't think there is anything you can say to me that will explain." I was trying to get my wrist free of his grip.

"Everything okay?" Josh came up behind me, sliding his arm around my waist.

I breathed a sigh of relief, and Matt released my wrist.

"Just trying to talk in private with Kate," Matt replied.

Josh didn't miss his meaning. "You know, I've been told I have horrible timing." But he didn't budge from my side.

Josh slid his fingers through mine, rubbing his thumb across them. The combined comfort and intimacy that I felt surprised me and distracted my thoughts away from Matt.

"Would you mind giving us a minute?" Matt's tone startled me back to the situation at hand.

"Actually, I would mind. If you need to carry on whatever this conversation is with Kate, I think I'll stick around." Josh stood up just a bit straighter with that statement.

"Hey, guys." Bridget walked up to the three of us, tensely standing there. Her discomfort mirrored ours. I could tell Josh's hold on my waist and his interlocking of fingers with mine were not lost on her.

"I think I'm going to excuse myself. I've been looking for Andy." I stepped back from the group.

"I saw her in the back by the pool tables," Bridget responded.

"Thanks." I smiled at her.

I found Andy and Drew at the back of the bar, where Bridget said they were.

"Are you all right?" Andy took my elbow.

"Yeah, I'm fine. Matt is an absolute ass. Whose friend is he?"

"Jason says he's cool. I'm with you, though. He's just a little intense," Drew stated.

"Beth's opinion seems to be a little off about him too," I added.

"She always sees the best in people, even if they are complete jerks. That's probably why she's friends with us," Andy smiled, clinking her beer with ours.

"Would you mind terribly if we went back to the house?"

"That's fine." They both nodded.

Drew went to close out the tab and then grab the car. Andy had gone to the bathroom, so I was waiting outside by the front door.

"Do you think we could talk for a minute without involving your boy?" a voice came from behind me. I turned around to see Matt approaching me. "Look, it's no secret that I find you attractive. I have made that clear, but all I am looking for now is to make the best of this weekend with the group and not have it be awkward between us."

"That's all I want too."

"Good, I'm glad we're on the same page." He moved forward and started outlining the spaghetti strap on my shoulder with his finger.

I jumped back. "I'm not sure we are. Look, I'll be civil, but that's it."

"Where do you get off acting all self-righteous?" His eyes flashed anger toward me.

"I'm not. I think you're drunk. Maybe you should go inside and find the others."

"Maybe you're just playing hard to get, and I just need to be a little more persistent."

"I assure you that I'm not and that you don't."

He placed his hand around my arm. "Look at how you're dressed. You want to be noticed. I'm doing what you want and noticing you."

"Matt, really, you need to go back inside." I pushed him away from me. He lost his footing and fell hard into the car behind him. He regained his balance and took a step toward me. I took a step back, and Josh was suddenly beside me. He threw a punch, sending Matt to the ground. He picked up Matt by his shirt and pulled him to his feet. "I think she's made it clear that she wants you to leave her alone. Do not come to the house tonight. You are not welcome. You can come get your stuff tomorrow, but tonight you should find alternative accommodations. There are plenty of hotels." He pulled a twenty from his wallet and pushed it to Matt's chest. "You shouldn't drive. Have someone call you a cab."

Josh turned back to me. "Are you okay?"

"I'm fine. What about you?" I took his hand. His knuckles were starting to swell. Bridget stood frozen in place about five feet away. Her eyes were glazed over. Josh followed my eyeline and pulled his hand back, shaking it. "I just need to get some ice."

Drew pulled up in the Jeep at the same time Andy exited the bar, both surveying the scene. "What happened?" Andy rushed over next to me.

"Is everyone all right?" Drew jumped out of the Jeep.

"We're all fine. Let's just go back to the house." I turned toward Josh, who was talking to the bouncer about getting some ice. Matt had sunken to the ground next to the door. He seemed to be waiting for a cab. "Bridget, do you want me to go with you to get the other car?"

She hadn't said a word since everything had happened. "No, I can get it. You should go with Drew and Andy."

"We'll wait here just to be sure you and Josh get off without any trouble," Drew said.

We walked through the side door and into the kitchen. "I think a night cap is in order." Drew walked over to the liquor cabinet. Bridget, without saying a word, walked past everyone and upstairs to the bedroom she and Josh were sharing. The door shut a few seconds later.

"I should probably follow." Josh looked almost apologetically at us.

"Josh, thank you for stepping in tonight, and I hope your hand feels better," I said quietly. My eyes were watering, but I forced back my tears.

"It was nothing." He was still holding ice to his hand. "I'm just glad nothing worse happened." He walked over to me and kissed my forehead. "Good night."

"Bridget, is something wrong?" We could hear Josh asking Bridget when he went into the room. Old beach houses were horrible for retaining sound within a room.

A mumbled voice replied.

"You didn't say a word the whole way back to the house."

"It's just a little too much drama for me." Bridget's voice had become louder.

"Maybe we should take our drinks out on the porch." Drew was trying to corral Andy and me out of the house.

"I want to listen," Andy hissed at Drew.

"He's probably right." I picked up my drink to follow him.

"I'm not saying that you shouldn't have stepped in when you did, but why does it seem that you are always coming to her rescue?" Bridget's words stopped me from moving.

"What did you want me to do?"

"I think you should have punched him, but earlier in the night when it started, did you have to have your arm around her? You were acting like she was your girlfriend. I felt like I was intruding."

I couldn't make out Josh's response.

"And can you honestly say she was fighting off Matt's advances?"

"That's not fair. You don't know the whole story with that guy."

"And you do?"

I strained, but still couldn't hear Josh's response.

"And you're always spending time with her. How many hours have you been spending together working on that project with the pictures?"

Guilt passed through me as I thought back to the other night and my almost-kiss with Josh.

"You mean the one for the wedding?" he questioned.

"Come on, Kate." Drew was holding open the door. "Let's go wake up Beth and Jason and tell them what a crappy friend they brought along this weekend."

Andy grabbed a throw blanket on her way out of the door. I followed, trying to ignore the conversation going on upstairs.

Beth and Jason apologized profusely to all of us. Jason kept repeating that Matt had been a good guy to get a drink with after work. He had no idea that he would do or say the kinds of things he did. In recounting the events, we felt as if we had regressed in time. The last bar fight any of us could recall witnessing was in college.

By the time we went back inside the house, it was silent. I curled up in bed with Buddy. I finally let the tears come that I'd been holding back earlier. I knew I was upset about the events from tonight, but also knew I couldn't blame my feelings entirely on that.

I wrapped the blanket around me as I got out of the bed. Buddy was wagging his tail, waiting for the door to be opened. Coffee was sitting out, but I didn't see any other signs of anyone being up. I opened the door to let Buddy out.

"Good morning."

I jumped about ten feet in the air and threw my hand up to my chest. "Sheesh, you scared the crap out of me!" I took a deep breath.

"Sorry about that." Josh was rocking back and forth in the porch swing.

"What are you doing?" I sat down next to him, letting his momentum move us.

"Just watching the sun rise." He held his coffee close to his chest, seeming to be lost in thought.

"I'm sorry about last night."

"What for? It wasn't your fault." Buddy was running along the water. He would slow down every once in a while to try to sneak up on birds, but his splash would cue them to fly off.

"I'm not sure that Bridget would agree." We both sat silently watching Buddy for a few minutes. "Did you work everything out?"

"She's upset. There wasn't much rational conversation."

"She'll cool down. Is she still asleep?"

"She left already." I looked to the driveway and saw his car was no longer there. Then I looked back at him and noticed the circles under his eyes. It didn't look like he had gotten any sleep.

Sunday passed quietly, paling in comparison with the events of the night before. Beth and Jason left early to get back to the city, so it was just the four of us. We spent a fair amount of time by the water. Andy and I alternated between soaking in the sun and wading in the water to cool off. Josh and Drew tossed a football, with Buddy running back and forth between them trying to intercept. After our fill of sun, we cooked a late lunch, trying to use up the rest of the food, and played cards on the deck. We all squeezed into Drew's jeep for the ride back. Josh used my pillow to ball up and sleep against. Buddy was squished between us, but he was so exhausted that he rested a good portion of his body on me. The conversation drifted from topic to topic, but we all avoided any mention of Matt or Bridget.

"What color do you think the elephant is?" Andy asked, flipping through her iPod to find a song she wanted to listen to.

"Why would the elephant be any other color than grey?" I looked at her quizzically.

"I figure if there's one actually in the room, it would be a bright color or something."

"I think there are several in the room, so you can probably have as many different colors as you want." I looked at the billboards passing by. The Houston skyline was becoming more visible as we sped along the highway.

"What the heck are you two talking about?" Drew looked at us before signaling to move into the next lane.

"Elephants," Andy responded, as if this was the most ridiculous question.

"Obviously. But why?"

"Because we're weird like that." Josh stirred next to me, forcing Buddy to shift and let out a cow-like moo. I petted his ear, and he closed his eyes and kicked out his back leg, which hit Josh.

Chapter 24

"How's the new apartment?" I picked at my salad. I felt like I had eaten quite a bit, but it barely looked like a dent had been made in the bowl. Somehow the lettuce seemed to multiply.

"It's good. It's a little small and we still have boxes everywhere, but I like it." Caroline took a forkful of her baked potato.

"And how is the adjustment of living with Shawn?"

"I think the only adjustment has been trying to merge the stuff from two people into one place. Otherwise, it doesn't really feel like much has changed. With him at school or studying all the time, I don't think we would see each other at all if we weren't living together."

"Does he study at the apartment much?"

"He has a few times. Some of the other med students from his study group have been over. But we really don't have that much space. I think Shawn feels bad that it forces me to the bedroom while they are studying."

After grabbing dinner with my sister and filling her in on the previous weekend, I went to Ben's. I was excited because he had asked to see me and it was a Friday night. It took a few minutes for Ben to answer the door. "Hey." I gave him a quick kiss, but he didn't seem to respond. "Long day?" I took in the open liquor cabinet and half-empty glass on the end table.

"You could say that." His voice was lifeless, and he returned to sit in the chair.

I sat down on the ottoman halfway across the room. I couldn't read his mood, which wasn't unusual. I tried to lighten it. "Dinner was good. I wish you had been able to make it. I would love for you to meet my sister." His eyes were transfixed on the glass in his hands. I continued, "I was thinking that next week we could—"

"Kate," he interrupted. He got up from the chair and moved to the chair-and-a-half. It still made me smile that he bought it. I turned toward him, and he took my hands. "You know it is serious when I want to talk about the relationship." He gave a wry smile.

"Okay." I could feel my palms become clammy. "Is something wrong?"

"I got a call today from someone I had been seeing," he started. "We were dating a while back."

"What are you talking about?" I was confused by where the conversation was going. "What does this have to do with us?"

I just waited.

"She's a client. Because of that we had been keeping it quiet. No one really knew, especially in the office." He ran his hand through his hair and looked up at the ceiling. "The point is that she called today. She's quitting her job and moving to Houston to give our relationship a real chance."

"What? Why would she do that? Have you been talking to her?" I shook my head. "This doesn't make any sense. I thought you didn't want a 'relationship.'" I used air quotes as I said the word and cringed at my own mannerism. "How long did you date her?"

"For a few years." He ignored all of my questions except for the last one.

His response shocked me. "But you just got divorced."

"That's true." The light was going on inside my head. The rumor about him cheating had been true.

"When did you stop seeing her?"

"I didn't, really. We had taken some space to figure things out when you happened."

"I don't understand," I mumbled.

"But now with her moving, I just don't feel right about us continuing to see each other. I want to try to make it work with her."

"What about trying to make it work with us? I thought things were going well. Was I completely misreading us?"

"No, you weren't. But she and I … I owe it to her."

"And you didn't think this was worth mentioning, when we initially got involved?" I stood up. "Actually, before we were involved?"

"I didn't think this would turn into anything." He was motioning to the space between us.

"Are you sure you weren't worried that it might hurt your chances of sleeping with me?" I asked, sarcasm filling my tone.

"Kate, you know you mean more to me than that."

"How would I know? By what you have told me the last couple of months? By what you are telling me tonight?" I wiped a tear from my cheek.

"I am sorry." His voice was shaking. Silence took over as we both just stared at each other. I was willing myself not to cry.

The phone rang. Ben grabbed it off of the coffee table. "Hello." There was a pause. "I have a friend over right now." I could feel my stomach sinking. "We're talking. I'll call you back."

"Who was that?" I didn't care that I was being nosy. I was pissed that he had even answered the phone.

"It was …"

"Her." I finished the sentence for him. For once, I could read him.

"Yeah." He looked almost sheepish.

"Does she know what kind of friend I am?"

"I told her that I started seeing someone. I also told her I would end it tonight." He looked at the phone. "She's making a big gesture, so I guess she wants to make sure I'm following through on my end."

My head hurt, and I felt like I was going to throw up.

"I know this may be the last thing from your mind, but we have to figure out how we will keep working together."

"Work," I repeated. "I just, I don't ..." I realized I wasn't forming an intelligible statement, but I didn't care.

"We need to make sure that no one can tell anything happened between us," he continued.

I was vaguely aware he was talking, but I couldn't focus on the words he was saying. *How could I have been so stupid? How could I have thought we were building a relationship? How could I have been so naïve?*

"Does that sound okay?"

"What? You may have been talking, but I didn't hear a word. I really can't think straight right now, much less focus on a game plan. My heart is breaking at the moment," I said without emotion in my voice.

I picked up my bag and headed toward the door. It was taking every ounce of me not to beg and plead, "What about us and what we have?"

⁓

I knocked softly before opening the door. "Hey," I said quietly.

The light from the hall streamed into the room, making my tear-stained face impossible to hide.

"What's wrong?" Andy groggily asked.

"He ended it," I said as I walked over and sat on the edge of the bed, tucking my knees up under my chin.

"Are you okay?"

"No." I gave a look that stated the obvious.

"Sorry, I'm still half asleep. Obviously, you're not okay. What happened?" She started to sit up in bed.

"He said there's someone else."

"Who?"

"Some woman named Nicole. He was seeing her before we started dating. She wants to get back together, so he ended things with me."

"Kate, I'm so sorry." She hugged me.

I woke up the next morning feeling like I had been in a bad car accident. I heard Andy's voice in the other room. She and Josh were sitting in the kitchen, immersed in conversation. I could hear my name and Ben's every once in a while.

"I'm sad. I've been crying. My nose is stuffy. I feel numb. All that said, I *can hear you*. Stop talking about me and talk *to* me." I rubbed my eyes with the heels of my hands.

Andy ignored my mood. "Good, you're up. Get dressed. We're going to brunch," she said as I stumbled into the room.

"I don't want to be the stereotypical weepy girl who can't get out of bed when a guy breaks up with her, but I'm not in the mood to go anywhere right now." I fell heavily on the couch.

"We're your best friends, and it's our responsibility not to let you wallow … at least in the apartment by yourself. Get dressed and you can wallow over brunch." Andy moved from the kitchen to the couch and dragged me into my bedroom. "Wash your face and get dressed. We're going."

I eyed Josh. He put up his hands in defense. "I'm playing catch-up. I didn't even know you were seeing someone."

"Are you going to get mad at me about it?"

"No, but it's not forgotten." Josh teased gently.

"Great." I flopped onto the couch.

"Uh-uh-uh. Up." Andy pulled me off the couch.

Andy and Josh finally dragged me out of the apartment to eat. I mostly pushed the food around my plate. I still was feeling sick to my stomach. "Let's go. I think you need to do something more active." Andy motioned to the waiter for our check.

"We're supposed to meet Caroline and Beth for the movie tonight. You know I love chick flicks, but I cannot see a movie tonight where Kate Hudson finds the love of her life in ten days."

"Obviously, I'm in favor of skipping a chick flick. I have to run up to my office for a few minutes. I'll give you a call after I am done and meet up with you." Josh gave me a hug before getting in his car and driving off.

"So what's next on the agenda? How about some skeet ball with screaming kids at Chuckie Cheese? Then we can get a palm reading. And there is a guy movie out right now that is guaranteed not to have anyone ending up with the love of their lives," Andy offered.

"Do you have a pregnancy test on our agenda?" I asked flatly.

She stopped midway in opening her car door.

"I'm two weeks late. Great timing, I know. I don't think I am. It's probably just stress."

"I didn't think to include it. But it's now next on the agenda. Let's be on the safe side and find out."

Andy came out of the drug store waving the plastic bag. "I got two in one so you can pee twice. Have you felt nauseous at all?"

"Just the thought of Ben is making me nauseous. The thought of peeing on a stick is making me nauseous. The thought of going to work on Monday is making me nauseous. Is that what you mean?"

"There's something ironic about peeing on a stick in the bathroom of Chucky Cheese."

"Probably not the message to send to kids."

We sat in the bathroom for the next few minutes in silence.

"I can't look," I stated when Andy pointed to her watch, indicating enough time had elapsed.

"Okay, I'll do it." Andy pushed herself off the wall and picked up the sticks. "I don't know."

I blew out my breath slowly. "What does that mean?"

"It means one says you are, the other says you're not." She pulled me up so I could see for myself.

"How is that possible?"

"Well, they're not 100 percent accurate."

"Obviously. So much for finding out. Now I feel even crappier."

"We'll figure it out." She gave me a hug.

"Hey," I said as I opened the door.

"I wanted to check in on you." Josh's eyes and smile could not have been more compassionate.

"Thanks. Come on in." I backed up so he could pass me. I moved to grab some more Kleenex before plopping back down on the couch. He sat down next to me and reached over and brushed the hair off my forehead.

I blew my nose, which at this point had become numb.

He smiled sympathetically. "How are you doing?"

"Great. Don't I look it?"

"I know you think you are somehow weak if you cannot keep it together because of a guy. That's not true."

"I think that I don't know what I thought I knew." I scrunched up my nose. "Does that even make sense?"

"It's okay to be upset. You were in a relationship with this guy. You had strong feelings for him, and it didn't work out."

"Do you want me to cry? Be a typical girl about it? I think I pretty much fit the bill."

"I want you to let out your emotions and not keep them bottled up. And if you want to talk about stereotypes, I'm a guy talking about feelings."

I let out a little laugh. "I just feel stupid, like I should have known better."

I rested my head on his shoulder. Josh was gently stoking the side of my face. We sat like that for a while, not talking. I looked up at him, and at that moment he looked down, tipped my face gently up to his, and softly traced my cheek. I leaned in to kiss him and he responded. I moved into his lap. And with that, he picked me up and carried me to my room, all the while kissing. He set me on the bed. I lifted my arms up and he pulled my shirt over my head. I fumbled unbuttoning his jeans. He lay next to me on the bed kissing me, first my lips, then moving to my neck and back to my lips.

He gently pulled back. "Kate."

"Hmm."

"Kate, open your eyes."

"What?"

"I wish you could see your face right now. You are going through the motions. You don't want this."

I sat up. "What do you mean?"

"I mean, you're doing this to avoid feeling sad, but tomorrow you'll wake up and it will still be there." He was sitting on the corner of my bed, facing the window.

"You didn't seem to have a problem going down the road a couple of weeks ago."

"That felt distinctly different."

"Is it because of Bridget?" I knew I was ignoring his point, but at the moment I didn't care.

"Are you even listening to me?" He stood up and buttoned his pants.

"Do you feel guilty?"

"I'm not Ben."

"What? I know you're not Ben."

"Do you?"

"I know you're not Ben," I repeated.

"If you're concerned about Bridget, would you really want to be the other woman?"

"Does it even matter?"

"It's not you."

"How do you know?"

"Because I know you."

"I'm glad somebody does."

I curled up on my bed, and Josh sat down beside me. I was fighting how tired I felt. Josh pulled the blanket over my shoulders and began stroking my hair. I gave up fighting it and let myself fall asleep.

Chapter 25

I woke up on Monday morning with a pounding headache. I swung my legs over the side of my bed. It was taking every ounce of pride that I had not to call in sick to work. Buddy followed me around all morning as I moved from the shower to the kitchen and back to my room. After the past couple of days, he had gotten used to getting back in bed. I threw on a black suit, which was normally something I would wear to see a client, not for being in the office all day. But a suit meant I didn't have to think about what to throw together.

"Do you want to ride in together this morning?" Andy asked.

"Sure."

"Have you thought about what you might say to him?"

"I think I'm going with an avoidance approach, just hole up in my office. If I'm at all lucky, he'll have to travel this week."

The next few days I did just that. I trudged through a pile of work and was fairly undistracted.

On Thursday night someone knocked at the apartment door. Andy was not home yet, so I got up from the couch to answer it.

When I opened the door, I saw Ben holding a T-shirt of mine.

"Can we talk?"

"No." I took the shirt from him and closed the door.

I leaned against the back of the door and took a deep breath. I wanted to know why he had come. I paused and then reopened the door. Andy was standing there with a sack of groceries and fumbling for the keys. "Good timing. Was that …" She was motioning over her shoulder.

"Yeah."

"What did he want?"

"I don't know. I told him to leave." I grabbed the bag from her and we walked inside.

The next night I opened the door to find Ben again. "You can't keep coming over like this." I looked at him; he looked tired and older.

"It's not the same," he said quietly.

I let out a little laugh.

"You are so distant at work," he continued.

"It's not going to be the same."

"Your light was still on when I went back to the office tonight. I was kind of excited, thinking you were there."

"You can't say things like that anymore."

"I'm just confused right now."

"Why are you confused? You made your choice. It wasn't me."

"I think I made the wrong choice."

Those were the words I had wanted to hear, but I wasn't sure how I felt. "You think?"

"This week has been horrible for me. I know I have handled it completely wrong."

"For you?" I repeated with exasperation. "Do you realize how self-absorbed you sound? You are talking all about you. How confused you are, how horrible you feel."

"Can we go inside and talk?"

"Fine, but I'm only letting you inside because I would rather not have my neighbors hear all the details of my life." I held open the door for him to pass through.

"I made a mistake. I was faced with a choice, and I chose wrong."

"And why are you realizing this now?"

"This past week I've been missing you." He reached for my hand, but I pulled back.

"You've seen me every day."

"It hasn't been the same. I've seen you in the office from across the room. Every time I came within ten feet of you, you would either leave the room or try to casually move to the other side of it."

"What did you expect?"

"I just ... All week things have been reminding me of you. I miss you. I miss the way I can smell your shampoo on my pillow. I miss the secret stash of tampons you had been keeping at my place. I miss the irritation I felt when you squeezed the toothpaste from the top of the tube. I even miss the hair that you seem to be able to mysteriously shed wherever you go."

"Ben," I said quietly, "why couldn't you have realized this last week? I feel like I have been pushing and pushing for this, but ..."

"And I realized something else." He had picked up my hand, and this time I let him take it. "I am in love with you."

"What?" No other words would come out of my mouth.

"Kate, I love you."

"You cannot say that now." I looked at him, wanting to believe what he was telling me. "Are you serious? What about Nicole?" I hated that I even had to say her name during a moment like this.

"I was trying with Nicole for the wrong reasons. I felt an obligation because we had been together for so long, but what I should have been trying was to give you and me a real chance. I'm just hoping you are willing to give us that now."

"I just don't know. I mean, last week I would not have hesitated, but your actions, they changed things. It doesn't sit lightly with me that at the first real bump we had, you walked away looking for something, someone else. And it doesn't sit lightly with me that you were with someone you didn't even mention to me."

"I know that I'm asking you to take a huge chance with me."

"I took a huge chance with you in the beginning of this. I'm not sure how to even quantify what you are asking of me now."

"Will you think about it?"

"I don't know if I can."

"I know we would have to start over, and I'm willing to do whatever I have to."

"I wish you had been saying this before, when I felt like I constantly had to pull emotions out of you."

"I know. I'm just hoping that I am not too late now." He was pacing back and forth in front of the coffee table. "Look, I'm leaving for a week. Why don't you take that time to determine if you can get back into a relationship with me?"

"Where are you going?"

"I'm heading out of town with my family. We are going up to the Cape. They have rented a house for a couple of weeks, and I thought it would be good to get away for a bit."

"When do you leave?"

"Tomorrow."

I took a deep breath. "Okay."

"Does that mean you will think about us?"

"It means I will think about it, but you should know that I'm not willing to say that I will definitely give you another chance."

"I understand. Can I call you while I'm gone?"

"Sure. I may choose not to answer, but you can call."

The next week passed quickly. Ben called every day and sent e-mails. I didn't answer or respond, but I did listen to every message and read every e-mail.

His first night back in town he came over to my apartment. He had been there for ten minutes, and I could not seem to stop moving. I unloaded the dishwasher, folded some clothes, and now stood in front of the mirror putting on powder and lip gloss. Ben followed me into the bathroom. He moved behind me and put his arms around my waist, burying his head into my neck. "I missed you."

I felt like I had been holding my breath since he walked into the apartment. "We need to get going." I snapped the cap onto my gloss and wriggled out of his hold.

"Where are we going?" He stepped back, allowing me room to exit the bathroom.

"My parents' house." Registering his confused look, I added, "For dinner." I could tell Ben was uncomfortable with this, and I hadn't asked him whether or not it was okay. I had put aside what I wanted for long enough and wasn't asking so much as telling him of my plans.

By the time we arrived at my parents' house, my mom was just taking the food off the stove and out of the oven and placing it into serving platters. They were getting ready to move from the kitchen into the dining room. I quickly introduced Ben to everyone. After the initial round of pleasantries, my mother shooed us into the dining room so she could finish the last-minute touches.

Ben filed out of the kitchen first and sat down in Caroline's chair. Caroline stopped when she entered into the dining room. Her abruptness caused Shawn to run into her. "What are you doing?"

I walked around her to see what had given her pause. I knew immediately what the problem was but tried to smooth it over. "Maybe we should mix things up a little. We always sit in the same places." I walked around to the side of the table where Ben was seated.

"I'm sorry. I didn't realize ..." Ben began to stand.

"No, it's fine." I put my hand on his shoulder to keep him from getting up.

"But I always sit there so I don't bump my elbow into Shawn when I'm eating," my sister protested.

"So sit in—" I almost said "Josh's chair" and stopped myself. "Sit in that chair and you'll be fine." I motioned to the chair.

"Really, I can move." Ben started to stand.

Shawn sat down. "Caroline, sit next to me." He patted the chair I had been motioning her to sit in.

She finally gave in, and I smiled gratefully at Shawn.

My parents, who had been in the kitchen, joined us.

"Well, how am I supposed to tell you two apart now?" my dad cracked as he noted the seating arrangements.

"I didn't realize there were assigned seats." Ben looked reproached as he said it.

I put my hand on his. "There aren't. We're just creatures of habit, and it's good to be shaken out of it every once in a while. And besides, Dad, if you get confused, just say 'hey, you' if the blond versus black hair isn't enough help."

"Maybe we should also change things up." My mom sat down in my dad's chair before he could.

"You want me to sit in your lap?"

"You're too big for that. I want you to go sit at the other end of the table."

"I can't believe you're knocking my weight. You know how sensitive I am about that." Dad sucked in his stomach.

"So sensitive that you'll have a big bowl of ice cream after dinner."

After the seating fiasco, dinner seemed to go downhill. Caroline did nothing to hide her displeasure at Ben's presence. And while Ben is normally smooth and composed with his clients, with my family he was not.

"Ben, I hear you were on vacation in the Cape. How was it?" Dad asked.

"It was nice. We had good weather and good food, really great seafood. You would have loved it." He looked at me.

"She doesn't like seafood," Caroline interjected.

"Oh, I didn't realize."

"It's kind of a big thing not to know about someone." Caroline didn't let Ben off the hook.

"No, it's not," I jumped in. I knew telling my sister had been the wrong thing to do if Ben and I were ever to work it out. At the time,

216

though, I didn't know Ben and I might be trying again. She was trying to protect me, and I knew it would be difficult for her to move beyond what I told her about him.

My mom must have pinched her under the table because she jumped in her seat. "Ouch."

"What's the matter?" Mom looked at her innocently.

"Nothing. I stubbed my toe on the foot of the table," Caroline replied.

Shawn and my father smirked, neither looking up from their plates.

I was trying to think up an excuse for us to leave. I couldn't get through much more myself and wasn't sure Ben could handle it. Caroline had laid it on thick for Ben, and he had politely taken what she was dishing out.

"So, Ben, I know you work with my daughter, but what is it that you do?" My father tried to redirect to a safe topic of conversation.

Ben began talking about one of his clients out of D.C. "They are a mid-sized sporting goods chain trying to move into another market."

"That's it." Shawn snapped his fingers. "I knew I recognized you. You're Nicole's fiancé."

The table went silent as we looked from Shawn to Ben.

"What are you talking about?" My sister's voice came out in a whisper. The color had drained from her face. I knew my own face mirrored hers.

"Remember I was up visiting my sister in D.C. a few months ago? She was hosting an engagement party for a friend of hers, Nicole Montgomery. I tagged along as her escort." He looked at Ben. "I've been sitting here trying to place you. You were one of the guests of honor that night."

I heard a tiny gasp escape from my mother.

I set down the fork that I had a death grip on. From the look on Ben's face, I knew Shawn was right. I placed the napkin on my plate. "If you'll excuse us." My voice was remarkably even.

Ben pushed back his chair to follow. He cleared his throat. "Thank you for dinner." His words were hollow and he knew it. This pitch was sunk and there was no recovery. Ben's normal charm for clients when a meeting was going poorly could do nothing for him now.

The embarrassment, anger, and sadness that I was feeling were all secondary to the foolishness. I had trusted this guy. I was vaguely aware of Ben sitting next to me in the car. I saw his hand move from time to time to signal changing lanes. I could not bring myself to look at him. The silence followed us up the stairs to my apartment and through the door. I walked into the kitchen and pulled out a bottle of water from the refrigerator. The water coated the emptiness I now felt. Setting down the bottle, I took a deep breath and fixed my eyes on Ben. Then I waited.

Ben was leaning against the sink. He was rubbing his hand across his forehead. Buddy was sitting at the edge of the kitchen, staring warily at Ben. He had stopped growling at him, but he still wouldn't let Ben pet him.

"So there's something I need to tell you."

I looked at him wryly. "You think?"

His eyes were downcast, and he did not raise them to meet mine. "We had been seeing each other."

"What are you talking about? Are you talking about Nicole? I've kind of guessed that."

"Yes, I'm talking about Nicole."

"Well then?" I sighed with frustration, "I think you need to just start talking, and I need you to be explicit."

"We were seeing each other. We were engaged. We weren't on a break."

My stomach was doing all kinds of acrobatics. "So I was the other woman?" I said, half in a question and half in a statement. My knees felt weak beneath me. I found a chair to sit down. I couldn't help but thinking of the irony that Josh's remark now held.

"I guess if you want to look at it like that."

"It was bad enough thinking you were going back to her, but now you're telling me you were with her the whole time that we were seeing each other? And you were actually engaged? I don't understand how you could do that to her—and to me, for that matter."

"There's more." His voice became quiet, almost a whisper. "The trip I went on was with her, not my family. She found out about us, and we were trying to work it out."

I sat in stunned silence.

"After we spoke last week, I intended to use it as a way to end things with her. I felt like I owed it to her to take the week and hash it out. It had been three years, we were engaged, and I needed to let her have the time to come to the realization about it being over."

"What you owed her—actually, both of us—was the truth. So why are you telling me about the trip now? Are you afraid I might find that out too?"

"I want us to start off in the right place, and if we're moving forward I want you to know the truth. You and I just happened. It turned into something I never expected. Things between me and Nicole had … I should have ended it then, as soon as I realized I had feelings for you, but I guess I was confused. The plans were already in motion and starting to pick up momentum. I wasn't sure how to stop it."

"I could have helped you with your confusion. If I had known about your engagement, I never would have become involved with you. I would have removed myself from the situation. You wouldn't have been confused because I would not have been an option." I stood up, pacing around the kitchen. "I don't understand. We spent almost every night together during the week."

"Well, she lives in another city."

"So on the weekends, when you were out of town, you were with her?"

"Yes. Or she was here."

She was here. "You would be in town with her. Didn't you think you might run into me?"

"I didn't think we would go to the same places."

"Wow, you are bold." I sat back down. "Now I understand why you freaked out about my leaving anything at your place." I couldn't help but want to know more. "But didn't you two talk on the phone or something? How was I never around when she called?"

"You always came over late. I made sure we talked before you came over."

"This is why you wouldn't commit."

"Kate, please know this was never my plan. I was caught off guard by our relationship and how I began to feel about you. "

I was holding my forehead in my hands. "This isn't right. If we were right, you wouldn't have been so confused about your feelings for me." Somehow the words just poured out of me, and I realized they had been pent up in me for a while. "If we were right, you wouldn't have started a relationship with me before ending yours with Nicole. From what I can gather, your plan was just to have an affair with me, never letting Nicole or me become the wiser."

"Kate, there was no plan. I let things happen that shouldn't have happened. I am truly sorry for that, but please can we work through this … this … situation?" He was grasping for the right word.

"You didn't give me an opportunity to choose whether I would get involved with you, given your *situation*. Well, now I'm choosing to *remove myself from this situation*." I added emphasis to the last words.

"What do you mean?"

"This isn't me. The way I've been with you… You actually think this would be okay with me, don't you? This is not me. Or, at least I'm not the person I want to be when I'm with you."

"What are you talking about? I like who you are."

"What is my dream, my goal?" I tested the words he just stated.

"You mean the promotion?"

"No." I shook my head. "Exactly, that's exactly it. You don't know, but that's my fault. I didn't let you know me. I didn't even share with you something that is so important to me—my dream of one day running my own company."

"Well, share it with me now. Let me know you now." He reached out for my hand.

"It's too late. I'm out," I stated simply.

"Wait, Kate. You don't understand." His voice rose slightly.

"I think you should leave. I do not need to talk anymore about this. I thought I saw something in us, but I was wrong. You are not who I thought you were, and I wouldn't be who I think I am if I stayed in a relationship with you."

"Kate, I just, there is something I—" he started to plead, his eyes searching mine.

"No, you need to go."

"Please just hear me out. I never planned for this to happen. And I know I have made it difficult for us, but I want to make it work." He stopped and looked at me searchingly. His voice changed in tone. "You're done, aren't you? I can see it in your eyes."

"Yeah, I'm done. You asked me to take a chance on you. I did. But this is more than I can do. I cannot build a relationship with someone I don't trust." I held open the door for him to leave.

"I hope you will change your mind." He touched my arm.

"I won't."

After Ben left, Andy peeked her head out of her room. "Are you okay? I'm sorry, I couldn't help but overhear."

"It's fine. I'm fine." I moved past her and into my room. I started going through my closet, removing clothes I didn't wear anymore.

"What are you doing?"

"Cleaning." I didn't look up from what I was doing.

"Okay. Well, let me know if you want to talk."

An hour later, I had made good progress in my room. I heard Josh and Drew come into the apartment and then a mumbling of voices.

"How are you?" Josh asked as he ducked his head inside my room.

"I'm fine. I'm relieved actually." I was busy moving around my room, picking up clothes off my floor, putting shoes back into their boxes, straightening piles on my desk.

"That wasn't exactly the response I was expecting." He came into my room and sat on the corner of my bed.

"I mean, I am sad, but I am also truly …" I paused, searching for another word that could describe how I felt. "Relieved. Yep, relieved. It's the only way I can describe it." I shrugged my shoulders.

"I have to say, you look like you're doing better. I can't say that I entirely understand your response." He had turned toward me. His eyes almost looked as if he were hurting for me.

I sat down in my desk chair across from him.

"What I went through the first time sucked. But part of the reason it was so horrible for me was that it was unexpected. I felt like it was out of left field, like someone had punched me in the stomach, and I wasn't ready for it or didn't even know it was coming. This time around I can't say that was the case. It was almost like I half expected something like this to happen. It was too good to be true. Things had worked out exactly how I had wanted them to and everything was going at the pace I had originally been wanting. At that point, I just had this weird sense of something. I mean, I believe good things can happen, but when something bad happens … and then to be so neatly wrapped up in a little bow. " I was fiddling with the strap on one of my shoes. "It was just more of the waiting game for when … when the other shoe would drop. And now that it has, I don't have to wait anymore." I let the shoe I had been holding drop to the floor. "How's that for dramatic effect?"

"You're putting on the brave face." He took my hand, rubbing his thumb across the top of it. "But you don't have to. I am here for you if you need to talk."

I squeezed his hand. "I know that. I really do. But I am done. I am done being sad about it. Ben wasn't who I thought he was."

"What do you mean?"

"Well, for one, he seemed to have a continuing problem of beginning a relationship before ending the one he was in. And I thought he was someone who could make me happy. But you know, all he really did was tie me up in knots." Josh suppressed a grin. "Okay, mister literal, I meant figuratively. The knots were in my stomach, but thanks for the visual."

"How do you think I feel?" He smiled.

"I also started to think when it came down to it that he didn't get me. I mean, my birthday gift … and then there was the chocolate milk."

"Chocolate milk?"

"It was nothing. It really was stupid. I just think I somehow was forgetting who I was. I wasn't willing to speak up for what I wanted or needed. I was blaming him for me being unhappy. I own that, though. I just need to move past it now and focus on what's next for me."

"In terms of what?"

"Whether I get some ice cream. Whether I go for a run with Buddy." He perked his ears up and I tugged on his tail. "Whether I keep working at the firm. Just a few light decisions."

Josh's look registered surprise.

"I don't know anything yet. So let's focus on the other two, a run and then ice cream. Interested?"

Chapter 26

I couldn't help getting the feeling that everyone was staring at me as I made my way from the elevator toward my office. It was too quiet when I walked by. The lingering of gossip in the air was palpable. Feeling self-conscious, I pulled out my compact from my desk drawer to make sure I didn't have something on my face.

"Bill wants to see you in his office in five." Angie, his assistant, popped her head in my office.

"Hey, Angie," I called after her. "Does it seem a little quiet around the office to you this morning?" She didn't hear my question, or if she did, she didn't respond.

I wondered if they were making promotion decisions today. I hadn't seen Simon, but I was sure he was lurking nearby. I gathered my notebook and walked down the hall. Ben's office light was still off. I was relieved, since I wasn't sure how to face him. Angie wasn't at her desk when I got to Bill's office, so I knocked lightly on his door.

Bill turned around from his computer. "Kate, please come in and close the door behind you." He got up from his chair behind the desk, sat down in the one of the two big arm chairs that face each other, and motioned for me to take the other one.

"How are you this morning?" I asked. I could hear my throat catch slightly. I tried to discreetly wipe the palm of my hand on the side of my pant leg. I still became nervous when summoned to his office at the end of the hall.

"It's been an interesting morning." He took off his glasses and rubbed the bridge of his nose.

"I was wondering if something was going on around here."

"I was actually hoping that you could help me with that."

"I'm sorry." I shifted in my chair. "I'm not sure what you mean."

"Well, you and Ben seem to be a topic of interest this morning."

I couldn't open my mouth to respond. It felt glued shut.

"It was brought to my attention that you two may have been involved in more than a working relationship. Now, Kate, there is no office policy against this. However, there are a couple of things that have me worried. The first being you. I want to make sure you were not put in a position ..." he cleared his throat. He looked painfully uncomfortable. "I want to make sure that Ben did not use his position inappropriately."

"No, he didn't." I couldn't meet Bill's eyes.

"Kate, I don't want you to feel pressured now. If you want to take some time to think about this. I know you are being caught off guard."

"You mentioned there were multiple things that had you worried."

"This all comes at a time when we are announcing promotions. The allegation has been made that a promotion was based on an inappropriate relationship."

"But I haven't been promoted."

"The partners all met last week and made our decision. I was going to offer you a promotion."

"Was?" My voice trailed off.

"Kate, you were our top choice. You still are our top choice. The promotion is yours. We just need to sort through all of the other stuff."

"What about Simon?" I asked, knowing the answer already.

"We are only making one offer this year."

"Is Simon leaving?"

"I would imagine he will be, but not before making some noise."

"And Ben, what will happen to him?"

"He's been put on immediate leave." He put his glasses back on. "I'm not sure he will be coming back."

"Am I getting the promotion because you are afraid I'll sue?"

He laughed. "Oh, I am afraid you might sue, but that's not why I am extending you an offer. Your work has been impeccable. In my mind, one has nothing to do with the other."

"This is what I wanted, what I was working for. But obviously, I didn't want any of the outside stuff to have an effect. I need to take some time, though. I need to sort through where I want to go from here."

"I understand. I'm just sorry it seems to be casting a shadow on the whole process."

"Me too."

Bill held out his hand to shake mine. I shook his, surprised that my hand was no longer clammy. He put his other hand on top of mine. "Kate, I'll wait to hear from you."

Simon was in his office. I decided not to confront him but went back to my office to grab a few things. He must have seen me pass because he appeared behind me a few seconds later.

"Going somewhere?" He perched himself in the chair across from my desk.

"Should I be asking you that question?"

His smugness disappeared for a second. "I'm weighing my options right now."

I logged off my computer and powered it down. "Even for you, this is low." I looked over to him.

"I'm not sure I know what you are talking about."

"Simon, you know exactly what I'm talking about. Do you really think I would do what you are telling people I did?"

"I just call it like I see it."

"And what is it you think you see?"

"I saw you two in the parking lot. I heard the tail end of your conversations. There was more than work between you two."

I flashed back to bumping into him after leaving Ben's office. "I have to assume this didn't quite turn out like you intended it to." I paused. "I thought you looked to Ben as a mentor."

"I don't know that I would call anyone that. I am where I am."

"And where's that, Simon? You are spreading rumors that you don't have any real evidence for. You aren't in line for a promotion. You've burned bridges. Is that what you were hoping for?"

"I would worry more about yourself than me. This will follow you around, not me. As soon as I leave this company, it's forgotten. If you leave—"

I cut him off as I picked up my bag. "Simon, I wouldn't want you to change now and start thinking about anyone other than yourself. I'll be fine." I walked past him and headed down the hall toward the elevator. I could feel eyes following me, but I didn't dare turn around. I entered the elevator and waited for the doors to close before finally turning around. I was counting the seconds until I would be out of the building and at a safe distance from any employees who happened to be on their way into or out of the building. Thankfully, no one I knew had gotten on the same elevator car as I had, and I managed to make it through the lobby without bumping into anyone. When I got to my car, I threw my bag in the back and quickly made my way out of the parking garage. A couple of blocks away from the building I pulled off the road and finally let myself breathe. The tears were streaming down my face.

Chapter 27

*I*t had been a week since the scene in my office. I hadn't talked to Ben since the day he walked out of my apartment. He finally had stopped calling the apartment. I was still keeping up with e-mail, so I knew he was transferred to another office. It had been such a short time, but it felt surreal to think back on my relationship with Ben. It was as if I were looking at something that happened to someone else.

With the time I now had, I threw myself into planning Andy's shower. I decided to make individual favors for each guest. Twenty-five people were coming. I had gone through Andy's pictures to find a current one of her and each person. I then used a program to create a picture of them when they were about five years old and when they were seventy-five years old. It looked like they had been friends since childhood and predicted what they would look like as older women. I used the three pictures to cover each side of a treasure box, with the fourth side containing their names. The shower was over brunch with the focus on food …no games, at Andy's request. Afterward Andy and I went to the park to take in the sun.

"This is beautiful. I just love days like this." The sun was shining without a cloud in the sky and it was only seventy-five degrees. "I think your shower turned out really well today." I took my wedges off to walk in the grass.

"Those favors were out of control."

"What can I say? I had a little extra time on my hands." I shrugged my shoulders.

"So, I have to ask. Are you ever going back to work? Or have you suddenly become independently wealthy and I was unaware of it?"

I smiled at her question. "I wish. Actually, I'm letting my paid vacation run out. I had about a month saved up in my vacation bank. I talked to Bill and he was okay with me using it while I figured everything out."

"I guess they would be when you could sue."

"I think he probably wants time and distance between me and Ben to let the office gossip subside."

"Well, have you come any closer to a decision?"

"No, I really haven't. I think I need to start exploring options so I am not just choosing between going back and not going back. I probably should look to see if I have any alternatives."

We walked a little bit more in silence. "Hey, Andy." She turned to face me. "Thanks for not lecturing me or telling me I told you so."

She laughed. "I'm pretty sure you knew that without me saying a word."

When Andy and I got back to the apartment, Josh and Drew were there. Andy started relaying the events of the shower to Drew and then showing him the gifts.

I changed and then joined Josh on our balcony. "What did you guys do today while we counted how many ribbons Andy broke opening gifts?" I pulled up a chair next to Josh's.

"Wait. Why were you counting ribbons?" Josh took one last pull from his beer to finish it off.

"To determine how many kids they are going to have."

"Oh, how very scientific of you," He scoffed at me. "We watched a few games, that sort of thing."

"I can't believe you still wear those." Josh eyed his old blue jeans that I was wearing.

"They're comfortable, and I've just now gotten them to fit perfectly." My legs were curled underneath me.

"I can tell—rolling them up at the bottom and rolling them down at the top." He chuckled.

"What do you care? It's not like they would fit you anyway."

"You're right about that. I can't believe they ever fit me." He paused before adding, "I was a bit lanky then."

"You were downright skinny." We laughed before drifting into a companionable silence.

Josh finally cleared his throat and shifted his chair toward me. "Kate, I've been wanting to talk to you." I turned my attention toward him. "Bridget and I are not seeing one another anymore."

"What? Why not? What happened and when?" I placed my hand on his arm. "I know, four questions at once, but are you okay?"

"I'm fine." He shook his head. "It was because of me. She wanted more, and I just couldn't get there."

"I thought you really liked her."

"I did, but nothing serious."

"When did it happen?"

"The night at the beach house. You know, after the fight at the bar."

"Seriously?" My eyes widened "How did I not know this? How have you not told me sooner?" I jabbed him in the shoulder. "I can't believe Andy didn't tell me."

He held his arm, feigning pain. "It's been a crazy few weeks for you. I thought it could wait."

I was flabbergasted, but he didn't offer any further explanation.

"So what about you and Ben?" Josh changed topics.

I mused over how quickly guys move through mourning the relationship. If it had been me and Andy, we would have dissected it for at least a few more hours. "That's it?"

"Yeah, that's it. So?" he redirected again.

"Definitely done."

"Are you over him?"

"I'm working on it." I smiled. I was watching the cars below. "How come you let me off the hook? I mean, why haven't you gotten upset with me for not telling you about him?"

"I guess I figure, what's the point? It won't change anything now."

"It might make me feel less guilty."

"You should feel guilty."

"You're right." I sighed. "Look at us, a couple of relationship casualties."

"That's what I wanted to talk to you about."

"I'm not sure I follow. Are you thinking we need to join some sort of support group?" I nudged him in the side. "You know what they say, all's fair in love."

"It wasn't fair to Bridget." Josh's tone was quiet and serious.

"What wasn't fair?" I was beginning to realize this conversation was difficult for him.

"My feelings for you." He repositioned his chair again so that we were knee to knee.

I sat for a moment, not being able to form any words. This seemed to be happening to me frequently of late. When I did finally speak, all that came out was "Josh."

"Look, I know it's been a while since we were together, and I also know that it didn't work out the first time around. But I also think we never really broke up."

"What?" I half laughed, not knowing what other reaction to give. "I seem to recall a definite breakup."

"There may have been, but how much changed?"

"Yeah, we were lazy for a long time."

"It changed, though, when you started dating Ben and I began seeing Bridget. And that's when things became weird between us."

I didn't respond.

"I hate that you couldn't tell me about Ben and how I only found out after the fact. And thinking about how he treated you, I can't believe you gave him a second chance, even if it was short-lived," Josh continued.

I couldn't tell him there may be more to it. "I think it's natural to be jealous when two people are as close as we are."

"It wasn't jealousy. It was knowing that you were with the wrong person." Josh pushed back his chair and walked to the balcony. "And what about your feelings toward Bridget? Were you jealous?"

"I don't know." I knew I didn't think she was the right person for him, but I couldn't admit that it was because I thought that I was the right one. "I assumed I was being catty—you know, territorial."

"And the … we almost …" Josh said quietly.

He didn't elaborate, but I could vividly recall the two instances he was referring to. "I'm not going to deny that we have an attraction toward one another, Josh." *Just tell him. It's not fair to go there if there's a possibility.*

"You're reducing it to a physical attraction. That's great, Kate." He looked away.

"Josh, I didn't mean to minimize it."

"You don't want to be with me, but you don't want me to be with anyone else."

"That's not fair."

"And it's fair to me?"

There was a silence while we both tried to figure out what to say next. Josh broke it first.

"And what about now? What is in your head after hearing what I've said?"

"Josh, everything is so muddled for me right now." I stood up and walked over to where he was standing. "You know how much you mean to me, how much I care about you …"

"Do I? What I know is when things don't go well for you, when it doesn't work out with some other guy, I'm the one you come back to. I've somehow become the shoulder you cry on over these jerks. I'm not really interested in that anymore."

"You're not interested in being my friend?"

He took a deep breath. "You're it for me, Kate. I haven't moved on because I don't want to move on from you. I want to be with you. You can't imagine how hard it was for me to pull back from you—or try to—the past couple of months."

"Josh, I'm still a mess right now. I'm trying to get myself together, but I'm not close to the point where I can even think about this. You and I would not be a casual thing."

"I'm not looking for a casual thing."

"And I am not sure that I could do something more."

"I'm not asking for you to come to some decision right now. I have had time to figure out where I am. I want you to have time to do the same. But you do have to do that, because I'm not willing to stay in the same place where we are." Josh didn't wait for my reply. He leaned down and quickly kissed my cheek, then whispered in my ear, "Think about it."

"I will." My voice didn't reach above a whisper.

He picked up his empty beer bottle and left.

Chapter 28

"*H*ave you talked to Josh?" Andy's room had become filled with different piles of clothes.

"No." I picked up a shirt from the pile on her bed and began to fold it. "What are all of these?" I motioned to the various stacks.

"I'm dividing clothes up into things I will need for my honeymoon, things I'll need right away when I move into Drew's, and things I won't need until winter." She tossed another shirt in my direction.

"How big is the bag you are taking with you?" I eyed her honeymoon pile.

"It's just preliminary. I intend to go back through it with another pass." She was standing in front of her closet. "I hate that some of my stuff has to go into storage. Even if I can't wear it, I like knowing it is there and looking forward to the season change."

"It won't be that long. You close on the house in six weeks." I turned around and ran to the restroom. A few seconds later, I excitedly screamed, "Yes, thank you, thank you, thank you!"

"Are you okay?" Andy called out.

"I'm better than okay. I just got my period." I smiled when I reentered her room. "It wasn't the right time or the right guy."

Andy gave me a hug and then returned to her clothing.

"Did you think I was going to drop the subject of Josh?"

"I kind of hoped." I plopped down on her bed. "I mean, I did just find out for sure that I'm not—"

"Well, you're not *pregnant*, and you did bring up the comment about the right guy. So ..."

"So I have been avoiding him. I don't know what to say, where to begin."

"What I don't get is how you can be surprised that you and Josh are in this place. It's not like the signs were hard to miss."

"What are you talking about?"

"You had to notice conversations that stopped when you came into the room."

"Sure, but I figured I was being narcissistic, thinking they were all about me."

"Well, you weren't. They were all about you. I can't tell you how many conversations Drew and I had with him or I had with him."

I thought back to seeing them on the street, and it was beginning to come together. When I didn't say anything, she continued, "Kate, you are not this naïve. You had to notice how much attention Josh paid to you, how bothered he was after he found out about Ben."

"You're right. I'm not naïve. I might be in denial," I attempted a tiny smile, "but I can explain his behavior."

"Oh, please do enlighten me. They say denial comes before acceptance, right?"

I ignored her rhetorical question and offered my explanation. "I attributed his response to Ben to disapproval. That was not an uncommon sentiment from my friends." I looked at her pointedly before continuing. "You, Josh, and Drew are best friends, so I didn't give it much thought or want to give it much thought, for that matter, when you all were talking ... or not talking. And as far as his paying attention to me, we are friends."

"And you didn't notice a distinct difference between your friendship with Josh and mine?"

"Andy, maybe I was being naïve in wanting to think that a girl and a guy could have an uncomplicated friendship."

"They can. Just not if one of them is in love with the other one."

"Josh is not in love with me."

Andy didn't respond. She just raised one of her eyebrows.

"Okay, I know there are feelings there, but it just seems like something keeps getting in our way. And, he and I both just got out of relationships with other people, in case you forgot."

"Can I just say it sounds like your grasping for excuses? You clearly are in a state of avoidance—avoiding Josh, his feelings, and I'm guessing your own feelings as well. This is where that denial you mentioned is definitely at play."

"Well, that's where you're wrong. I know I love him. He's Josh. But in terms of more, I just don't know." I paused. "There's so much history there. I hurt him so much."

"I think you hurt just as much from the relationship ending … whether you want to admit it or not."

"You're right. And I don't think he or I could go through that again and come out the other side. I stand to lose so much with him not in my life, even if it's just as a friend."

"You take risks at work. You went after a company that everyone else had written off. And what happened?" She didn't wait for my response. "It paid off. You should think about applying that risk-taking behavior to your relationships."

"It was risky getting involved with Ben."

"Not really." Her response stunned me. "I think you knew on some level that it wasn't going to work from the beginning. You played it safe by getting into a relationship with Ben. I saw it more as a distraction, one where you weren't really investing yourself or your feelings."

"Thanks for telling me now," I muttered, staring off at the wall behind her.

"You weren't ready to hear it before," Andy responded simply. "You were holding back with Ben. But you would be all in with Josh. And you know that's the difference."

I gave some thought to what she was saying. Then expressing my fear, I stated, "I keep getting stuck on the question of whether it is too soon to even be thinking about it."

"It's Josh. Just talk to him. Tell him where your head is."

"I can't. He made it quite clear where he stood, and I don't think he wants to hear any of my doubt. And *doubt* isn't even the right word. I don't want to jump into anything until I am ready and I can do everything within my control to make sure it is going to work."

"You can't guarantee that it will work, and I don't think he is expecting you to."

"But I want a relationship to have a chance. I don't want us not to work out because I wasn't ready with where my head is and everything."

"Well, where is your head right now?" Andy pulled out a suitcase. She looked back and forth between its size and the size of the pile.

"I was thinking about a first date. Maybe asking him to your wedding. I'm assuming he doesn't have a date," I said in more of a question than statement.

"I assume not. I mean, he sent in his RSVP for two when he was still dating Bridget. I haven't gone back to him to see if that changed." She sat down on the bed. "I think it's a great idea. You should ask him. Besides, there will be less pressure for the date since so much will be going on and all your attention will be on me." Andy dramatically fluttered her eyelashes.

"Don't worry. That day will be all about you."

"Day?" She mocked disappointment.

"I meant the weekend. The whole weekend."

I helped Andy sort through her closet and reduce the pile for the honeymoon over the next couple of hours. I reminded her that she would be in a swimsuit lounging around a Grecian isle most of the time, which helped shrink the size of it quickly.

Afterward, we both changed into our pajamas and plopped onto the couches to watch a movie. At some point, I must have stumbled into my room half-asleep, because the next thing I knew Buddy was tugging at the sheet. I stubbornly rolled over. "Buddy, let's sleep in a little longer." Talking caused Buddy to jump on the bed and stare at me. His wagging tail was shaking the bed. "That's not really what I had in mind." I pulled my hand from under the sheet and petted his head. "Okay." He sprung from the bed, stretching fully, tail wagging. I threw on boxers and flip-flops and opened the door to my room. Buddy bounded forward, grabbing his leash from the table by the door. I threw my hair in a pony tail, and we went downstairs to the grassy area next to the apartment building.

From the sidewalk I could see the window to Josh's apartment. The blinds were closed, so I couldn't tell if he was there. I was still working up my courage to ask him to the wedding.

"Buddy, what do you think? Should I ask him today?"

I kept busy the rest of the morning, picking up around the apartment, returning some personal e-mail, and paying bills. I then ran out of things to do, so I changed my clothes, trying for casual but cute. I grabbed my keys to lock the door behind me and walked up the flight of stairs to Josh's apartment. My hands were feeling clammy. I could not think of a time when I had been nervous to talk to him. As I lifted my hand to knock on the door, I felt like my heart was going to pound out of my chest. "Kate, pull yourself together," I muttered to myself. I knocked on the door.

The door swung open. "Bridget, um, hi." I tried to mask my surprise.

"Hi, Kate. How are you?" She didn't move back from the doorway.

"I was looking for Josh." I managed to get the words out.

"He ran out to grab coffee. Do you want to come in and wait?" She still wasn't budging from the doorway.

"Thanks, but that's okay. I'll get a hold of him later."

"Okay." She smiled. "See you."

"Bye." I turned to walk back to my apartment and could hear the door close behind me.

"What the hell?" I was holding onto the rail as I descended the stairs.

"Who are you talking to?" I turned the corner on the stairs to see Josh walking up holding two coffees.

"No one. I didn't see you."

"Are you coming from my place?"

"Yeah, I was just dropping by, but Bridget said you were out making a coffee run."

"Do you want to come back up?"

"Thanks, but I was going to take Buddy out for a run." I moved down the stairs past him. "I should really go do that. I'll see you later." I kept walking, not waiting for him to respond.

Chapter 29

I was sitting in a coffee shop, probably the only non-coffee drinker there. I had ordered a bagel and juice and found a table in the corner by the window. It was close to ten in the morning, and the crowd that had settled in was mostly those who would camp at the tables for hours, much like myself. I took comfort in knowing that I didn't have to rush to finish my bagel for the next person to get my table.

"Kate." I glanced up, unsure whether I had heard my name. "Kate." This time I was certain and swiveled in my chair in the direction of the voice. When I turned, I saw Chase walking toward me. I had not seen him since my date with Oakie.

"Hi, Chase." I thumbed the corner of the page and closed my book.

"It's been a while, what—eight, nine months?" He was fiddling with the top of his coffee.

"About that I think." I smiled.

"Do you mind if I join you?" He glanced at the chair across from mine.

"Not at all." I slid my bag off the chair across from me onto the floor. Chase slid into it.

"So how are things going?" He set his coffee on the table and looked at me with an earnest expression.

"Well, thank you. And how about you?"

"Good. They're keeping me busy. I don't think I mentioned when we met that I work for Baker, Allen, and Cooling."

"No, I didn't realize."

"You're still at Smithson, York, and Associates, right? I heard you were offered a promotion in the firm. Congratulations."

I was surprised he knew that I worked for them. "Thank you."

Without my asking, he offered, "It's a small world. When the announcement went out, I recognized your name. So, you're a partner now?"

"I'm weighing my options."

"Well, I don't know if you would be interested, but we are looking right now. I would be happy to make a call so we could have a more formal conversation and you could meet some of the senior partners."

"Really?" I was taken aback by his offer. *You don't even know me.*

He must have read my expression. "I think I'm a good read of people. We're always looking for talent, and I think you would be a good fit. Think about it anyway." He stood and reached into his wallet. "Here's my card. If you're interested, give me a call." He handed it to me.

I took it. "Thank you, Chase."

"Thank you for letting me interrupt you. Give my offer some thought."

"I will."

"Well, I hope to talk to you soon."

"Bye." I opened my book but couldn't focus. The words seemed to be swimming on the page in front of me. I closed the book and picked up the card, looking it over.

I didn't want to think about work or lack thereof, and I couldn't bear running into Josh at the apartment. I made a quick stop and used the back way into the building. I grabbed an overnight bag for me and Buddy and then drove the forty minutes to my parents' house. On the drive, it occurred to me how funny timing could be and how things can work out. Who would have thought that a sucky date with Oakie could result in a potential job opportunity? My mom would love if that turned out to be the case. She almost said as much when I called to briefly mention running into him and let her know I was on my way.

I let myself in the back door to the kitchen. "Mom, Dad!" I called out. I set my stuff on the counter and unleashed Buddy so he could roam.

"Hey, sweetie." Mom came into the kitchen carrying a load of laundry. "I'm glad you're here."

"Just thought I could use a home-cooked meal and some time with my parents."

"Well, let me just throw this into the washer." She picked up the basket again. "It's a nice afternoon. Why don't you go out to the porch and I'll join you in a minute?"

I nodded my head. "Is Dad here?"

"Yeah, he's doing some work in the study."

I picked up my bag and set it on the bottom step of the stairs to take up later. Then I let myself out the front door. Buddy followed behind. My parents had installed an invisible fence a year or so ago, and Buddy had been trained to know the perimeter in the front yard. I watched him sniff the grass and trees and then trot off to sniff grass in another part of the yard.

"Do you want to talk about it?" Mom sat down on the swing next to me.

"I don't know." I was pushing my foot off the porch so the swing moved slowly back and forth.

She didn't say anything before taking a drink from her iced tea.

"I was thinking I might stay over tonight, if that's okay."

"I was thinking you might be, seeing the bag you brought with you. But you know it's always okay. I enjoy having you around."

Buddy was lying on the porch, watching the birds fly in and out of the yard. He had given up on chasing them but was still keeping a close eye in case one of them stayed on the ground too long.

"Kate, your father and I are really proud of you."

"I know. I'm not sure I deserve it, but I know." I sighed. "I feel like I made a mess of things."

"It sounds like you have options with work. Maybe you should call the man who gave you the card just to learn more about it."

"I don't even know if it's an opening at a comparable level to where I am now, or if I would have to start all over."

"No reason to speculate. Call him and find out."

"You make it sound so simple."

"Darling," she tucked hair behind my ear, "calling *is* simple. It's the decision that will be hard."

"I feel so naïve." I knew I was jumping around, but I didn't care.

"I don't think trusting someone is naïve."

"Even if he didn't earn it," I said, half to myself and half to my mom.

"I don't think it could ever be a bad thing to believe the best in people. Every now and again it may not work out, but I think it is a positive trait. I would hate to see you stop trusting people because of one man who was dishonest. Maybe I'm naïve myself, but I do believe people are inherently good and if given the opportunity will do the right thing. Maybe you just need to be more careful in who you give your heart to."

"The same could be said about me with Josh."

"What do you mean?"

"Do you think I'm selfish?"

"Of course not. Why do you ask?"

"I was thinking about Josh and wondering if I was being selfish in wanting our friendship to stay the same. I just worry that I was careless with his feelings and now it is too late. On top of that, I feel guilty about not telling him about Ben. There was no reason not to."

"Maybe the fact that you were wanting your friendship to stay the same was reason enough. You knew talking about Ben would change it. And there's so much history between you two that I'm not sure it's too late." She paused, then asked, "Do you know what you want?"

"I think so, but I thought I knew what I wanted before. I don't want to be careless with his feelings. If I was before, I definitely do not want to be again."

"I think the fact that you are worrying about his feelings shows you are not careless."

"I think he is back with Bridget. I lost my opportunity with him."

"Things have a way of working out the way they are meant to."

"Mom, what is that supposed to mean? If he ends up with her, that is the way it was supposed to be? I should just let things work themselves out?" I looked at her in exasperation.

"Kate, you can't control everything." She smiled and patted my knee.

"Do you think I should say something to Josh about how I feel?"

"I can't tell you that."

"Why not?"

"Because you need to do what you think is best."

"I wish I had recognized what a great guy he was before. I mean I knew it, but I just didn't see it."

"Sometimes we have to go through experiences that lead us to where we should be."

"I just don't want to look back and regret not saying anything to him. I guess I would rather tell him and risk him saying it's too late than to never know. I just hate that I might be hurting someone else in the process."

We sat silently together. I was lost in thought.

"I'm going to tell him, but if I do am I being selfish? Agh!" I shook out my hands. "Okay, I'm not going to tell him. I'm not going to tell him," I repeated. "If he's decided he wants to be with Bridget, then I'll support him and be happy for him."

"Do I need to be here for this conversation?" Mom teased.

"Probably not." I let out a light chuckle.

Mom stood up from the swing and turned to me. She pushed my hair back and kissed my forehead. "In that case, I'm going to start dinner." She paused. "Why don't you go rile your father from his study and you two can keep me company in the kitchen?"

"Okay." I stood and patted my leg for Buddy to follow. He stood up, did a full body stretch, and then trotted inside after me.

"Hey, Dad" I knocked softly on his study door before walking in.

"Hey, kiddo." He looked up from his computer.

"Mom wants us to keep her company while she cooks."

"You sticking around for dinner?"

"Yeah. Actually, I'm going to stay the night." I was dragging my finger across the books that lined the shelves of the room.

"Really. Might you be up for golf in the morning?" He raised his eyebrows.

"I would, but I promised Andy I would be back early. I'm helping her stuff wedding programs."

"Sounds like fun." He rolled his eyes. He then pushed his chair back from his desk and stretched as he stood up. "You could always strike out on your own. It'd be hard at first, but you might enjoy it." I was surprised by his statement. "And if you needed some start-up cash, I'm sure we could help with a loan. Food for thought anyway." He led the way from the study to the kitchen.

The next morning I pushed myself out of bed and stumbled down the stairs into the kitchen. I sat down at the breakfast table, where my father was reading the newspaper. He slid a section of the paper toward me. Mom walked over to me and kissed my forehead. "Good morning, sweetie. Are you hungry? I'm making pancakes."

"Sure." I reached for the section of the paper Dad had pushed toward me.

"Coming right up."

"I feel like all I do is eat when I come home."

"You're lucky. I never see this much food unless you or Caroline come home, and then it usually is for you. Do you see me sitting here?" Dad asked Mom.

"I do. Are you checking my vision? Your father, always concerned about me."

"I was just wondering if I might get some breakfast this morning."

"Feel free to help yourself."

"Why does Kate get special treatment?"

"I don't get to see Kate all of the time."

"So if I leave and come back, I might get some breakfast?"

"You might."

"Could you like each other a little less this early in the morning? No offense. It's a bit nauseating."

"We'll try, dear."

I watched my parents playfully tease each other. I dipped the last of my pancakes into the syrup I had poured on a small section of my plate. "I should probably get going." I took my plate to the sink to rinse off the leftover syrup.

Mom helped me and Buddy out to the car. "It's no wonder I struggle with my romantic relationships. You two have the perfect marriage. How could I possibly find anything to measure up?"

"Sweetie, nothing is perfect. Not even your father and me. And you don't have anything to compare yourself to. You just have to find what's right for you." Mom gave me a hug and handed me some Tupperware with a casserole and a pasta dish that I could heat up later in the week. "I love you, sweetie."

"I love you, too, and thanks for the food." She stood and waved as I backed out of the driveway.

"I'm back." I let Buddy off his leash as he began his sniff of the apartment to make sure nothing had changed since he left. "I'm ready to stuff programs."

"Hey." I walked in to see Andy sitting on the floor with the materials for the programs sprawled out in front of her. "Where were you last night?" she asked without glancing up from the papers and ribbon she was sorting out.

"I stayed out at my parents'."

"And how are they?"

"Good, the same."

"I sat down on the floor next to her. So what do you need me to do?"

She picked up the outer sheet, inserted two pages, and tied the whole thing together with a bow. "That's it."

I sat down next to her. "Easy enough. How many are there? And why didn't you hire someone to do this?"

She was shielding the pages from Buddy as he sniffed around and settled into a spot nearby. "I thought it would give me some sense of accomplishment." She laughed. "It seemed a good idea at the time. On the bright side, it gives us time to bond."

"We could have been bonding over pedicures." I picked up the loose sheets of paper and began to collate them, following the process that Andy had used. "So what would you think about going out on our own?"

"What are you talking about?" Andy's expression furrowed as she remained focused on folding a program.

"Starting our own business." I could tell I caught her attention. "We're good at what we do. We could do it for ourselves—decide on the clients we represent, the ideas we pitch."

"Are you being serious?" She looked up at me.

"It was just an idea I have been mulling over."

"Well, to be honest, I am not sure this is the best time to ask me about something like that." She set down the ribbon and leaned back against the couch. "I'm not sure I could juggle another major life event."

"I know you have the wedding, a house closing, probably not the best time to start our own company."

"We would get to choose our own name," Andy offered.

"Something that highlights our assets—like Buxom Brunettes," I remarked without any attempt at keeping a serious face.

"Hah. Neither of us could be called buxom. What about Brains, Brawn, and Beauty?"

"I think the name could use some work. But seriously, it was something I wanted to throw out there for thought."

It took us five hours to finish folding the four hundred programs and tying ribbons through them. I suffered only one paper cut during the process, and Andy raised her voice only a little when I got blood on one of the programs. Even though we didn't talk much more about starting a company, I knew the conversation was enough for us both to be toying with the idea.

Chapter 30

The phone rang. A few seconds passed before it rang again. "Come on, Caroline. Pick up." Another ring. One more and I knew it would go to voice mail. I was resigning myself to leaving a message when my sister's out-of-breath voice greeted me. "Hello."

"Should I even ask why you are breathing so heavily?" My question masked my gratefulness at not having to leave the message.

"Ha-ha. I couldn't find my phone. I was running around the room throwing clothes out of the way." Her breathing started to slow.

"Where was it?" I asked, stalling for time and courage.

"In the bottom of the laundry basket," she stated as if this was perfectly normal.

"Why on earth?"

"Who knows?" I could picture her shrugging her shoulders.

"I'm assuming it was with dirty clothes."

"No, clean actually." Reading my mind, she explained, "And it wasn't washed. Shawn must have found it and set it there when he was folding clothes."

"Must be nice to have someone find what you lose."

"Surely you didn't call just to give me a hard time."

"No, while I am enjoying it, there was a reason." I was twisting a paperclip into an unnatural contortion. "I was hoping you could do me a favor ... I want to meet Nicole. And I was hoping you could set it up for me."

There was an extended silence before Caroline spoke.

"Kate, why would you want to meet Nicole? Don't you think it would just," she was struggling with what to say, "I mean, don't you think it would make things worse?"

I closed my eyes. "I don't. I think it would give me closure, and I'm hoping it would do the same for her."

Caroline proceeded to give me every reason possible for why I shouldn't meet Nicole. I didn't budge, and in the end she conceded and said she would contact Shawn's sister for me.

A couple of days later, I received an e-mail.

Hi Kate,
I'll be in Houston for work on Thursday.
Let's meet for a drink about six at Harrison's on Main.
I'll only expect to hear from you if that won't work.
Nicole

I must have read everything possible into the three lines. Each scenario ended with me thinking about the wronged woman. I just wasn't quite sure who that was.

I positioned myself at a table that was removed from other people but still had a view of the door. A red-haired, petite woman entered, and I knew it was her. She must have felt me looking at her. Her eyes locked with mine, and she walked toward me.

"This is completely weird, isn't it?" I laughed nervously, hesitating with whether to stand and deciding against it.

"I'm here too." Her expression was compassionate as she regarded me. "I was curious too." She took the seat across from me, setting her bag to the side.

"It's more than just the curiosity. Obviously, that's there." I paused before continuing, "I feel like I need to apologize."

"So we're going to get right to it." She motioned to a waiter, then turned back to look at me. "Why? You did nothing wrong. Not that I didn't want to blame you. I tried, but then I realized I was directing my anger toward the wrong person."

I shook my head. "I should have known, though. But I don't think I wanted to, not really anyway."

She laughed, and I immediately felt at ease. "I should have known. I mean, I knew his past and believe me, he's no saint. But I ignored it. Saw what I wanted to see."

"And what was that?" I asked.

"You know as well as I do that his divorce wasn't all that long ago. But I justified it. He told me he was separated and the divorce was a formality. Now I have to wonder."

She paused to order a drink from the waiter. I nodded to indicate the same for me.

When he left us, I asked the question that had been on my mind. "So how did you find out about me?"

She twirled a straw in her hand, then shrugged her shoulders. "By accident really. I needed to send an e-mail. His computer was right there, so I thought, *No big deal*," Nicole stated. "Was that ever an understatement. To get to my work e-mail, I was going in through my company's Web access. He already had Internet Explorer opened, so I clicked on it. He had left his personal e-mail account open, and there were quite a few from you with subject lines that caught my attention." She smiled.

I knew most of them were mild, but a "hey there" or "when you coming over" would have caught my attention too.

"I think I'm making it sound like it was no big deal. That's what perspective gives you. But at the time, my stomach sunk. I knew without opening them, but I had to be sure." She drew a deep breath. "I also knew that I was crossing a line of trust that I wouldn't be able to go back over. But in that moment that I hesitated, I already didn't trust him. So I opened one, then another, then another. By that time he came back in the room. He saw the computer, and the look on his face was the only confirmation I needed. But you know what? I didn't trust my instincts. I let him charm me."

"What do you mean?"

"I don't think I've ever seen someone try to spin so fast, and I let him. I knew he wasn't telling me the whole truth, but I wanted to believe him."

"Dare I ask?"

"He went with the whole being lonely since we lived in different cities. It was a fling, if that, and didn't mean anything." She rushed on, "I don't mean to hurt you by saying that."

"It's absolutely fine … at least it is now." I prompted her to go on.

"So we had this vacation planned. The thought being we would use it to get back on track. I mean, this had been three years of my life and what I had been thinking up until that point would be the rest of my life. I wasn't sure I could just throw it all away. I started rationalizing it—we all make mistakes. I did a better job of stating his case than he did. All he had to do was sit and watch me play out the conversation. So we went, and I was miserable. I couldn't get over the betrayal I felt and didn't think I could start off a marriage with doubt. Relationships and marriages are hard enough without adding a rocky foundation to them."

"You sound so pulled together."

"Yeah, now. This took intensive therapy to get here. I also know that if I am over it so quickly, there were other things that were wrong." She swirled the ice in her drink. "So how did you find out?"

"I would like to say that it was me, that I wised up. But I guess it was when you found out. He told me he wanted to start seeing you again. At that point, I didn't know the extent of it. It was after your vacation, the one I thought was with his family. I gave him a second chance—

actually took him to meet my family. It took my sister's boyfriend and the coincidence of him attending your engagement party for me to find out that you were his fiancée."

"I guess evidence for how small a world it can sometimes be."

"I just wish I had heard that little gem of information without my whole family having to witness it." I smiled wryly.

"It could be worse. Believe me, I wish mine was limited to family. Calling off a wedding fuels rumors and speculation that you can't even imagine until it's happening to you."

"I'm so sorry." I was realizing how my own humiliation paled in comparison to what she had been through.

"It's okay. It's shown me who I can really count on and made me thankful for those people in my life."

"Nicole, I have to say, you're incredible. I don't know what was wrong with Ben to look for anyone other than you."

She shrugged off the compliment.

"So what now?"

"Well, first of all, returning engagement and wedding gifts. And, needless to say, I have terminated my contract with Smithson, York, and Associates. I'll be looking for a new marketing firm. That's why I'm in Houston, to meet with our local office and strategize. Any recommendations on a firm?"

"Well, Baker, Allen, and Cooling is solid if you are looking for another boutique kind of firm. Then there's me."

"What do you mean?"

With everything between us, I was feeling comfortable, more like I was talking to a friend, not the woman who unknowingly shared the same bed. I genuinely liked her, so I took a chance. "I think I'm going to start my own firm."

"Really?" she responded with surprise to my candor.

"It's something I've wanted to do, and all of this has given me the push I needed to reexamine what I want from my career. I'm still trying to decide if now is the right time, but I don't know. It feels right."

"Well, if you're serious, I can set up a meeting for you."

"Really?" It was my turn to act surprised.

"I can't promise anything, but I can get your foot in the door. You'll have to do the rest."

"That would be unbelievable. I don't know what to say. Thank you, Nicole." I took a sip of my drink. "Not to seem ungrateful, but can I ask why?"

"Probably the same reason you told me. While I wasn't certainly expecting it, I do like you. So regardless of the messy situation Ben created, at least maybe a friendship can come from it."

"I hope so."

"To finding friends in unexpected ways." Nicole raised her glass. I met hers with my own.

Chapter 31

The wedding party had already started to trickle into the church for the rehearsal. Andy was waiting with her bridesmaids in the foyer. The wedding planner was running late. "I cannot believe we are waiting on her. What am I paying her for? Drew is going to give me such a hard time for this."

"I talked to the minister and he's ready. He said he could give the nod to the quartet if you want to start without her."

"I think you're right. Let's start. Otherwise, we'll be off schedule for dinner."

"Hey." I squeezed her arm. "Just remember, nothing can start without you. If you want to wait, we'll wait. This is the one time people will wait for you."

"Are all the guys up front?"

"I think so." I peered into the church. "Yep. I can see Drew and his brother standing up with the minister. And Jason and Josh are sitting in the front row talking to your dad. Do you want me to grab him?"

"She says she's two minutes away." Caroline snapped her phone shut and walked over to us.

"Good. I'll get the guys lined up and grab your cousin and father."

"Okay. Caroline, could you get my mom? I think she's outside pacing in front of the church."

The music started and we began our walk down the aisle. Andy's cousin Lindsay was the first one down the aisle, followed by Caroline, and then me. I walked up the stairs of the altar and was directly across from Josh. Instead of looking at him, I turned to face the door where Andy would enter. We ran through the entrance and exit a couple of times, making sure we were standing in the appropriate places, with the proper amount of space between us.

Drew's brother, Scott, walked back down the aisle with Lindsay. It was hard not to be amused by Scott. He was trying his best to act interested, but he was only fifteen and was a little bored by his surroundings. Jason walked out with Caroline, and then Josh extended his arm for me. "Don't trip," he whispered.

"Thanks for the concern."

"That's why I offered my arm."

"I think you have to as the guy I am paired with."

"You're pretty busy tonight."

"I'm just trying to make sure everything runs smoothly for Andy."

"If I didn't know better I would have thought you were avoiding me."

"Why would I do that?"

"That's what I was trying to figure out."

"You're just being paranoid." I forced myself to playfully jab his stomach and tried to ignore his abs, which I could feel through his dress shirt.

"You know, you're not supposed to outshine the bride," he whispered in my ear.

I felt his breath on my neck and a tingle run up my back. I reminded myself, *He's with Bridget.* "I'll pass that along to Caroline." I smiled and dropped his arm. "I should go and see if there is anything Andy needs help with."

At the restaurant, I was seated with Caroline, Shawn, my parents, Andy's cousin, and her parents for dinner. I was happy Andy had arranged the seating so that her guests were primarily to one side and Drew's were to the other. Because Josh was the best man, it meant he would spend most of his time on the other side of the room. I knew that he was seated with Jason and Beth and some of Drew's family. With the distance between our tables, I was able to avoid him most of the night. I even managed to excuse myself from the table when I noticed him making his way over, presumably to say hello to my parents.

A clinking began to resound in the room. "Excuse me, everyone. I'd like to make a toast." Josh cleared his throat. He looked so handsome, and even more so by the subtle nervousness that I could detect in his voice. "I think I've had a chance to meet just about everyone here tonight, but for those of you I haven't met, I'm Josh. I have the honor of serving as Drew's best man." He began his toast with a few harmless anecdotes about how he and Drew had become friends, then turned more serious to talk about Drew and Andy. "They truly complement each other, and not just in the fact that Drew always tells Andy her butt looks cute in those jeans." There was a soft chuckle. "But also in how they love each other. They do it as best friends—seeing each other for who they are and unconditionally liking and loving one another." His eyes fell on me, and I immediately looked away.

When Josh finished his toast, I knew it was my turn. I stood up from the table, clutching my wine glass. Shawn tapped his own with a fork to gain everyone's attention. "Hello, everyone, I'm Kate Hayden, and I have the privilege of not only being Andy's maid of honor, but also her best friend and roommate. This night is bittersweet for me. I am so happy for Andy and Drew joining their lives together and making this amazing commitment to one another, but I am a little sad because I know this is the last night that I will go back to our apartment and stay up late and have our girl time. It's my understanding that after tomorrow Drew expects Andy to live with him."

"I think as far as Andy is concerned that is still up for negotiation." Laughter filled the room at Drew's comment. I continued with my toast, adding some anecdotes and my own view on why they were meant to be, and then I raised my glass to the happy couple. I took my seat and let out my breath slowly. After my toast, a few more friends and family members stood to tell their own stories and give their best wishes to them.

With the toasts finished for the evening, each of the tables was engaged in their own conversations, which were keeping a low buzz going in the restaurant. A few of the guests were mingling between the tables, but I had settled in at my own.

"So, sweetie, just out of curiosity, were you planning to go back to work?" My dad directed the conversation to my career.

"I was thinking I might become a woman of leisure."

"Become? I think you already have become one."

"Okay, maybe *continue* would be the better word," I conceded.

"And how are you going to keep yourself in the lifestyle you have become accustomed to?"

"I can live a simple life." My answer held an air of indignation.

"Have you looked down at the shoes you're wearing?" my sister chimed in.

I looked down and smiled at my glossy Prada pumps that I had bought just yesterday. "Okay, so I might struggle in the shoe department." Then I added, "I called Bill this morning, and we had a good conversation. I told him that I didn't think returning was the best thing for me to do, and he was very understanding. We left it on good terms, and he said his offer was open in case I changed my mind." The looks around the table registered surprise. "I haven't completely lost it, and don't worry, I am not planning on moving back in with you two." I looked at my parents. "I have an interview set up with Baker, Allen, and Cooling for Tuesday, so we'll see how that goes."

"I am sure it will go well." My mom squeezed my arm.

"I'm so glad you convinced me to buy these cute flat sandals and switch them with my heels halfway through tonight," Andy said as we climbed the stairs to our apartment. "My feet are exhausted, but I cannot even imagine what they would feel like if I had been in my three-inch heels all night. I never knew it could be so tiring to stand around and talk all night."

"I can't believe you didn't want to stay in the cush suite tonight." I was using the hand rail to pull myself up the stairs.

"And miss our last night in the apartment together? No way."

"You know, it's not like we can't have sleepovers."

"I know, but it won't be the same. I'll just be visiting." She turned the key in the lock and opened the door. "It's so weird not to have Buddy meet us at the door."

"I know. It makes the apartment feel kind of empty. I just thought he would be better off at my parents' house today and tomorrow. We were barely here today, and then tomorrow he would have been alone for most of the day too. This way he is getting spoiled at his grandparents' house."

"Should we have a glass of champagne before we go to bed?" Andy asked. She was already walking to the kitchen to grab the bottle we had put in their earlier in the week.

"I think we should." I took off my heels. "Josh's toast was pretty good," I remarked, failing to sound nonchalant. I knew Andy would see right threw it.

"I thought so. A little funny, a little sappy, just the right combination. He couldn't take his eyes off you, though."

"I couldn't bring myself to make eye contact with him." I hid my face in my hands.

"I noticed. Have you talked since you ran into Bridget at his place?"

"No, not really." I shook off the thought. "Enough about me. So, are you nervous?"

"I think I would describe it as nervous excitement. It feels surreal. I cannot believe it is finally here and that I will be marrying Drew tomorrow. I am joining myself to someone for the rest of my life, knowing we are going to get the name joke every time we meet new people."

"Now that's true love." I pulled out some cake from one of the bags we brought home from the rehearsal dinner.

"Oh, you didn't."

"I did."

"I have to fit into my dress tomorrow."

"I do too, and your dress cinches you in and could hide an extra pound. Mine does not. But it is too good to pass up." We carried the champagne and cake into Andy's room and took in the bare surroundings as we lay across her bed. "This is depressing," I said with a forkful of cake in my mouth. Andy and I traded the fork to eat the cake and drank half the bottle of champagne before we curled up in her bed and fell asleep. We woke up to multiple phones ringing. Andy was reaching out blindly at the alarm. I told her it was the phone and she stopped.

"Who could be calling this early?"

I rubbed my eyes and took in the time displayed on the clock. I jumped out of bed, knocking over what was left of the champagne. "You need to get in the shower. We're late."

"What?" Andy was now fully awake. "What time is it?"

"It's okay. I'll tell Caroline and Lindsay to start with their hair and makeup and we will be there soon. The good news is you don't have to do either of those. I just need ten minutes myself and then I'm ready to go." I answered the phone to Caroline's screeching and held the phone away from my ear. "We're on our way," I said into the phone without waiting for her response. If my head had not been pounding, I would have taken the moment to point out the irony of Caroline being on time and me not setting an alarm for the morning of my best friend's wedding. "I should be fired as the maid of honor," I muttered as I patted dry the spilled champagne.

"Ten minutes." Andy was dragging herself to the bathroom. "Can you do me a huge favor and start a pot of coffee?" I nodded and set up the coffee maker, trying to remember the step-by-step instructions Andy had once given me on how to brew coffee.

By the afternoon of Andy and Drew's wedding, the church parking lot was already filled with cars, and I recognized most of them as the wedding party. I knew it would be a pain later when we all realized we had multiple cars to get to the reception. Earlier in the day, Andy and I had been in the same car, but after we had finished at the salon, she decided to ride with Caroline so she could go ahead and get to the church. Her nerves were starting to wear, and she just wanted to be settled at the church, even if she did have to wait for a few hours. After waking up late this morning, Andy wasn't taking any chances. Lindsay followed them to the church, and I went to pick up our dresses from the boutique. They were slightly behind in their alterations and didn't finish the last of them until this morning. I pulled the dresses out of my car and walked up the steps of the church. My makeup and hair were done, but I was still wearing a tank top, and Juicy sweat bottoms with flip-flops.

"You look nice," Josh said as he walked across the church corridor.

"Thanks." I smiled and kept walking, trying not to trip over the bottom of the bridesmaid dresses I was carrying.

"Are we not talking?" Our backs were toward each other.

I turned around. "I responded."

"Barely."

"What did you want me to say?" I sighed as I said the words.

"What's the deal? You avoided me all last night. Except for the walk down the aisle you stayed a good fifty feet away from me and even would walk away if I got anywhere close." He was shifting back and forth on his feet, with his hands stuffed in his tux pockets.

I paused, hesitating with what to say next. "It wasn't fifty feet."

"Is it really necessary to be so literal? You know what I mean."

"Why did you say anything to me?" I asked. I was nervous in even asking the question and wasn't sure I wanted to hear his answer.

"Would you rather I didn't speak to you at all at the wedding?"

"That's not what I am talking about."

"Then what?"

"You know." I fumbled with the plastic covering the dresses.

"Are you asking why I told you how I feel?" He finally turned toward me. When I met his eyes, I could see a sadness.

"Yeah. Why did you bother telling me? You couldn't even give me a little time. You're already back with Bridget." I draped the dresses over the table, looking down and letting my eyes fall from his.

"Kate, it's been weeks."

"So what? Have your feelings changed in a couple of weeks?"

"No." His voice was strained, but he was trying to keep it hushed.

"So then what's the deal with Bridget?"

"What does it matter?"

"I just don't understand how you could tell me that stuff and then get back together with her."

"I can't wait around for you forever. It's not like last night was the first time you avoided me. You've been avoiding me for the past couple of weeks. That's not to mention the topic of us almost … You won't even touch that with a ten-foot pole. What did you expect me to do?"

"I guess I expected you to … I don't know. Never mind, it's fine." I moved to pick up the dresses.

Josh moved toward me, catching my hand to stop me from leaving. "Clearly it's not fine. Can we talk for a minute? This is not how we work." He was holding my hand.

"Look, I know I'm being selfish, but I just thought maybe you would wait."

Josh let out a sigh. "What am I waiting for?"

"Do you remember when I came by the other day? Passed you in the hallway?" I pulled my hand away.

"Yeah."

"And Bridget was at your apartment?"

"Yeah."

"I came by to ask you to be my date today," I said quietly. Then I took a deep breath and continued. I could hear my voice shaking. "I was going to tell you that there was a lot that I don't know right now. I don't know where I am going with my job. I don't know where I am going to be living in a couple of weeks. But what I do know, what it took me a while to figure out, was that I wanted to ... that I want to be with you." It felt like my words just hung in the air. "It's just that I want to be ready. I want to have a clear head, and I want to get rid of the baggage I'm carrying with me right now." I shook my head. "But with you back with her ..." I trailed off. "I want you to know that I will be supportive of your decision."

Josh chuckled softly and moved toward me, sliding his hands around my waist. I could feel my breath catch. He then lifted his hand to raise my chin and lowered his head to kiss me.

I forced myself to pull back, the confusion on my face transparent. "What about Bridget?" I could feel my heart pounding and was sure that he could feel it too.

"I'm not with Bridget." And with that he began kissing me. This time I didn't resist but let myself fall into it.

After a few minutes, I finally pulled myself back from him. I couldn't help but smiling. "I should get back to Andy and the other girls." Josh was holding onto my hand. He was smiling broadly.

"I'm glad we talked." He winked.

"So what now?" I asked.

"We'll figure this out. We don't have to do it right now. After all, it is Andy and Drew's day."

"Don't let Andy hear you say that. She expected the whole weekend to be devoted to her." I picked up the dresses, putting them over my arm. I stopped and tilted my head. "But what about Bridget? If you didn't get back together, then why was she there?"

"She came by to talk. She wanted to see if there was a chance, but I told her I couldn't be with anyone right now because of the way I felt about you."

"Was that before or after you had gone to get coffee?"

He scratched his head. "Before, I think."

"I guess that would explain her icy reception of me when I stopped by."

"Yeah, we got into it pretty heavy when I got back. She was convinced we were together and I was lying to her. As far as I knew, you had no interest." He moved back toward me and gave me a quick kiss. "I'm glad that I was wrong."

"And I'm glad I was wrong."

"Hey."

"Yeah?"

"I'm sorry you didn't get your chase scene."

I smiled. "I think it was my turn to put myself out there."

The wedding ceremony went by quickly. I was so intent on Andy, making sure the train of her dress was not folding oddly and handing her bouquet to her at the right time, that the vows went by in a blur. I stole a few surreptitious glances in Josh's direction. He would catch my look and smile or wink in my direction. When he held out his arm to walk me back down the aisle, I held onto it tightly. It was hard to believe just twenty-four hours before that I had been trying to keep my distance from him.

At the reception, the wedding party mingled among the guests, leaving my throat and feet tired from all of the talking and standing. I finally had a chance to sit down and slipped my feet out of my heels, hiding them under the skirt of the table. Caroline was already seated at our table and was watching Andy and Drew cut the cake. They were smiling at each other and totally lost in the moment. I glanced around the room, looking at all of our friends. Caroline followed my gaze across the room.

She leaned over. "You know, he's been waiting a long time."

"I know, I know." I slid my shoes back on. I got up from the table, smiling at Caroline's I-told-you-so look. As I crossed the room, Josh saw me coming toward him. "Hey." I reached out my hand for his, "Wanna dance?"

"With you?" He took my hand. "Of course."

We walked to the dance floor, and he took me in his arms as the music slowly played in the background. I leaned back from him to be able to look him in the eyes. "I know it took me a while to get here, but I'm here now."

He pulled me into him. "I wasn't going anywhere." He whispered into my ear, "At least not until we danced. But you know, I was thinking, maybe we could plan a first date."

I pulled my head back. "That would be good."

He cupped my chin in his hand and went in for a soft kiss. As his lips pressed against mine, I sighed. I felt happy, and I rested my head on his shoulder as we moved around the dance floor.

"So this is what you two have been up to?" Andy gingerly fingered the book that Josh and I had given to them. We had pulled Andy and Drew aside, wanting to catch a few minutes alone with them before they left the reception.

Andy's eyes were tearing up as she turned each page to see a different set of pictures. "This is amazing." She squeezed Drew's arm. "I love it."

He opened his arms to envelope her. "This is really great, guys. Thank you." He looked over Andy's head, first at me and then at Josh, his eyes clearly expressing his gratitude.

"I'm not sure which gift I like better." Andy had a twinkle in her eyes.

"You are comparing this with other gifts?" I reached out as if to take the book back.

"Hmmm. Well, there is this." She held the book to her. "But there is also the two of you being together."

"Okay, okay. I think you are on sentimental overload," Drew cut in. "Although, can I just say it's about time?" He patted Josh on the back.

"We know." He smiled at me. Then we all hugged before Andy and Drew got swept back up into the festivities.

"How soon do you think before we can leave?" Josh whispered in my ear. The look in his eyes was playful.

"I think we are here until the end. But don't worry, the night is still young." I gave him a quick kiss before pulling him back onto the dance floor.

Printed in the United States
147998LV00002BB/8/P